The Gemini Connection

Julie Hamstead

Copyright © 2024 Julie Hamstead
All rights reserved.
No part of this publication may be reproduced, distributed, or transmitted in any form or by any means, including photocopying, recording, or other electronic or mechanical methods, without the prior written permission of the author, except as permitted by U.K. copyright law.

This is a work of fiction. Names, characters, organisations, places, events, and incidents are either from the author's imagination or are used fictitiously. No identification with actual persons (living or deceased), places, buildings, and incidents is intended or should be inferred.

Book Cover by Ariadne Tomé
ISBN: 9798879625615

DEDICATION
*For my father,
who always believed in me.
1936~2023*

Prologue

Evie sat alone in the apartment, staring out of the window. Silent tears streamed down her face as she looked out onto the Boulevard Saint-Michel, the towers of Notre-Dame visible in the distance. She looked down at the letter in her hands, the ink smudged by her tears. At least she now knew the truth. She began to read it once again....

Chapter 1

Two months earlier

Jackson groaned as he reached across the monitor for his pen.
"You alright mate?" Harry asked. "You don't look so good this morning."
"Bad Chinese last night I reckon," Jackson grimaced, "just got terrible gut pain. I need some water."
He rose slowly out of his chair and moved painfully across the office to the water cooler. Reaching for a cup he winced as the pain once again seared through his right side. This really was not great; he could feel sweat trickling down his back despite the air conditioning keeping the office cool. He shuffled back to his desk and slumped back into his chair. This day couldn't end soon enough as far as he was concerned. Chewing down hard on his pen every time another bolt of pain gripped him, he studied the jumbled words in front of him for what felt like the millionth time.
Turning back to Harry he pulled a face. "Stanners is not going to be impressed with our progress."
"I think you mean lack of progress," Harry replied.

The Gemini Connection

Right on cue the two men heard the booming voice of Stanners, "Update now, my office."

Jackson swallowed hard; the pain was getting worse, and he was starting to feel nauseous. The short walk across the room to Stanners' office felt like a mini marathon; by the time they got there his dark curly hair was stuck to his forehead and neck as more and more beads of sweat broke out over his whole body.

Entering the office, Stanners greeted them with, "Don't sit down gentlemen, this won't take long."

Looking Jackson up and down he did not even attempt to hide the disgust on his face. Clearly the lad was hungover, and it infuriated him. "You look like shit Jackson; turn up like this tomorrow and I'll have your balls for dinner."

Compared to the pain that was beginning to consume him, Jackson found the thought of losing bits of his anatomy quite mild in comparison. With a bit of luck his boss would choke on them.

"Sorry Sir, not feeling so good today, food poisoning I think."

Stanners raised his eyebrows in a quizzical fashion but decided against commenting further. Turning to the report he was holding in his hands he glanced at it and then fixed the two men with his steely gaze. "So, these messages are coming from a burner phone, but you still can't trace the sender. Have you at least managed to locate the intended recipient?" he demanded to know.

"Yes Sir," replied Jackson trying to hide the sigh that accompanied his words. How many times did he have to tell him this?

The Gemini Connection

Stanners was due to retire at the end of the year and it could not come soon enough for Jackson. He respected him for all that he had achieved over the years but, in his opinion, Stanners' time was over. He was fast becoming a relic from a time when MI5's intelligence was gathered only from sources in the field, not via computers operated by, as Stanners called them, virtual youths. Unlike some who spurned modern advances in favour of the old methods, Stanners was a peculiar mix of someone who viewed advancing technology with suspicion and contempt whilst simultaneously expecting it to be capable of rivalling only God for its capabilities.

"Our friends at GCHQ picked them up first, then asked us to get involved. The messages are all in a code with no discernible pattern, we can't break it," Jackson continued.

"For pity's sake boy," Stanners exploded, "if we could break Enigma and beat the bloody Nazis more than half a century ago how the hell can we not break this one?"

Jackson took a deep breath. "Because it uses a mixture of letters and numbers that defies analysis. There are no vowels, only consonants and every so often they are broken up by a number. With codes like Enigma, once we had understood the method, we could break it. It followed the same rules, day in and day out. These messages don't, every time we think we have a breakthrough it falters."

"Well, find the person who is supposed to be receiving them and damn well bring them in," Stanners demanded.

The Gemini Connection

Harry looked across at Jackson who seemed to be struggling to speak. "We could Sir, but we don't know who or what we are dealing with yet. If we do that we may play right into the hands of a hitherto unknown group and arouse their suspicions. We reckon we need to start tracking this person first, see who they might lead us to."

"Fine," said Stanners, "but move quickly. Who is this person? Are they already known to us?"

"No Sir," Harry replied, "it's not making much sense at the moment. The messages were all sent to a young woman with no known connections to any groups, political or otherwise. We have a name as of yesterday – it's a young doctor in London, a Dr Evangeline Longshaw."

"Right, she's already under surveillance I take it?" Stanners looked from one to the other of them. "How far have you got with background checks and such like?"

Jackson opened his mouth to answer but as he did so, he felt a twisting knot of pain tear through his abdomen dragging him down into an abyss of unconsciousness. He dropped unceremoniously at his boss's feet, but not before managing to vomit all over them as he fell.

~~~~

The Gemini Connection

Dr Evangeline Longshaw ran down the Underground steps and flung herself into the tube train. The train was quiet; that was one advantage of doing the night shifts if nothing else. Alighting at the Westminster stop she came out into a beautiful summer's evening and walked across the bridge towards St Thomas' Hospital. Unable to pronounce her own name as a child she was Evie to all who knew her, even her hospital lanyard said; "Dr Evie Longshaw".

She was hoping for a quiet shift but knew that was a forlorn hope for a London teaching hospital. Training in anaesthetics, she often joked she was drawn to it because it was as difficult to spell and pronounce as her own name. Arriving at the hospital entrance she disappeared inside, unaware that her every move was being tracked via the CCTV cameras dotted throughout the roads, stations and buildings of the capital city.

Evie caught her breath as she climbed the stairs up to the fourth floor of the hospital. She tried to always use the stairs, seeing them as her equivalent of going to the gym. She found it ironic that now she could finally afford a gym membership, she had neither the time nor the energy to go. She walked down to the changing rooms and changed quickly into her theatre scrubs before heading off down the corridor to her department's coffee room to see what delights awaited her in the long night ahead.

The Gemini Connection

Jeremy, Evie's junior colleague, looked up and grinned as she entered the room. He was watching an old episode of *ER* on the television. "Here they are again saving the world at Chicago County General," he told her. "Do you know that in just 30 minutes they have performed two successful lots of CPR, tackled a fire on level three and defused a bomb in one of their ambulances?"

"Why do you watch it Jem?" Evie smiled, "every night shift I do with you, you give yourself borderline hypertension watching it!"

"It's how I stay up to date Evie, I view it as contributing to my continuing professional development. Might start logging it in my CPD diary."

"Yeah, right," Evie laughed, "that will go down well at your appraisal."

"Right my bright young underlings, how are we all doing tonight?" Noel Carter, their consultant and boss, breezed into the coffee room. "Ah Jem, buffing up your knowledge courtesy of our transatlantic friends again I see. Well, in the real world we've got a couple of emergency ops already lined up. The orthopods need to pin an ankle; the ENT crew have got a fishbone to extract from some poor beggar's throat and I've just had a call from the general surgeons. They've a suspected burst appendix who they need to get to theatre ASAP, he's the priority case. Jem, go and see the ankle and the fishbone. Evie – your chance to go solo again if you're happy? Go and prep Mr. Appendix and let's get him sorted first."

The Gemini Connection

As Evie scanned her staff pass through the acute surgical unit's entry system and went in, she did not need to ask which patient was Jackson Bridges. In the bed in the far corner was a young man groaning in pain who was clearly 'Mr. Appendix.'

"Hello Mr Bridges, I'm Dr Evie Longshaw. I'm the anaesthetist on call this evening and will be popping you off to sleep for your operation."

Jackson moaned as more pain held him in its grip. Why did her name sound familiar? Deep inside his tunnel of pain he grappled to remember but couldn't dredge up anything from his memory. "I don't care what you do, just make this pain stop."

Evie ran her eyes quickly through his charts and wrote him up for a pre-med and pain relief. "Let's give him this and then get him straight up to theatre," she said, handing the drug chart to the nurse. "I'll let theatre and the surgeons know we are good to go."

Back in the changing room Evie pushed her long auburn hair under her theatre cap, pulled on a face mask, swapped her shoes for theatre clogs, and walked down the corridor to anaesthetic room three.

Jackson was being wheeled in and the pre-med was clearly taking its affect.

"Hi, how are you doing?" Evie asked him.

Flat on his back, looking up at the ceiling, all Jackson could see was a bright light and a face looking down at him that, to him at least, appeared to be shrouded in some kind of veil.

"Shit, are you an angel? I must be dead. Am I dead?" he questioned Evie.

The Gemini Connection

"No, you're not dead," Evie replied, "you do however have appendicitis and need it taking out."

"No," groaned Jackson, "please don't do that. My boss is already having my balls for dinner."

"Okay." Evie was used to her patients rambling although this was slightly outside the norm. "Nothing bad is going to happen to you," she promised him, "I'm just going to send you to sleep now."

Evie slowly administered the intravenous drug that would send Jackson off into a dreamless sleep. His last thought as his eyes closed was, *she has such pretty eyes*. He thought he said this to her as he drifted off but his actual words, somewhat slurred and to Evie's amusement, were, "Don't let them take my balls, he'll eat them."

Chapter 2

"Good to have you back," Harry greeted Jackson as he walked into the office.

"Ah, did you miss me then?" Jackson replied. "I would say thank you for the grapes and the flowers and the chocolates...but wait, you didn't bring me any!"

"But I did smuggle that can of lager in for you mate!"

"Which you drank because I was still nil by mouth, remember?" said Jackson in exasperation.

"Oh yeah, sorry about that," a totally unrepentant Harry grinned.

Jackson pulled out his chair and sat down, wincing slightly at the memory of how much pain he had been in when he last sat there. He had only been away from his desk for ten days, but it felt much longer. Harry had been covering for him during that time; out of office e-mail replies, or putting work projects on hold, were not an option in their line of work.

"So, bring me up to speed H; where are we at with our coded messages?"

"Not much further really, we've been keeping tabs on this Evangeline Longshaw but so far nothing much to note. She lives a pretty normal life as far as we can tell.

We've found nothing to link her to the far right, the far left, Islamic extremists, home-grown terrorists, nothing. The most radical thing she ever appears to have done is sponsor a Snow Leopard through the World Wildlife Fund. She supports various animal charities so am guessing she's a big animal lover." Harry sighed and sat back in his chair. "Stanners wants to bring her in but, so far, he's been vetoed from above. We're not supposed to even have the technology we're using to intercept these messages, let alone be using it, so HQ want to tread very carefully on this one."

"Maybe we are just missing something," Jackson replied. "Her name sounds familiar, why do I already know it?"

"We'd just identified her the day before you collapsed on us?" Harry answered. "Don't you remember?"

"Not really, that day is a complete blur to me."

Harry grinned. "Well, Vivian was in seventh heaven looking after you."

Vivian was Stanners' secretary, or personal assistant to be more correct. As old school as Stanners, nothing happened in that office without her knowing about it instantly. Her calm demeanour hid nerves of steel that had seen her through many years of working in a job not even her closest friends knew about. The young men she had once worked with had mostly grown older alongside her, but she knew by heart the names of those who hadn't. And not just their names, she remembered the anniversaries of their deaths too and always said a silent prayer and lit a candle for them in St Stephen's church near Victoria station on her way home. Now the office was full of men young enough to be her sons, had she had any, and she affectionately thought of them as 'her boys'. They spent their days wreaking havoc in the world from behind a computer screen and Vivian had spent many hours trying to understand all their terminology and acronyms. There had always been a rumour of a liaison between Vivian and Stanners sometime in the past, but Vivian had wisely kept her own counsel on the matter, choosing to ignore the gossip.

When Jackson had collapsed in an ungainly heap at Stanners' feet, it was Vivian who had rushed to his side and cradled his head in her lap as they waited for the ambulance whilst uttering soothing reassurances to him. Harry had found this hilarious and wasted no time in relaying it all to Jackson.

"The older woman mate, they lurve you. I reckon old Vivian has the hots for you."

"Show some respect," Jackson responded only half-jokingly. "I don't remember you rushing to help me."

"Yeah, well I don't do vomit, you know that."

Jackson was about to ask Harry why then he frequently drank enough beer to sink a small battleship, usually accompanied by a large doner kebab, only to throw it all up again if he 'didn't do vomit' but was interrupted by Stanners, bellowing from his office that he didn't have all day to hang around and wait for his latest update session.

As Jackson and Harry entered his office Stanners was fighting with an unruly bundle of papers that flowed across his desk and onto the floor.

"Vivian," he shouted, "need some help in here."

The Gemini Connection

Vivian came into his office, a wry smile on her face, and began collecting and sorting the papers. Despite the fact e-mail was the preferred mode of communication in the office, everybody knew Stanners abhorred trying to read information from a computer screen. He needed proper paper he could scribble over and carry around with him, including into the toilet if necessary. Patience was not one of his virtues and he would repeatedly press the Print button in frustration at the seeming inability of his computer to respond instantaneously. This always ended with him having multiple copies of every document and it had become Vivian's job to sort and sift it all on a daily basis until he finally had something usable.

"Right," he began, "as Mr Bridges is gracing us with his presence again after his holiday on the Costa del NHS let's go back to where we were two weeks ago and pick up from there."

"Okay, a couple of weeks ago we began intercepting phone messages from an area within Syria, near the Turkish border," Harry began excitedly. "Using the GSM Stingray System, we collected the IMSI and ESN of a mobile sending repeated messages to a number here in the UK. Thanks to the FISHHAWK software, plus a bit of PORPOISE analysis, we've been able to grab the messages out of the ether and hold them whilst we attempt –"

Stanners cut Harry off. "I don't understand a bloody word of what you just said. What happened to just bugging a phone and listening in?"

"Which bit didn't you get Sir?" Harry asked.

The Gemini Connection

"You lost me after the word phone," Stanners replied tersely.

Seeing the colour rise in both Stanners' and Harry's faces Jackson felt it wise to interject. "If I may," he began, "in essence we plant a device, just suitcase sized, in an area we want to keep an eye on. The device acts like a cellphone tower and gets all the local mobile phones to connect to it. We can then effectively eavesdrop on calls, messages, voice mails, everything. Most communications are innocent, and we simply forward them to the real tower. Anything that piques our interest we can hold on to. The software works so fast that neither caller nor recipient even realises there has been a transmission delay."

Stanners gave Harry a quizzical look. "Why the hell couldn't you tell me that?"

Harry muttered something incoherent and, pretending the pencil in his hand was Stanners' neck, broke it viciously into two behind the cover of his laptop.

"Anyway," Jackson continued, "we have now intercepted three messages written in some sort of code and all sent to a phone registered here in the UK to a young woman. We were just beginning our surveillance on her when I got sick."

"Don't remind me," Stanners grimaced, "cost me a small fortune getting my shoes professionally cleaned after you pebble dashed them. Anyway, tell me about this girl, what do we know?"

Harry began reading from his computer screen. "Dr Evangeline Longshaw, known as Evie. Born in Hastings on 23rd May 1994, so 28 years old. Her father was a local GP there but died from cancer five years ago. Mother is an English professor at Sussex University, specializes in American poetry. No siblings, educated privately. She went to Roedean no less. Bit of a highflyer, studied medicine at UCL, London and collected various merits and awards along the way. Always worked in London since graduating, training in anaesthetics, currently a registrar at St Thomas' Hospital."

The penny finally dropped with Jackson. "That's why I already knew the name. She put me to sleep when I had my op."

Stanners stared at him in disbelief. "Are you telling me that you were anaesthetised by this girl and didn't even realise who she was? We'd been talking about her that same bloody day!"

"To be fair I was in a lot of pain Sir, and I only saw her once before the op. I was out of it really."

"Boo hoo, save it for Mummy," Stanners barked, "you lost a good opportunity for some more intel there."

Jackson and Harry exchanged a look; Stanners was incorrigible where work was concerned. It always came first, no matter the cost or the situation.

"So, her student days," Stanners was now looking at Harry again, "anything of note? Was she in any dodgy societies? Been arrested at protests?"

"No, nothing," Harry replied, "there is literally nothing."

"Relationships then? Suspicious partner or friend? There must be something, innocent young women don't just receive coded messages from a part of the world known to harbour anti-western terrorists, by accident."

"Again, doesn't look like it," Harry replied. "One serious boyfriend in her student days, he's off the scene now. She lives in hospital owned accommodation with a couple of other medics; looks like she recently started seeing another doctor called Matthew Reed, known as Matt, about eight or nine months ago. He's a surgeon, same hospital, nothing of note in his background. I don't know, maybe we've got this completely wrong. Maybe the messages are legit but were sent to the wrong number? Or maybe it was just a kid playing with his mum's phone, writing gibberish, and sending it off to a random number."

Harry paused; Jackson was looking thoughtful. "I could buy that if it were a one-off, a single message sent once. But the same type of message sent on three separate occasions? That isn't a child playing around with a phone, that's someone trying to get in contact with somebody else."

"I agree," Stanners said. "Well, looks like we have our way in thanks to your appendix Jackson. You're ideally placed to 'bump' into her again, meet and greet her, get to know her."

"I don't know Sir; we didn't exactly meet under normal circumstances. I can't pick up where we left off."

"Oh, I don't know," Harry mused. "You flat on your back, naked, with a beautiful young woman hanging over you? Reckon you need to pick up exactly where you left off!"

"Oh, shut it," Jackson exclaimed, "and anyway, I had a theatre gown on!"

"Gentlemen, much as I would love to sit here and discuss your sex lives, or lack of, get out of my office and formulate a plan for getting Jackson into this woman's life. Oh, and before you go," Stanners reached across his desk and handed an envelope to Jackson, "this is for you."

Jackson was stunned; had Stanners finally shown a soft underbelly and actually sent him a Get Well card? Bemused, Jackson opened the envelope and pulled out the piece of paper inside. No such luck, it was instead the cleaning bill for Stanners' shoes.

Chapter 3

Evie flopped down into the chair in the coffee room with a huge sigh. It was 6am and she couldn't remember when she had last had anything to eat or drink. Sometimes it felt like she lived in this hospital and never left it. Her back and feet ached, and she was longing for a warm bath and her bed.

"Is it me," she asked Jem, "or is it always utter carnage when we are rostered together? I have lost count of how many people we've anaesthetised this shift!"

"No, it's not just you," Jem replied, "I reckon they know we make a dream team so store up their emergencies just for us!"

"Who's 'they'?" Evie laughed, "the patients or the staff?"

Like a self-fulfilling prophecy, before Jem could even answer, their emergency bleeps went off.

"Crash team to labour ward," the ominous call rang out.

"Oh, you have got to be kidding me!" Evie groaned, but she and Jem were already out the door and running down the hospital corridor before she had finished speaking.

The Gemini Connection

They burst onto the labour ward to be greeted by a scene of frenzied activity. Ross Sinclair, the obstetric doctor in charge, saw them arrive and shouted across the hubbub of activity.

"Evie, we've got a 36 weeker with a massive antepartum haemorrhage. Wheeling her into theatre now, get her under."

Evie ran down into the operating theatre grabbing a cap and mask on her way. She was horrified by what greeted her – a young, heavily pregnant woman clearly bleeding out and rapidly losing consciousness. There was no time for a calm chat with her patient first.

"What's her name?" Evie shouted above the chaos.

"Sarah," somebody shouted back.

"Sarah, I'm Evie and I'm going to send you off to sleep, okay?"

There was a faint nod from Sarah and Evie just heard her say, "My baby…"

"Jem, get a second cannula in her and get more fluids in. Have we got O neg on the way?"

"Yes," bellowed Ross from the scrubbing room, "just hurry up and get her under!"

"What do you think I'm doing?" muttered Evie under her breath. She had occasionally clashed with Ross before in this theatre. What he knew about obstetrics would fill endless textbooks; what he knew about anaesthetics would barely fit on a postage stamp. As far as he was concerned, she could take a mallet to the patient's head to knock her out so long as he got the go ahead to start operating the instant he was ready.

Evie swiftly administered the initial drugs to render her patient unconscious and deftly intubated her.

The Gemini Connection

Attaching the tubing to the anaesthetic gases whilst simultaneously watching the monitors she called out, "Good to go."

The theatre nurse began carefully and methodically wiping iodine solution over the swollen belly of the woman causing Ross to look at her in utter disbelief.

"Sod that Sister," he said as he grabbed the bowl of iodine and flung its entire contents over the woman's abdomen. "She's bleeding out and we've lost the foetal heart, just pass me the bloody scalpel!" Without waiting for the surgical drapes to be arranged over his patient, Ross barked at his junior to pull the pregnant belly upwards so he had a clear incision point.

Evie was becoming increasingly worried. "Her BP's dropping Ross and I'm pouring fluids in."

With swiftness and dexterity a master swordsman would have envied, Ross was already through the abdominal wall and into the uterus. He could see the baby's head through a sea of blood and began pulling on it whilst shouting at his junior to push down hard from the top of the pregnancy bump. With a final tug from Ross the baby was delivered into the waiting hands of the paediatric team, but it was blue and horribly silent.

Evie's attention remained with her patient, and she stopped herself from looking over to where the team was working hard to resuscitate the baby. Ross likewise switched himself off from what was happening just over his right shoulder and concentrated on the task in hand; at least now he was only operating on one person and not two.

The Gemini Connection

"Massive placental abruption," he told Evie, "But some is still attached. Hopefully enough to have kept baby going...."

As if to prove him right the unmistakable sound of a baby's first cry rang out across the theatre, followed quickly by sighs of palpable relief.

"58 seconds," Evie said to Ross.

"Sorry, what?" Ross asked.

"I timed you," Evie said. "From you picking up that scalpel to placing babe in the paed's arms was 58 seconds. Well done."

"How's her BP doing?" Unable to take the compliment, Ross kept his attention on the new mother.

"She's stable, you've all the time you need now," Evie replied.

"Well, it's going to take me more than 58 seconds to stitch her back together," Ross said drily but Evie noticed that he finally allowed himself a little smile as he announced, "Drinks are on me tonight."

~~~~~

"Now I know why people say third time lucky," Harry remarked to Jackson, "looks like you're on."

Jackson followed the direction of Harry's gaze and, sure enough, Dr Evie Longshaw had just walked through the door. This was the third time the two men had staked out The Camel and Artichoke pub frequented by the St Thomas' medics of a Friday night. Hacking into the hospital's computer system to find out when Evie was on and off duty was easy. Ascertaining that her cohort of colleagues had an informal arrangement to meet in this pub most Friday evenings was just as simple. What was not so straightforward was knowing when Evie was actually going to go. A combination of sheer exhaustion from long shifts and a need to study for her next set of exams meant she only went there occasionally. Twice already Harry and Jackson had rehearsed their roles and set themselves up in the pub, only for her not to show.

It had taken some persuading to get Stanners to agree to their plan. As far as he was concerned all Jackson had to do was go up to her, say "Hi, remember me? Let's go for dinner," and she would acquiesce and then tell all before they had even finished dessert.

"Do you think that actually worked in his day?" Jackson had mused to Harry.

"Dunno," Harry had replied, "maybe. I guess you could try 'You put me to sleep, let me buy you dinner to say thank you.'"

"Could you be any cornier?" Jackson had grimaced. "How exactly do you suggest I progress things from there if by some miracle she said yes? Ask if she's got any known food allergies or likes and dislikes and follow it up with 'Oh and by the way, do you happen to know any jihadi extremists?'"

"Got it," Harry had said, warming to his theme. "Go up to her and say 'Hi there, the name's Bridges, Jackson Bridges. Same initials as James Bond only I'm licensed to thrill.'"

Jackson had stared at him incredulously. "You're an idiot!"

"Yeah, but you love me mate!" was Harry's reply.

Eventually a more sensible plan was drawn up that Stanners conceded might work and he agreed to sign off.

The Gemini Connection

So now here they were, with Evie sitting to the right of their table, and Jackson had a sudden feeling of apprehension about what he and Harry were about to do. Evie was laughing at something the group was discussing and the man opposite her, presumably another medic, appeared to be demonstrating how to tip an imaginary bucket or bowl upside down. Goodness knows what that was about. As Jackson watched her, he couldn't help thinking that those bright eyes he had first noticed when she sent him off to sleep might soon be very dulled.

Chapter 4

"Don't spook her before we've even started!" Harry admonished Jackson. "You're staring at her."

"Well, I guess that would fit with me appearing to recognise her if nothing else," he replied, still gazing at Evie before he turned to Harry and said, "I'm not sure I can do this."

For once Harry didn't come back with witticism or sarcasm. "Stop seeing her as the pretty doctor who looked after you and start thinking of her helping to plan the next act of terrorism on a London bridge. That should help ease your conscience."

"She doesn't exactly look like a would-be terrorist though, does she? You must admit this is all pretty weird. I wonder if...." Jackson broke off as he saw Evie stand up and begin to make her way to the bar.

Harry looked at him. "It's now or never mate. Look at it this way, either this is all a complete farce, and those messages were never meant for her. After tonight we'll be leaving her alone to live her life. Or if they were meant for her.... Well then, I don't think she can be quite such a little Miss Innocent. We need to know one way or the other."

"You're right," Jackson conceded, "here goes."

He weaved his way through the crowded pub towards the bar. It had become busier since he and Harry had arrived earlier, although the balmy summer evening meant many punters had spilled out onto the street.

Evie was already ordering when he sidled up and positioned himself next to her. Pretending to ignore her at first, he studied the sticky cocktails menu lying on the bar.

"Two more jugs of Pimms please Davy," Evie was saying. Clearly, she was on first name terms with the barman, Jackson thought, probably because the pub was a popular haunt for the St Thomas' doctors.

Swallowing hard Jackson turned towards her. "Hi, excuse me, I don't mean to bother you, but I think I know you, well not exactly know you as such. I think you might have anaesthetised me a few weeks ago?"

Evie stared up at him blankly for a moment then frowned a little, clearly trying to remember him.

"I'm Jackson Bridges."

Evie still looked blank.

"I had my appendix out," Jackson continued.

The mention of the appendix triggered Evie's memory. "Oh hi, yes, I remember now. Sorry, it's very clichéd isn't it? For doctors to remember people by their medical condition rather than by their names? It was in the evening, wasn't it? You were my first case of the night shift. How are you now?"

"Pretty good thanks. I hope I didn't disgrace myself in front of you. That entire day and evening is all a bit of blur to me."

"I'm surprised you recognised me," Evie replied, "you were in so much pain. You must have a good memory for faces. Between the pain and the hefty pre-med I gave you I wouldn't really expect you to remember me."

Great! Jackson thought, was he about to fall at the first hurdle, did his story already sound suspicious?

"I think I recognised your voice too," he added, hoping this would give his explanation more gravitas, "just now, when you ordered your jugs of Pimms."

Evie laughed, "It's not all for me. It's been quite a day, but I wasn't planning on drinking two jugs by myself in a single sitting."

"Are they fellow medics?" Jackson enquired, nodding his head towards her group of friends, despite knowing full well they were.

"Yes, we all work at Tommy's," Evie replied.

Jackson struggled with what to say next; he was infinitely more comfortable behind a computer screen.

"So, are you feeling back to normal now?" Evie was asking.

"Yeah, great thanks but I have to admit I've never known pain like it."

Evie smiled at him, wondering whether he remembered what he had said to her as she had sent him off to sleep.

As if reading her mind Jackson said, "I have a horrible feeling I said something completely inappropriate to you, I hope it wasn't too awful."

"It happens all the time, I'm used to it," Evie laughed. "I've had everything from declarations of undying love to death threats. It's amazing how many people say they're going to kill you if you let them die."

Jackson shuffled uneasily. "Dare I ask which category I might have fallen into?" he asked.

Evie grinned. "Neither actually. If I remember correctly, you kept telling me not to give your boss either your appendix or your balls because he'd have them for dinner."

Jackson gulped; this wasn't good – what else had he said? If he had been talking about Stanners, he could have said other things too.

"I'm guessing you have a bit of a tyrannical boss," Evie continued. "I'd sent you off to sleep before you could say anything else about him. What do you do?"

Jackson relaxed a little. "I'm a computer geek," he began, this was the easy bit – he and Harry had rehearsed their back stories.

"Always stay surprisingly close to the truth, it makes it easier to remember," Stanners had told them.

"I work in cyber security."

"Oh, computer viruses and things like that?" Evie asked.

"Kind of, I deliberately try to hack into things to see how secure they are. The banks are always getting us to see if we can get into their data bases, see how easily they can be accessed, that kind of thing really."

"So, you're a bit like a legal bank robber then?" Evie teased, tilting her head slightly, "except you don't need to leave home or wear a pair of tights over your head to do it?"

Jackson laughed, "I guess that kind of sums it up."

"Here you go Evie," Davy the barman was handing two large jugs of Pimms across the bar to her.

"Thanks Davy, put it on this," Evie said, pulling her phone out of her jeans pocket and extracting a credit card from its case.

Jackson was relieved to see her pull out her phone; if this plan was going to get off the ground, they needed her to have that phone on her.

When Stanners had announced he wanted Jackson to weave his way into Evie's life he had taken some convincing that his old-fashioned blunt approach wouldn't work. The world had moved on since Stanners first joined the service and the setting of what amounted to little more than a honey trap, which might have been common in his early career, wouldn't work now.

"Besides," Harry and Jackson had told him, "whilst technically honey traps were still legal, they were fraught with so many difficulties over what was and wasn't admissible in a court of law that they caused more problems than they solved."

Their entire case around Evie centred on whether or not she was the intended recipient of the coded messages. If she wasn't, then there was nothing to be gained by pursuing her. However, if they were meant for her, and crucially if she understood them, then it was a different ballgame and one they needed not only to be playing but to have control of.

When Harry and Jackson had first suggested to Stanners that they wanted to send her the first of their intercepted messages he had looked at them incredulously. "Are you completely insane? You want to deliberately pass on a potential terrorist message? Can you imagine how that would look if the press got wind of it? 'Intelligence services intercept crucial texts between unknown terrorists but, because they can't understand them, decide to pass them on anyway so they can see what happens?'"

"It would be a bit more controlled than that," Jackson had explained through slightly gritted teeth. "We would observe her as she received it, see how she reacts, follow her, keep her under tight surveillance. Any hint of trouble and we can bring her in, but she might lead us to people we know nothing about. We know it's a risk, but it's a measured risk."

"Yeah, it's like that American geezer," Harry interjected. "Oh, who was it? The one who said that in intelligence there are the things you know, and you know you know them which is great; then there's the things you don't know but you know you don't know them so that is still kind of okay; but the real worry is the things you don't know, and you don't know you don't know them. Well, this girl and the messages – we don't know anything about the unknowns, we don't know what we know about what we don't know and even less about what we don't know about what we don't know...." Harry's voice tailed off as he realised Stanners was looking at him as if he was ready to paper the office walls with him.

"What on earth are you talking about? Are you an intelligence officer or the next poet bloody laureate? If I wanted you to wax lyrical at me, I'd sign you up for a poetry degree with the Open University. Better still, next time you want to go off like that warn me in advance so that I can have my letter opener ready to slit my wrists!

Or preferably your throat," he added. "Ye gods, what do they do when they train you these days?"

"Well, it makes sense when you analyse it," Harry muttered, "you just need the right kind of brain."

"What the –" Stanners exploded but before he could finish his sentence, which would have included most of the expletives known to man, Vivian bustled into the office.

"Now boys, play nicely," she began, "remember there's no I in teamwork."

"Well, where these two are concerned there's no I in Intelligence either," Stanners bellowed.

"Actually, there's two but that's beside the point," Vivian replied. "They're right of course you know William," she continued, ignoring the smirks on Jackson's and Harry's faces.

They only knew that Stanners' Christian name even was William because Vivian would use it when she was seeking to mollify him. She was the only person Stanners allowed to use it but somehow 'William' just didn't fit with their boss's gruff and belligerent persona, in their minds at least.

"I think their plan may just work," Vivian continued. "And I think you'll find that the American geezer," she looked in Harry's direction, "was Donald Rumsfeld, speaking in 2002. Although the concept of unknown unknowns is much older of course originating, I believe, in the 1950s when two American psychologists first developed it as a problem-solving technique." And with that Vivian swept from the room leaving all three men open mouthed and speechless.

The Gemini Connection

In the end Stanners had conceded that he could see a tiny spark of potential in their plan and gave it the green light which was how Jackson had found himself talking to Evie Longshaw in The Camel and Artichoke one Friday night.

"Is this a regular haunt for you?" Evie was saying as she finished paying for her order.

"Not until recently," Jackson replied, thinking that really was a true statement.

"My mate there," he pointed towards Harry who had been watching and surreptitiously recording their entire encounter at the bar, "has just started working near here and suggested it." A less true statement this time.

"Well, good choice," Evie said. "It was nice to see you again." And with that she started to make her way back to her table.

"Thank you," Jackson called as she walked away.

"What for?" she asked.

"For saving my life of course!" Jackson said with a grin and then gave a mini bow.

Evie laughed. "All part of the service."

Jackson sat back down next to Harry. "I really can't believe she's some sort of terrorist sympathiser. She just seems so.... nice."

Harry groaned, "Nice? That's a bit bland, isn't it? My last girlfriend dumped me when I told her she was nice!"

"She dumped you because you're a commitment phobic, parrot faced slob!" Jackson retorted.

"Hey, I have a classic Roman nose thanks very much! But yeah, the rest might be true!"

Jackson laughed but quickly fell back down to earth when he remembered why they were there.

The Gemini Connection

"Okay," Harry was saying, "let's hope our Evie is someone who checks her phone a lot."

"She's put it on the table in front of her," Jackson noted. "She should see she's received a message."

"Are you ready then?" Harry asked.

Jackson looked at him and gave a virtually imperceptible nod of his head.

"Okay, here goes nothing," and with that Harry pressed Send on the encrypted phone in his left hand.

Jackson turned his gaze towards Evie, everything now depended on her reaction. If she looked confused and simply threw her phone down again, or better still showed it to the people she was with, then it was highly likely she really had been the unwilling recipient of misdirected texts. If, however she displayed a suspicious reaction….

Jackson didn't have long to wait; he saw her reaching for her phone as the screen lit up when the message arrived and realised he was willing her to simply look bemused.

Please don't react, please don't react! he found himself thinking, praying even. However, his prayers that day were not going to be answered. To Jackson's dismay, as Evie unlocked her phone and read the message, she clasped her hand over her mouth. The colour drained from her face and, without a word to her friends, she stood up and ran from the pub.

Chapter 5

Stanners cradled the whisky glass in his right hand, swirling the contents round in time to the classical music playing softly in the background. He hadn't turned the lights on, there was still just enough light from the setting sun to illuminate the room. Every so often a little drop of liquid spilt from his glass onto his trousers, but he didn't care. He may have been holding a whisky glass, but the drink within it was not alcoholic. He'd been dry for twelvex years and, as those years had ticked by, he had realised he missed the feel of the crystal glass in his hand almost as much as the contents. He now filled it with a drink of his own concoction; a mixture of dark, espresso coffee and orange juice that masqueraded as a coffee liqueur. He'd tried various non-alcoholic spirits, but they were all so unpalatable it was enough to drive a man to drink, which rather defeated the purpose.

In the beginning he had tried the odd AA meeting, but they were not for him. How could he open up and share the reasons behind his drinking when there was so little he could say about the reality of his life? He would only have had to lie. And once you start lying, you must remember your lies. That never happened with the truth he reflected. You don't have to remember the truth; it doesn't change with your mood or perish in the harsh light of day. But lies? Lies beget more lies, until eventually you don't know where reality begins and ends. He had learnt that the hard way, when someone else had paid the ultimate price for his folly; when he had forgotten which lie to tell. He might have been exonerated at the subsequent enquiry, but he had never exonerated himself.

That was why he had told Jackson and Harry to keep their back stories close to the truth. "Don't invent jobs and lives with no resemblance to your own, you'll never remember them," he had told them. "The closer your lies are to the truth the more convincing you are, the less suspicious your actions."

He hoped they had heeded his warning. He knew what they thought of him of course, the ancient relic who couldn't be pensioned off soon enough. In his working lifetime he had seen so many changes, too many in recent years. As was always the case in his era, MI5 came looking for you, not the other way around and he had entered the service straight from university. With a first-class degree in maths, he had been taken aback but then intrigued, when MI5 came knocking on the door.

His scant background knowledge of the services came only from Bond films or John Le Carré novels, and he couldn't see how he fitted the image of either James Bond or George Smiley. Two radically different, fictitious individuals but neither with attributes Stanners saw in himself. But MI5 were not looking for another Bond or Smiley, they saw his potential for something else entirely. With his analytical working style, quiet self-assurance and solitary lifestyle he was the ideal raw material for them, and they offered him a post in what they referred to as their Development Department.

He had masterminded ways for MI5 to gather information. He wasn't an inventor, he left it to others to make the gadgets. His forte was plotting and planning when and how to listen in to conversations; to steal information whilst it was floating in the air. Very little could be gleaned from bugging the home phone of a suspected Soviet sympathiser or IRA supporter; it was obvious to all that it was the first thing MI5 would do. No, find out instead which bars they most like to drink in, and which table they like to sit at, and at which point in the evening they have drunk just enough alcohol to let their guard down. Then move your man – or woman – in to listen into their conversations. Get all of that right and you could gather some very interesting intelligence.

Stanners had risen rapidly through the ranks, appearing infallible until the technological world began to explode around him. In less than a decade the fundamental mode of human communication changed, and he had struggled to keep pace with this brave new cyber world. Jackson, Harry and their ilk spent their days hacking into phones and computers, finding back doors to spy on the miscreants who mistakenly thought they were hidden from view. They could intercept and gather more information in one hour than he had managed in a month when he had first started with the service.

He grudgingly admired Jackson and Harry but, if truth be told, he also envied them. It was this envy that spilled over to cause the gruff belligerence he showed the two men, the mask he hid behind. The truth was he felt increasingly irrelevant to the modern world. He had always planned to work until he was 65 but he knew he was losing his grasp. It wasn't just advancing technology that was defeating him though. Over the last few years, he had dropped the ball on several occasions, and he didn't really know why. Information that used to be at the tip of his fingers seemed to disappear into the ether, often and unfortunately in meetings with his superiors when he would be unable to find something on his computer he was convinced he had read only the day before. Or the opposite would happen, he would deny all knowledge of a project development only to look back on his computer and find e-mails about it he was sure he had never received. This was why he now printed off every piece of correspondence he received, even if it did usually fall to Vivian to gather it all up and put it in some semblance of order for him. He was starting to look like a fool, and it was only a matter of time before somebody in an office somewhere in Whitehall decided he was a liability and should be let go. Better to announce your retirement and attempt to leave with your head, if not held high, at least still on your shoulders, he had decided.

Stanners swirled the liquid around in his glass again and wondered what progress Jackson and Harry were making, if any. It was thinking back to his early days in the service that finally led him to concede that their plan might just work. He might not understand the complexities of how they had intercepted those phone messages but one thing he was sure of, people didn't fundamentally change even if technology did. Get this girl on her own territory, with her friends around her and her guard down, and something might just give.

～～～

Harry looked at Jackson as Evie ran from the pub. "I think that counts as a reaction."

Jackson nodded his agreement. "More than I was expecting if I'm honest."

"Come on, let's see what's happening out there."

Harry grabbed their bottles of beer, and the two men made their way to the pub's door. As they walked out into the warm night, they could see Evie a little way down the road. One of her friends had raced after her and was now standing with her arm around her. Evie allowed herself to be led to a nearby bench and, as she sat down, she dropped her head into her hands.

Harry and Jackson inched closer, trying to give the illusion of only being interested in their beers when in reality they were trying to hear what was being said.

They could just make out Evie's voice saying, "I'll be fine Christine, I just suddenly felt dizzy. Honestly, please go back inside."

"I'm not going to leave you in the street Evie, I'm sure you'll be okay in a minute."

Evie lifted her head from her hands and managed a weak smile; she knew she would not be okay in a minute. Or in an hour. Or anytime soon. She needed to be alone, she needed to process what she had just read on her phone.

"I think I'll call it a day Christine; I need my bed. Could you grab my bag and give my apologies to the others?"

"Of course, and I'll get Matt as well."

"Oh, please don't," Evie called out, but it was too late, Christine had already darted back into the pub.

Minutes later a rather sullen young man emerged from the pub and made his way to where Evie was still sitting on the bench. He virtually threw her bag at her, and Jackson and Harry were startled to hear him say, "I didn't realise you couldn't handle your drink Evie, not the greatest attribute in a woman."

"Wow," Harry murmured to Jackson, "this must be the new boyfriend. Seems utterly charming."

Jackson raised an eyebrow in agreement but remained silent.

Evie meanwhile just stared at Matt. "Are you for real? It never entered your head that something else may have happened, that I might be ill or something?"

"Oh, come on, you've clearly had a bit too much, you were fine earlier."

"If you're just going to stand there and lecture me on how much alcohol a woman should or shouldn't drink, then don't bother."

"All I'm saying is you should know when to stop. It's not a good look."

"Oh, just sod off!" Evie exclaimed.

"Nice one," Harry said approvingly, "she stood up to him. She needs to dump him."

"Will you stop giving me a running commentary?" Jackson hissed at Harry, "I'm standing right here!"

"Sorry mate, but looks like her words had the desired effect," replied Harry as Matt stomped past them and back into the pub.

Jackson looked at Evie, still sitting on the bench clutching her bag and looking deathly pale. "Ready to improvise a bit?" he said to Harry and, without waiting for an answer, started walking towards Evie. He pretended to walk right past her and then doubled back.

"Hiya, I don't mean to intrude but are you okay?"

Evie looked up at him. *Wow, those eyes,* he thought, *she really has the most incredible eyes.*

Evie blinked, not sure at first who was talking to her and then recognised him as the man from the bar. "Oh, too much Pimms I think," she tried to laugh but Jackson noticed how shallow her laughter was. "Shouldn't have had a jug to myself," Evie continued trying to sound jovial but was not succeeding. "I think I just need to go home." She stood up but swayed a little as she did so.

"Woah," Jackson said as he instinctively reached out to steady her, "need a hand?"

Evie looked confused and bewildered. "No, yes, not really. I don't know what I need."

Jackson threw Harry a glance; the phone message had clearly had a profound effect on her.

He seized the opportunity to ingratiate himself a little further with her and, nodding at Harry, said, "This is my mate, Harry, and we're going in that direction if that's any help to you." He pointed down the street knowing full well that Evie needed to go in that direction to get the tube.

"Thanks, but I'll be alright," she began, but even as she said it the weight of what she had read on her phone crushed her again. "Actually, I'm not sure I will be," she said weakly.

"Tell you what," Harry said, warming to Jackson's theme, "why don't we walk with you until we find a cab and then we can pack you safely off home."

"Thanks," said Evie, "if you're sure you don't mind."

The three of them made their way down Lower Marsh Street in silence.

As they drew closer to the river, Jackson ventured a question. "Do you live far from here?"

"Sorry, what?" Evie was miles away.

"I was just asking where you lived," Jackson replied.

"Oh, in Pimlico," Evie explained.

"With friends?" Jackson wondered how far he could push her right now.

"Sort of, we're all NHS staff so…" Evie's voice tailed off again, she was clearly utterly pre-occupied.

As they rounded a corner Harry spotted and hailed a black cab. He glanced at Jackson who gave a slight nod of agreement; for now they just needed to send her home and then regroup with Stanners. They knew perfectly well where Evie lived but had to go through the motions. They bundled her into the cab and, leaning towards the driver, Jackson asked, "What's your address?"

"Err, Bessborough Place in Pimlico," she said, "number seven."

"Sure you'll be okay?" Jackson asked, getting ready to close the cab door.

"I'll be fine, really, thanks for your help," Evie replied.

"No problem, you take care. You still look a bit like you've seen a ghost!" Jackson said, trying to sound lighthearted.

As he said this Evie looked up at him. "Actually," she said, "I think I did."

Chapter 6

Stanners didn't believe in hanging around. When Harry had let him know about the evening's events, he demanded the two of them get themselves to his house ASAP.

"Does the man never sleep?" Harry grumbled as he and Jackson made their way back to Jackson's car, parked down a side road near the pub.

"Apparently not," said Jackson.

"It's 11 o'clock, I could have been schmoozing up with a beautiful woman for the night."

Jackson looked at him. "I think the key word there is 'could' mate, you've got to find one who will actually tolerate you to some small degree first."

Harry pouted. "I'm not that bad."

Jackson laughed out loud. "Not that bad? Wasn't it about this time last year that you managed to double book yourself onto a date with two different women in the same place at the same time! As I recall one slapped you in the face and the other one chucked her drink in it!"

"Well, that's how I like my women," Harry replied nonchalantly.

"What? Emotional and upset?" Jackson queried.

"Nah, feisty and in pairs!"

"And you wonder where you're going wrong," Jackson sighed as he opened the car door.

Harry settled himself into the passenger seat and immediately began rooting around in the glove compartment. Finding a packet of sweets, he started popping them one by one into his mouth.

"Do help yourself," Jackson said but the irony was lost on Harry.

"Ta, I love a Fruit Pastille. Anyway, where women are concerned, we can't all be like you, Saint Jackson of the Bachelorhood," Harry teased. "You're way better looking than me, I could easily fix you up with one of my exes and you'd be in there."

"Gee, thanks for such a wonderful offer, I'm sure the ladies of your acquaintance would be thrilled to know you're auctioning them off to the highest bidder!"

"Seriously though mate," Harry said as they drove across the river and towards Lambeth, "you need to lighten up a bit. Have some fun, get out there. Apart from anything else, if you're going to try and impress our young Evie, you could do with some practice first!"

"I don't need practice and I don't need to impress her. It's work, nothing more, nothing less. If she's anything like Claire, she can stay at arm's length thanks very much."

As he said this, Jackson's face clouded over. Claire had been his fiancée, his fiancée, in fact, right up until three days before their wedding when she had announced she was in love with someone else and couldn't marry him. That was two years ago, but the pain was still raw although sometimes Jackson couldn't decide if it was his heart or his pride which carried the largest wound.

"Ah mate," Harry said, a little more gently, "not all women are Claires."

Jackson pulled the car up outside Stanners' home and switched off the engine. He turned to Harry, "Maybe, maybe not but I'm never going to let myself find out, okay? It's just easier that way."

Before Harry could respond, Jackson was out of the car and up the path, ringing Stanners' bell.

"Come in," Stanners said as he answered the door in his usual gruff manner, "You know where the kitchen is, make us some coffee."

Jackson was used to this; no wonder Stanners' own marriage had lasted just four years. He probably barked orders at his wife until she finally decided enough was enough and walked out. At least, he assumed she was the one who did the walking out. The only reason he knew Stanners had even been married was because Vivian once mentioned it. Stanners had never said a word about his ex-wife, but he never talked about anything to do with his private life.

Jackson retrieved three mugs from the cupboard and spooned some coffee granules into them. He knew exactly where everything was, he'd lost count of the number of times he and Harry had come over to this house and worked halfway through the night. *We don't even get paid for it*, he thought to himself.

He wandered into Stanners' sparse living room with the coffees. The place was so impersonal it seemed impossible that he had lived there for more than twenty years. There were no books or magazines lying around, no plants, not even empty pizza boxes or the odd beer bottle. In fact, there were no signs of any kind of life outside of work. Jackson felt an involuntary shudder as he realised this could well be him a decade or two down the line.

The only thing there were several of in the room was computers, five in fact. Stanners, with his well-known hatred of technology, would insist on a new computer whenever his current one ran into problems or malfunctioned in any way. The concept of letting the chaps in IT fix it was as alien to him as if they had asked him to walk on water. Even when in possession of the new one, it was Vivian who had to come round, set it up and transfer all his files over from the mainframe computer. She knew all his passwords and could clone herself as him, in the cyber world at least, at a moment's notice. Completely irregular of course, if not downright illegal, but, if nobody knew, then Stanners figured it wasn't really a problem.

He would moan to Vivian that at his age he shouldn't be expected to understand how it all worked but she would brusquely remind him that she was a mere two years younger than him and yet she knew how to navigate herself round a computer and the IT guys would be happy to teach him. Stanners' response to this was usually to sigh, loudly, and then ask her to remind him what IT stood for.

"Well, that's not a normal reaction," Stanners was saying as Jackson put the coffees down on the low table, devoid of anything bar a single coaster. Harry was showing Stanners his phone footage of Evie receiving the message and then running from the pub. "Talk me through everything, don't leave anything out."

When they had finished recounting the details, Stanners nodded his head. "Nice touch, the taxi and asking for her address. Gives you a bona fide excuse for having it. Use it, get yourself round there tomorrow." His last comment was directed at Jackson.

"And do what exactly?" Jackson asked. "She's clearly fragile after tonight. I can't just show up, uninvited, and start asking questions."

"Why not?" Stanners retorted, "it's either that or I'll bring her in."

"With respect Sir," Jackson began, trying to be patient with this infuriating man, "I don't think we have enough to bring her in. We certainly can't have her arrested based on what we know so far."

"I know that!" Stanners barked, "but we could bring her in for a little chat. Confront her with what we know so far."

"Which isn't very much, Sir," Jackson replied, with exaggerated emphasis on the 'Sir'.

Stanners and Jackson locked eyes, not for long, but long enough for them to realise neither intended to give in to the other one.

Harry, never very good at reading the mood of a room at the best of times, was blissfully unaware of the rising tension.

"Got it," he quipped. "Buy a huge box of chocolates, dress up all suave and sophisticated and swing in through her bedroom window. Leave said box of chocolates on her bedside table along with your calling card and then bingo, she'll call you. Or maybe one of those baskets of fruit, you know, in case she's counting the calories…."

Stanners and Jackson stared at him in disbelief.

"You've been watching too many television adverts you fool," Stanners bellowed. "Nobody is swinging anywhere, not with chocolates, not with fruit. We're MI5 operatives not chimps at the bloody zoo."

There was a moment's silence until Stanners startled them both by bursting out laughing. Jackson and Harry looked at each other uneasily; Stanners was not known for his sense of humour.

"I must have done something very wrong in a past life to end up lumbered with you two buffoons! Still, you're entertaining if nothing else."

Before either of them could even think of a reply, Stanners' focus switched back to work again and the sliver of insight into another side of him was gone.

"Right, clearly that message meant something to this girl. If she was an innocent member of the public who received it by accident? She would have ignored it or shown it to her friends at the pub, wouldn't she?" He didn't wait for either of them to answer. "Her reaction was dramatic; it doesn't fit with someone who was expecting a message either. It was too extreme, too emotional, too spontaneous. You're monitoring every single second of this girl's life. I take it you've always got access to her phone? Has she tried to reply?"

"We agreed we wouldn't let the caller number through with the message," Harry reminded him. "She couldn't reply even if she wanted to."

"Hmm," Stanners said. "We need to get closer to this girl. I want you both back here at 7am. I'm going to get

Vivian here, ask her the best way for Jackson to wheedle his way into this girl's life. She's a woman, she'll know."

Jackson thought that it was far more likely Vivian would tell Stanners what he could do with his sexist, old-fashioned approach but decided it was wiser to keep his own counsel, for now at least.

Harry, however, had only heard 7am. "Bit early for Vivian Sir, on a Saturday," he said hoping he was doing a convincing job of feigning concern for her.

He wasn't, Stanners saw straight through it. "Yeah, you're right. Make it 7:30 then."

~~~~~

It took Evie three attempts to get her key in the front door when she arrived home that night. Her hands were shaking so much she struggled to line it up with the lock. When she eventually managed it, she virtually fell into the communal hallway as she pushed the door open. She realized now she had not paid for the taxi home nor had the driver asked her for money. She could only assume one of the young men who had hailed it for her had also paid. She hadn't even thanked them for helping her.

She stumbled up the stairs to her own flat and succeeded in opening its door on her first attempt this time. The flat was in darkness, and she was grateful that both her flat mates were out; one was working nights; the other had gone away for the weekend with her boyfriend. She sank down onto the sofa then immediately got up again. She went into the kitchen, opened the fridge, and poured herself a glass of wine but absent mindedly left it sitting on the kitchen counter and

The Gemini Connection

went back to the sofa. She kept turning her phone over and over in her hands; she wasn't sure if she felt elated or terrified at the thought of reading that message again. Perhaps it wouldn't be there, and she had imagined the whole thing; maybe she was having some sort of hallucination brought on by lack of sleep and sheer exhaustion.

She remembered her missing glass of wine and went to retrieve it. Collapsing back onto the sofa for the third time since getting home, she took a large gulp of it then, holding her breath, tapped her phone's screen. It bounced back to life, and she stared hard at the Message icon before hitting the button that would open her text messages.

It was still there. She hadn't imagined it. She read it again and again. There was no mistaking what it said or who it had to be from, but how could it have arrived on her phone now, this evening? Could messages get lost and only find their way to your phone weeks, months or even years after they were first written?

It made no sense, only one person could have sent this to her. The one person who knew that writing it in this way, in this manner, would make it indecipherable to anyone but her. But that was impossible, nobody could text from beyond the grave. Or perhaps they could. Because the only person who could have written this message had been dead for two years.

Chapter 7

Evie looked in exasperation at the young man standing on her doorstep with a large and extravagant bouquet of flowers in his arms. She couldn't help thinking that if he really knew her, he would have realised that a few simple freesias would have been far more suited to her taste.

It was Sunday afternoon and she had barely slept since Friday. Her entire world had shifted since she received that message. She had spent most of Saturday searching the internet for answers to questions such as *Can texts be delayed by months or years?* and *Can texts arrive two years after they were sent?* She had discovered this could happen, it was highly unlikely, but it was possible. She desperately wanted to reply to that message and ask, *Is this really you? Where are you? How are you? How can you be alive?* but she couldn't because the message came from a No Caller ID number. She agonised over going to the police but felt sure they would dismiss her and attribute her crazy claims to unresolved grief. In the end she tried to dismiss the possibility the sender could still be alive and reassured herself that an aberration in the cyber world accounted

The Gemini Connection

for the long delay between the message being sent and her receiving it.

With so much on her mind the last thing Evie wanted or needed was this idiot standing in front of her and telling her to go and pack, he was taking her to Paris. Without even waiting for an answer, he had pushed past her and was already making his way into her flat.

"I can't just pack and leave," she said, "I'm due back at work tomorrow or had you not thought about that?"

"No problem," came the reply, "I've had a word with Noel, and he took a bit of persuading I have to say, but he finally agreed you could take the next three days as annual leave and then you're rostered off anyway for the next two."

"I can't believe you went and talked to my boss behind my back," Evie exclaimed.

"I know, so don't say I don't care, okay?" he said, clearly assuming she was complimenting him. "I explained you were a bit stressed, and I had this conference in Paris to go to so it would be good for you to come too, have a bit of a break. We're going to be rubbing shoulders with some of the best cardiac surgeons in the world and who knows? Play my cards right and I might just set myself up for a consultant post."

Evie exploded. "Let me make myself a bit clearer. When I said I couldn't believe you spoke to Noel I wasn't praising you! How dare you Matt? How dare you go behind my back and decide what I should and shouldn't be doing like I'm some little woman at your beck and call."

The Gemini Connection

Matt did not look in the least bit abashed. "I was only thinking of you Evie. I may have been a little less than supportive Friday night, I just didn't know what to make of the fact you ran out like that. It didn't look good, you not being able to take your drink."

"Good for me? Or for you?" Evie cried. "Which is it Matt? Are you really thinking about me or is this all about you and what looks good for you? You didn't want a girlfriend throwing up in the street because, heaven forbid," she threw her hands up in the air for effect, "somebody might judge you for your poor taste in women."

"I'm sorry Evie, I really am," Matt replied. "I'm just trying to do a nice thing here. Look, they're not expecting you at work tomorrow now and I've got you on the evening flight with me; it was the last seat in business class too. We'll be staying in a five-star boutique hotel, just by the Pont Neuf. Think about the shopping, the food, the ambiance."

He pronounced the word *ambiance* with an exaggerated French accent as he started dancing Evie round the kitchen. "Look, I'm speaking French already."

Evie felt the little remaining strength she had drain out of her; she was too tired to argue anymore. On reflection perhaps Matt was trying to make up for his appalling lack of support on Friday night. It was not lost on her that two strangers had been more attentive than her boyfriend, helping her and seeing her safely into a taxi home. Maybe the one who'd lost his appendix on her watch, she couldn't remember his name, felt he owed her something although, if he did, that was so unnecessary. She would not have recognised him in the

The Gemini Connection

pub had he not spoken to her. That's just how it was in her branch of medicine; the briefest of chats with each patient as you sent them off to sleep, one after another, through endless shifts. She rarely saw them again once they were awake.

As for Matt, she knew he was very good at his job, excellent in fact, and it was clear he would become a leading light in the field of cardiothoracic surgery. Unfortunately, Matt knew he was one of the best and, as his surgical skills grew, so did his pride and arrogance. However high he was ascending within the surgical world; Evie couldn't help thinking his character as a man was moving in the opposite direction. She had initially been attracted to him because he seemed to attack life with a zeal she had found exhilarating, but she was starting to realise it hid an intensity and dominance she had not spotted in him at first. And it was showing itself again now, with his insistence she go to Paris with him.

She knew he wouldn't take no for an answer and when he said, "You're coming to Paris with me Mademoiselle, end of!" she caved in and quietly said, "Okay, yes, I'll come to Paris," as he continued to waltz her out of the tiny kitchen and into the lounge.

~~~~~

When Stanners rang Vivian at 1am Saturday morning, telling her she was needed at 07:30 and the reason why, she reacted exactly as Jackson had anticipated. Without mincing her words, she made it abundantly clear that she was not the department's resident agony aunt or relationship advisor and that if he wanted her to take on that role, she expected suitable training and a substantial pay rise first.

When her phone rang on Sunday morning, and she saw it was Stanners yet again, Vivian almost didn't answer but the fear of not being completely on top of her own game made her take his call. A slightly contrite Stanners told her he was meeting with Harry and Jackson at 11am because of developments and it would be very useful if they could have her perspective and help with the latest situation. Her curiosity got the better of her and, in the end, she acquiesced to his request.

She arrived at Stanners' home promptly at eleven but there was no sign of Harry or Jackson. Quarter past, then half past eleven came and went, by which time Stanners was turning the air blue with the expletives he was using to describe their tardiness. Vivian sighed as the phrases *in my day* and *when I was their age* were interspersed with various descriptions of what he would do to their anatomy when they finally did turn up.

"William," Vivian began in her most soothing voice, "you were no different at their age and you know it. You used to run rings around your old bosses, all of you did. They're only doing the same. You ask so much of them, when do they get to live their lives outside of work?"

Stanners looked at her. "Vivian," he said gravely, "when you do the work we do, there is no life outside of the service. How can there be?"

"That is only your perception because you made it so. You chose to make this your entire life, these boys haven't. And good for them I say, one day they might have wives and families and why shouldn't they? They don't want to end up like you," she paused before

The Gemini Connection

adding, "or me. It could have been different you know, but you would never let anyone in. Janey didn't walk out because of the hours you worked, she walked because you wouldn't let her into your life. You wouldn't tell her the truth, you should have."

Stanners shuffled uncomfortably. "You can't let people in, not even your own wife. Our work is too covert, you know that."

More than you realise, Vivian thought but, before she could say anything more, the doorbell rang.

"About bloody time," Stanners muttered and went to answer it.

Harry, who had been nonchalantly leaning on the front door, fell into the house when Stanners opened it.

"Sorry we're late Sir," Jackson said, coming up behind Harry, "but the traffic was bad."

"Really?" Stanners asked. "On a Sunday morning? If you're going to make up excuses, at least come up with something plausible, like, oh I don't know, your hair was on fire, or you woke up dead!"

Harry resisted the urge to come out with 'Whatever!' and settled for muttering something unrepeatable under his breath as he and Jackson made their way down the hallway.

Jackson didn't even wait for Stanners to say 'coffee' and instead headed straight into the kitchen, but Vivian had beaten him to it. As he walked in, she turned and smiled at him.

"Here, strong coffee and some Danish pastries I picked up en route. We'll need something to keep us going with old grouchy balls in there."

The Gemini Connection

"Oh, thanks Viv, you're the best," Jackson said, "don't know what we'd do without you."

Vivian had made four coffees which she was now placing on a tray along with the food.

"Let's go and check they haven't killed each other, shall we?" she said with a wink as she and Jackson made their way into the lounge.

Harry's eyes lit up when he saw the pastries and he dived in without waiting to be asked.

"Do help yourself Harry," Vivian said wryly passing him a plate and paper napkin.

"Yep, have done ta," Harry said between mouthfuls, completely missing her sarcasm.

Jackson sighed and reached for one himself; sometimes working with Harry was akin to having your mischievous kid brother as your partner. They exasperated you and made you laugh in equal measure, but you knew you would take a bullet for them if circumstances dictated. For all his buffoonery and idiotic ideas, Harry Rivers was one of the best computer geeks MI5 had ever had. He had breezed out of university with a first-class honours degree in computer science plus a sound knowledge of every pub within a three-mile radius of his student digs. He had done his Master's degree virtually in his sleep whilst working as a computer coder and, by the age of 25, was bored rigid by his work. It was Harry's boss who had suggested he look at MI5's website, in particular the job vacancies page. Harry was surprised; it had never occurred to him that an outfit such as MI5 would advertise for people. He had said as much at the time, but it turned out his boss was right – MI5 no longer recruited clandestinely behind closed doors.

The Gemini Connection

Now, you could search for jobs with just a few clicks of your computer mouse and that was how Harry found himself working for MI5. Over the last seven years Harry had found his niche and he was in his element hacking into supposedly impregnable sites, and unleashing chaos, if necessary, at the touch of a button.

He sat now in Stanners' living room with two laptops precariously balanced on his knees, tapping away on their keyboards whilst simultaneously managing to demolish a Danish pastry and gulp coffee at the same time.

"Scrote bag has booked an extra flight to Paris this evening for our Evie," Harry said. "He was going anyway to a medical conference, but he booked her in too, first thing this morning."

"Scrote bag?" Vivian asked. "How charming, could you expand a little on that Harry?"

Unfortunately, Harry had just shoved another enormous piece of Danish pastry into his mouth and couldn't answer without spitting it out everywhere, so it fell to Jackson to say, "I think he's referring to Evie's boyfriend, real name Matthew Reed. From the little we saw of him on Friday evening he's not the most pleasant of individuals. He certainly didn't seem to care much about her."

"Hmm," Stanners murmured, "any background on him we need to know about?"

"Not really," Harry had swallowed his last piece of pastry and was able to talk again. "He's a rising star in the surgical world, got his name on about seventy billion papers etc. etc. but from our point of view he's just a bit of a tosser."

"Eloquent as ever Harry," Vivian sighed, "thank you for that delightful résumé."

"So why am I here?" she asked, turning towards Stanners. "This had better not be another attempt to use me as some sort of resident matchmaker. You surely can't still be thinking that you can somehow get rid of the boyfriend and wheel in one of these two instead?"

"That was his idea," Harry said, pointing his head towards Stanners, "not ours."

"Oh yes, because your ideas were so much better!" Stanners exclaimed sarcastically. "As I recall you thought breaking and entering into her home to leave chocolates or fruit was the ideal way to ingratiate yourselves."

Jackson looked at Vivian. "His idea this time," he said, nodding in Harry's direction.

"What a surprise," she replied, raising both eyes heavenwards as she did so.

"We want to know if she talks about this message to scrote face," Harry explained, "I mean Matt," he corrected when he saw the disapproval on Vivian's face.

"It's easy enough to do when she's at home or at work," Jackson explained, "we've already got listening devices all over the place. We're reading her e-mails, monitoring her internet use, controlling her phone. We know she's been googling all manner of things about the possibility of receiving text messages a long time after they were first sent. We're wondering what the implication of that is."

"So where do I fit in? Why do you need me?" Vivian queried.

"We weren't banking on her suddenly jetting off to Paris, she's supposed to be in work tomorrow, so now we've got to shadow her there. The problem is the plane," Harry explained. "All gadgets have to be switched to flight mode, there's no CCTV and we can't use listening devices. So, we need someone on that plane, sitting close by, who can record everything she says the old-fashioned way."

"Are you saying I'm old?" Vivian asked Harry, fixing him with a steely look.

"'Course not Viv," Harry replied and, completely oblivious to her glare, helped himself to yet another pastry. "These are great," he said, munching away, "you're just less likely to stand out on the plane at your age."

Jackson did his best to hide the loud guffaw he nearly let out. You could always count on Harry to just say it as it was. Vivian leaned back in her chair and crossed her arms firmly across her chest. Harry looked up and gave her one of his characteristic impish grins. Vivian shook her head at him, but Jackson noticed the affectionate smile she couldn't quite hide as she did so.

"Very well young man, talk me through what I need to do," she said.

"You won't be alone Vivian," Stanners interjected, "Jackson will also be on the plane. I want him in Paris the whole time this girl is there so he's going too."

"I am?" said Jackson, looking up. "I didn't know you wanted me there as well. You didn't ask me to go."

"I don't ask, I tell," Stanners replied, "and I'm telling you now. Harry, find them somewhere to stay."

The Gemini Connection

After just a few clicks on one of his laptops, Harry looked up and grinned at Jackson. "Just found a great place on Airbnb; Boulevard Saint-Michel, says you can see Notre-Dame out the windows. Looks like you're going to Paris mate."

Chapter 8

Stanners nearly keeled over when Harry had told him how much the expenses claim would be for a rental apartment in the centre of Paris, in the middle of August, plus business flights. "Who the hell flies business class from Heathrow to Paris?" he demanded to know. "You're only on the plane an hour!"

"Plonkers with too much money, that's who," Harry replied scornfully.

"I've never flown business class before so I shall relish it, however short the flight," Vivian said.

"Huh, well he doesn't need to go business, stick him in the cheapest seat you can find," Stanners demanded of Harry whilst pointing at Jackson.

Jackson grimaced but said nothing.

Harry busily tapped away between his two keyboards. "Shall I see if I can get him in the hold along with the luggage?" he enquired innocently of Stanners.

"Yes, if you can do that!" was the gruff reply. "What on earth are you doing with all that tapping?"

"I've just hacked into Air France's website; the flight was full in business class, so Monsieur Dubois in seat B2 has just had his booking transferred to Monday's flight by yours truly. He'll turn up this evening but, *zut alors*, his dozy secretary booked him on the wrong flight."

"Excuse me young man," Vivian exclaimed, "but why does it have to be his dozy secretary who booked him on the wrong flight? Perhaps Monsieur Dubois could have accidentally booked himself on the wrong flight."

"Nah," Harry replied, "I can tell it was his secretary, she booked it two months ago."

"How on earth do you know who booked it and when?" Stanners wanted to know.

"Err, because I can see the e-mail URL the booking was made from and then it was dead easy to geolocate it," Harry spoke slowly, further infuriating Stanners, who had not understood a word of this.

"You don't need to talk to me like I'm an idiot," Stanners barked.

"Oh, I think I do!" muttered Harry under his breath.

"What did you just say?" Stanners began but Jackson, seeing the rapidly rising tension, intervened.

He swiftly grabbed the one remaining Danish pastry off the plate and threw it at Harry as a warning shot. "Here, stick this in your mouth, it'll help you focus!"

Harry deftly caught the pastry in one hand as he continued tapping on one of the laptops with the other. "All done," he declared a few minutes later. "Miss Vivian Harding is now booked in seat B2 with Dr Evie Longshaw and tosspot across the aisle in B3 and B4 respectively. Jackson, you're at the back in steerage, next to the toilet."

The Gemini Connection

~~~~~

At 6pm that same evening Jackson was sat at Gate 73 in Heathrow's Terminal 3 waiting to board the Air France flight to Paris. Vivian was making the most of her time in the business class lounge and had not yet arrived at the gate. He had severe misgivings about this whole endeavour and had tried, and failed, to get Stanners to consider finding someone else to take his place.

Earlier in the day he had hung back as Vivian and Harry were leaving Stanners' house. "Sir, with respect, I'm not sure I'm the right man for this. Do you not think one of the guys with more undercover experience would be better? It's never really been our remit. If my path ends up crossing with Evie again, I'm not sure I can keep up the pretence of not knowing anything about her."

Stanners looked at him closely, as if scrutinising his very soul. Jackson shifted slightly from one foot to the other feeling increasingly uncomfortable with the lengthening silence. He wondered if Stanners was about to respond in his usual brusque manner, perhaps losing his temper and telling him to 'grow a pair' or something of that ilk but Stanners surprised him.

"Jackson, it's because you feel this way that I know you are the right man for the job. Trust your instincts; remember, if you are talking to her, stay close to the truth with the mundane and ordinary, just cover up the day job. We do it all day, every day, it's in our blood. You're more practised than you realise, plus you are the one with the unique connection with her thanks to your appendix, better than anything we could have engineered. Although it's a shame it wasn't Harry being put to sleep by her, preferably for a frontal lobotomy," he added.

"Talking of whom, don't you think Harry is better suited for this than me? You see how he wins Vivian over again and again; he's a natural, always chatting up the women," Jackson pleaded.

Stanners laughed with derision. "And look where it gets him! He only gets away with it with Vivian because she looks upon him as some sort of half human-half puppy hybrid she can't help but love, despite the antics. If I let Harry loose near her, he'll start yapping away at her on some obscure topic he's plucked out of thin air and before we know it the girl will be throwing herself into the Seine just to escape! Trust me, you are the right choice."

Jackson gave a little shrug of his shoulders, but Stanners continued. "This trip will probably prove to be an utter waste of our time and resources, but we can't let a potential terror suspect go off to another country without some degree of close monitoring. If you find yourself face to face with her again just be consistent with the backstory. Remember, it takes two people to make a lie work, the one who tells it and the one who believes it. So long as she believes you, you don't have to worry."

Now, waiting at the departure gate, Jackson busied himself with his computer, creating the illusion he was completely preoccupied with some work-related spreadsheets. The truth was that he had a constant flow of information streaming into a discrete hearing device in his left ear courtesy of Harry who had hacked into the various CCTV cameras throughout the airport.

"She's in Duty Free looking at perfumes now, not buying anything. She doesn't look very happy though. Scrote face is splashing out on some posh crap in the Men's Fragrance section. Won't cover up the stench of being a loser though mate!" he directed at Matt.

"You do know he can't hear you right?" Jackson hissed into his collar where a small microphone was hidden.

"Shame," Harry continued. "They're off into the business lounge now; hey there's Vivian. Blimey look at all the free food you get in there, Jackson you're really missing out."

"I'm quite happy with my Starbucks thanks," Jackson interjected. "It's like listening to a shopping channel on permanent loop with you in my ear! Just tell me what I need to know, save the descriptions of duty-free goods and food stuffs for someone who cares!"

Jackson sighed and leaned back in his seat. The last time he had been to Paris had been with Claire, six months before their intended wedding. He really had not seen it coming when she turned round after their wedding rehearsal and said she couldn't go through with it. When she finally confessed the whole sorry tale to him, something in him had died and he had vowed to never allow himself to be hurt and used like that again. It was why he was so uncomfortable with the thought of acting out a deception with Evie. The irony was not lost on him that he should be fine with the idea, he did it all the time for work. His work was similar to Harry's, but not identical. Whilst Harry was the one constantly accessing the dark corners of the virtual world, it fell to Jackson to imitate the people in them. He was adept at creating online personas and masquerading as a fellow activist or anarchist or incel, whatever was needed at the time, and was able to deftly extract information from his unwitting cyber bedfellows.

In his work world Jackson felt no qualms about what he did. He was alongside fanatics at best, sociopaths and psychopaths at worse. He got an immense amount of satisfaction when he saw meetings disrupted and plans thwarted thanks to what he and Harry did all day. But dealing with another person, face to face, was different. He had wanted to spell out to Stanners that he didn't want any woman in his life, neither his private life nor his work life, but he knew it would not have been well received. Above all, he certainly did not want to enter into any kind of relationship based on deception.

Claire had deceived him. Unbeknownst to Jackson, she had been having an affair with a married man all through the final year of their relationship, a married man who repeatedly refused to leave his wife for her. In the end she had convinced herself that announcing her own marriage would force her lover's hand, so sure was she he wouldn't want to lose her to Jackson. It was a high-risk strategy that seemed to pay off; the day before their wedding rehearsal her adored lover had appeared on her doorstep, suitcase in hand, saying he had finally left his wife for her and begging her not to go through with the wedding. Claire spared little thought for Jackson, so elated at the success of her plan was she. But her triumph was short lived. Just three short months after her cancelled wedding to Jackson the lover returned to his wife, as married lovers often do, and dropped out of Claire's life completely. She had tried to reignite her relationship with Jackson but, instead of the jovial and affable young man she had been engaged to, she found a cold, detached stranger who refused her every advance and turned her away.

"Harry to Jackson, OVER, do you read me OVER?" Harry's voice interrupted Jackson's thoughts. "Is this formal enough for you, OVER, or would you prefer me in shopping channel mode, OVER, ROGER and OUT."

"You're an idiot!" Jackson grinned as he shook his head slightly.

"Evie and Shrimp face making their way to the gate. OVER."

"Shrimp face? Is that the name for him now?" Jackson asked.

"Yeah, you should have seen how much Sushi the man put away at the help yourself buffet, I'm more a fish and chips man myself. With loads of vinegar, and salt, reckon it's because my nan was a northerner, Yorkshire born and bred, they like their chips up there –"

"For pity's sake, put a sock in it!" Jackson interrupted him with a hissed whisper, "I don't need the culinary preferences of your entire family downloaded into my brain."

"Ah, you love me though mate, don't bother to deny it," was the irrepressible reply.

"Hello again, it is you, isn't it? Mr Appendix?"

Caught completely off guard, thanks in no small part to Harry's genealogical food ramblings, Jackson looked up to see Evie standing in front of him, smiling and looking down on him.

The Gemini Connection

"I'm sorry," she said, "yet again I've forgotten your name."

"Jackson, and yes, it is me."

"I wouldn't usually approach former patients so forgive me, but I just wanted to say thank you, for getting me home on Friday. I still owe you money for the taxi, or your friend. I think one of you paid?"

"Oh, please, don't worry about it. Harry paid and he's as rich as Croesus," Jackson said and smiled slightly as he heard a "What the f…" in his earpiece from Harry.

"Well, thank you again. Are you going to Paris for work?" Evie asked but before Jackson could reply, Matt had come up alongside her.

"Who's this then?" he demanded to know.

"Oh, a friend of a friend," Evie said in reply. "He was at university with one of my flat mates, weren't you Jackson?"

Evie looked at Jackson as she said this, and her eyes were pleading with him to agree to this complete fabrication. He heard a "whoa" from Harry in his ear but kept his countenance and answered in a calm and measured way, "Yes, that's right. Hi, I'm Jackson Bridges."

As he said this, he held out his hand towards Matt who completely ignored it.

"Well, come along Evie, we have priority boarding. No need to slum it with the economy passengers," and, with no further acknowledgement of Jackson, he took Evie by the arm and swept her away.

Evie turned and looked over her shoulder at Jackson and mouthed the word *sorry* towards him.

The Gemini Connection

"Did you get all of that?" he now asked quietly of Harry.

"Yeah, what an arrogant git. But why did she lie like that?" Harry wondered.

"I have absolutely no idea," Jackson replied, "but I think we need to know."

Chapter 9

Evie wanted the ground to open up and swallow her when Matt was so rude to Jackson. As he led her away, grasping her firmly by the arm, Evie was relieved that Jackson had played along with her explanation of how she knew him.

She did not want Matt to know who Jackson was for several reasons. He certainly would have rebuked her for approaching a former patient, whatever the circumstances. For Matt didn't see patients as people, to him they were conditions and diagnoses that required his surgical skill and prowess to put right. The thought of them being actual people, with personalities and lives outside of their hospital bed, was an anathema to him. Evie talking with a living and breathing ex-patient would have filled him with abject horror and he would have viewed it as unprofessional.

But Evie had other reasons for not saying who Jackson really was. Any mention of how he and his friend had helped her on Friday night might have led to conversations with Matt she didn't want to have. She had briefly, very briefly, debated confiding in Matt about the message on her phone but had quickly dismissed the thought. It was too complicated to explain and even if she had tried to, she knew he wouldn't understand. She never talked about the person behind the mystery message with anyone – not family, not friends, not colleagues. They all knew about him of course but respected the fact that she could not bring herself to speak of him. The only person she might have shared her sorrow and pain with was her mother, but they were not close and, after her father's death, the gap between them grew even larger. Evie desperately wanted to talk to someone about the message, but there was no one she trusted enough. The irony was that the one person she would have trusted, would have trusted with her very life, was the sender of the message.

~~~~~

Vivian settled herself into her seat on the plane and made a point of studiously ignoring Jackson as he walked past her to his own seat at the back of the plane, next to the toilet as Harry had so gleefully announced. Vivian was thoroughly enjoying herself, which was more than could be said for the girl across the aisle from her. Vivian thought Evie looked pale and drawn and not at all how a young woman being whisked away to Paris by her boyfriend should look.

Like Jackson she too had an earpiece in although, much to her indignation, hers looked like a regular hearing aid. "Exactly why young man do I have to wear this when Jackson has such a discreet, state of the art, hearing device?" she had demanded to know of Harry.

The Gemini Connection

"Cutbacks," Harry had replied. "I couldn't get the guys in tech to cough up another expensive one for you. And you don't need the microphone bit, you're going to be too close to Evie to be able to use it."

Had he stopped there, Harry's explanation would have satisfied Vivian, but unfortunately, in true Harry style, he didn't. "And you're old enough to look like you might need a hearing aid," he had added unhelpfully, earning himself a cuff round the ear from Vivian.

"Right, start the recording device as soon as you taxi back from the gate," Harry was now telling Vivian. "The minute you begin take off I'll lose you."

Vivian placed what appeared to be her mobile phone on her lap and settled back into her seat. It was probably a good thing she didn't have a microphone as she would only have drawn attention to herself by telling Harry she did not need to be told, for the fourth time, to start recording at take-off. The boy really did think she was senile.

She smiled to herself. One of the few good things about getting older was that you became increasingly invisible. Nobody noticed you as a middle-aged woman going about her business the way they did when you were in your twenties or thirties. Vivian had been an active field operative in her time, something Harry and Jackson were completely unaware of. Even within the service, things remained classified between departments, and sometimes even colleagues, for years. She had loved what she did but the events of 2005, when she and Stanners had fallen foul of the lies and pretence they had built around themselves, had irrevocably damaged her. She had tried and failed to go back into the

The Gemini Connection

field, but it had no longer held the same attraction or intrigue for her, and she had become sloppy at times. Disillusioned field operatives were too much of a liability, the service had told her, and when she was offered a London-based desk job instead, she took it. She had debated leaving the service altogether but her feelings for Stanners ran too deep and she wanted to remain close to him.

The plane began to taxi back from the stand and as it did so, the cabin crew began their usual safety announcements. Vivian glanced across at Evie who was paying no attention but was instead staring blankly across her boyfriend and out of the window, her right elbow on the arm rest and her chin resting on her hand. In Vivian's opinion it was a poor show that he had not given Evie the window seat choosing instead to take it for himself. Chivalry still counted in Vivian's world and this chap clearly did not have it.

~~~~

At the back of the plane, Jackson was counting down the minutes until take-off so he could finally have a break from Harry's inexhaustible commentary. Realising the cabin crew were doing their safety checks, Harry was now reciting his own version.

"To fasten your seatbelt, you insert this there…and release it like this. Quite frankly if you don't know how to do this you shouldn't be allowed out of the house, let alone onto an aircraft. In the event of a loss of cabin pressure, please put your own oxygen mask on first and then look for the most beautiful babe near you and help her with her mask. If she has an idiot of a boyfriend with her, disable his oxygen supply at the same time. Yes, I'm talking about you Matt Reed in seat B4!"

Jackson groaned as Harry continued. "If we end up in the sea, please put your life jacket on like so. Although we might all be drowning, the cabin crew rely heavily on sale commissions to pay their bills, so we will still pass amongst you as we bob around in the English Channel with a selection of drinks, snacks, and duty-free goods. Please activate the light on your life jacket or blow into the attached whistle if you wish to purchase anything."

"Have you finished?" Jackson hissed into his collar.

"For now," was Harry's reply, "see you on the other side! Roger, over and out."

~~~~~

"No, it's too warm, take it back."

Yet again Evie wanted the ground, or in this case the emergency exit, to open up and swallow her. Who insisted on tasting the wine first on a one-hour plane journey and then refusing it? Probably the same kind of man who bought the largest and most expensive bouquet of flowers in the shop just hours before whisking you off to Paris she reflected. She had not even had time to put them in a proper vase. Instead, she had left a hurried note to her flat mates: 'Gone to Paris with Matt, all very last minute. Flowers from him, feel free to enjoy (or dump in the bin!)' and thrown them into the kitchen sink with as much water as the small sink could hold.

The Gemini Connection

Having rejected the wine, Matt had settled for a gin and tonic instead and was looking thoroughly pleased with himself. "So, what are you going to do with yourself whilst I'm working away each day?" he asked her.

"Oh, I don't know," Evie replied. "Paris in August is very hot; I may go to the Louvre or some of the churches. At least they will be cool."

"Sounds rather boring to me," Matt said tersely, "would you not rather make the most of some designer shopping? Coco Channel? Christian Dior?"

This man really does not know me, Evie thought to herself. "I'm quite happy with the clothes I have thanks," she said out loud.

"If it's money that is worrying you, I'll give you my credit card," Matt offered.

Evie sighed. "I want to see Paris again; I haven't been since I was a teenager. I can shop anywhere."

"Suit yourself," Matt retorted, "but we shall dine in style tonight. I've booked a late table at the Paris Ritz."

Of course you have, Evie thought. She would have preferred a relaxing bath followed by room service, ideally eaten in bed whilst wrapped up in a fluffy white robe. She closed her eyes and pretended to doze to avoid further conversation, completely unaware that the pleasant looking older lady across the aisle had recorded their entire conversation and also scribbled down "Paris Ritz – tonight; Louvre & churches" on a piece of paper hidden in her book just in case the recording was muffled.

Chapter 10

"Bonjour Jackson et bienvenue à Paris."

As the plane landed at Paris Charles de Gaulle airport Harry's cheery tones once again flowed into Jackson's ear.

"You're still there then!" Jackson groaned.

"Bien sûr, naturellement," came the voice in his ear. "So, I'm just downloading Viv's recording," Harry said, reverting to English. "Looks like our girl Evie said nothing of note really. Shrimp face wants her to go shopping, she wants to see things. He's taking her to the Paris Ritz tonight, what a piece of work! I'm just hacking into their CCTV cameras."

"What about their conversation there, can we listen in?" Jackson asked.

"Ce n'est pas un problème," Harry answered, "our French buddies have it all under control. They've already done their hotel room and are on their way to sort out adding a recording device to their table as we speak. Nos collègues français sont magnifiques."

"Can you talk as incessantly in French as you can in English?" Jackson wanted to know.

"Mais oui," was the cheery reply.

Vivian and Jackson settled themselves into the apartment Harry had found for them on a side street just off the Boulevard Saint-Michel. To call it compact and bijou was an understatement. The description about the view was accurate though, you could indeed see the towers of Notre-Dame from all the front facing windows because the apartment was on the fourth floor of the old building, something Harry had completely missed, along with the fact it only had one bedroom and there was no lift.

"It's a good job I do my best to stay fit," Vivian puffed as she and Jackson made their way up eight steep flights of stairs, two between each floor. "I'm going to kill Harry when we get home."

Looking quickly around the small apartment it became clear that Jackson would be spending the next few nights tossing and turning on the rather uncomfortable-looking sofa in the lounge. If Vivian needed any help dispatching Harry upon their return, he would be the first to volunteer, he thought to himself.

As Jackson set up his computers, connecting one of them directly to Harry's, Vivian realised she would have to tackle those stairs again if they were going to eat and went back out. She returned with a baguette, ham, cheese, a bottle of red wine and a couple of ripe peaches for dessert.

"Grumpy pants probably won't sign off a dinner out," she told Jackson. "He's probably still lying down in a darkened room trying to recover from how much this little jaunt has cost already!"

"Indeed," replied Jackson, "if we'd known Evie was going to leave the country 48 hours after we sent that message we would have waited. Everything was well set up back home to monitor her every conversation – at home, at work, we had eyes and ears everywhere. Now we are at real risk of her saying something vital to the boyfriend about that message and it will be in some back street of Paris and we'll miss it!"

"Well, it is what it is," Vivian said soothingly, "you can only work with what is in front of you at the time. You can't be expected to see into the future."

"Would you like to try telling Stanners that?" Jackson asked her with a quizzical look.

"Only when the flying pigs go over his office," she replied with a smile.

As the evening unfolded, both Jackson and Harry were bored rigid as they watched, and listened where possible, to Matt and Evie's first night in Paris. It was impossible to hear their conversations as they made their way through the city though they were able to watch them via the multitude of CCTV cameras dotted around the streets. However, from what they could see, it became increasingly obvious that Evie walked mostly in silence whilst Matt did all the talking.

"She doesn't look like she's going to be confiding in the boyfriend anytime soon," Jackson commented to Harry.

"Probably can't get a word in edgeways," Harry replied.

The Gemini Connection

Jackson laughed out loud. "That's rich coming from you. Right, looks like they've arrived."

Once Evie and Matt were seated at the Ritz, the two men were able to listen in again, but the entire conversation seemed to revolve around Matt and who he was hoping to meet, and therefore impress, at the conference. This was followed by a myriad of details about the paper he would be presenting and how cutting edge it was, none of which was either of interest or made any sense to Jackson and Harry. Matt had then finished the evening by encouraging Evie to use the conference's social functions to network further amongst their peers.

"There are some top cardiac anaesthetists attending," he had told her. "Try and get alongside them, drop my name in as you talk all things gas!"

"I wish someone would gas him," Harry muttered to Jackson.

Evie hardly spoke during their meal and what she did say was of little substance. There was no opening up to Matt about her own worries, no mentioning of the message she had received just two days ago. Every so often she would nod at Matt or manage a small smile, but the rest of the time she seemed distracted by her own thoughts and in a world of her own.

They hailed a cab back to their hotel and Harry quickly hacked into its two-way radio but to no avail as, once again, there was nothing much in the way of conversation between the pair. Knowing Matt and Evie's hotel room had been bugged left Jackson feeling very uneasy about how much he and Harry might continue to see and hear once they returned. Legally they were on firm ground monitoring Evie, but morally Jackson was not so comfortable, and this total invasion of her privacy did not rest easy with him. However, he need not have worried. Within half an hour of returning to their hotel Evie was curled up in bed sound asleep, or at least pretending to be.

Throughout all of Monday, Harry and Jackson followed Evie's progress on their screens as she went up to Montmartre and visited Sacré-Coeur; they watched her sip coffee in a pavement café and buy a simple lunch from a kiosk in a shady area popular with the locals. She had jumped on and off the Metro with ease and then spent her Monday afternoon wandering in the Louvre.

"All that boring art," Harry yawned, "why doesn't she go up the Eiffel Tower or something?"

"Philistine!" Jackson retorted, "I bet you wouldn't know the Mona Lisa if it hit you in the face!"

"Actually, that's my favourite pizza, but I always ask for extra pepperoni – and no mushrooms!"

"Please tell me you're joking," Jackson laughed. "And by the way, couldn't you have booked a place with two bedrooms? You try being six foot two and sleeping on a sofa that's no more than five foot long. I'm aching in places I didn't know I had!"

"Mate, you try finding somewhere in Paris, in August, with twelve hours notice. You're lucky you and Vivian didn't end up on a park bench."

"Fine, point taken," Jackson grumbled.

"Anyway, why can't you bunk up with Vivian? Or get her to take the sofa, she's short," Harry replied unhelpfully. "I bet she wouldn't mind."

"Remind me to teach you the meaning of the word chivalrous when I get back," Jackson retorted.

The Gemini Connection

"I know what chivalrous means," Harry said gleefully, "it's when a walrus gets really cold and starts to shiver. It becomes a Shiverwalrus."

"And remind me to buy you an English dictionary whilst I'm at it, you moron!" Jackson laughed.

"I'd rather have un joli morse français," Harry replied.

"And what the hell is that when it's at home?" Jackson asked.

"A lovely French walrus...obviously!"

"How on earth do you suddenly know so much French?" Jackson wanted to know.

"I've got google translate on speed dial," Harry said, and Jackson did not need to see him to know he was sitting there with his impish grin all over his face.

~~~~

Monday evening yielded no success for the team either with another interminable dinner conversation, this time with conference delegates, dominated by Matt as he preened and plumed himself like a peacock strutting its stuff. He wasn't averse to pausing every so often to flirt with the waitresses, despite Evie being right beside him.

"What does she see in him?" Jackson pondered.

"No idea mate, but she doesn't look happy, does she?" Harry replied.

Jackson leaned back in his chair and started munching on a piece of fresh baguette Vivian had just passed him after returning from another of her grocery shopping sprees. Harry was right, Evie looked deeply unhappy. Her smile didn't reach her eyes and she seemed like a shadow of the girl who had been laughing and smiling in the pub on Friday night until the moment they had let that message through and onto her phone. Given that she had been with Matt for some time, her countenance now surely had more to do with that message than her pathetic excuse of a boyfriend. Why she was with him Jackson couldn't fathom, but he was certain that the profound change in her had been caused by the message and not the behaviour of her boyfriend.

Back in London, Stanners was becoming increasingly agitated at the thought of justifying to his superiors why he had sent not just one but two of his staff to Paris for what was increasingly looking like zero gains. *If only something would give*, he thought, *something needs to happen to make this all move forward*. He was starting to think he had been right all along when he had wanted to bring this girl straight in and start questioning her. Yes, there was logic in following her for a while to see who or what she might lead them to, but this was rapidly becoming the proverbial wild goose chase and an expensive one at that.

Fortunately for Stanners, someone, somewhere, must have read his mind that evening and decided to grant his wish. For the very next day, Evie's world was shattered yet again, putting in motion the series of events that would leave them all reeling.

Chapter 11

Stanners looked incredulously at the detritus surrounding Harry. "Are you keeping the fast-food industry going single handedly?" he asked, fixing him with a hard stare. "It stinks in here!"

Harry surveyed his desk area which was littered with the assorted packaging from at least five different takeaways. "Well, I've been here since Sunday evening boss, a man's got to eat."

"He also has to shower occasionally," Stanners countered.

"Yeah, I've been washing myself down in the gents," Harry grinned.

"That explains the shower gel and towels littered all over the place in there then. Good grief boy, your mother isn't here to clean up after you now, sort this mess out," Stanners barked.

"Well, I kind of need to keep monitoring these screens until nine, that's when Jackson takes over."

"It can't come soon enough," said Stanners, wrinkling his nose and slamming his office door shut as soon as he had entered it.

The Gemini Connection

Jackson and Harry had been taking turns to do six-hour shifts monitoring Evie, having quickly realised there was little point in the pair of them doing it simultaneously. Nothing of any note had happened and the only threat to life they had uncovered was the risk of them dying from extreme boredom watching interminable footage on computer screens.

Harry looked at his watch, 8:15am, only another 45 minutes to go then he would go home, have a proper shower, and eat some decent food. At least that was his plan but, just after 9am, Stanners walked back past Harry's desk to find him fast asleep with his head on it, his forehead inches away from a wrapper that declared 'The best burger in town'. Ironically the 'r' was hidden by a fold in the paper, so it read rather differently. Stanners sighed but couldn't help thinking that the alternative wording fitted young Harry rather well.

~~~~

Evie was very hot and very tired. By early Tuesday afternoon she had walked what felt like the length and breadth of the city and, despite multiple stops for a cooling drink, wasn't sure she could go much further. She was currently sat in the Jardin du Luxembourg, resting in the shade, and watching the people around her. Couples came and went in front of her, entwined in each other's arms and oblivious to the world around them. Evie couldn't help thinking that she and Matt did not seem to be *that* sort of couple. They had been together for just over eight months, but Evie wasn't sure she even liked him very much anymore, let alone loved him.

The Gemini Connection

Whether he had changed since the first heady days of their relationship, or she simply had not noticed just how narcissistic and selfish he could be, she didn't know.

They had first met the previous November when their on-call rotas had coincided, and they had both been crash called to the A&E department one Friday evening. The patient was a young motor bike driver who had collided with a car and been flung off into the road. By the time he had arrived at the hospital he was unconscious, and his vital signs were collapsing. Evie and Matt had met at the door into the resus room but there was no time for the usual 'after you, no, after you' pleasantries. They were confronted with a white-faced junior doctor who looked completely out of her depth. "I'm so sorry," she was saying, "but I'm on my own here, I can't find my consultant and the reg is already tied up. I don't know what to do."

Several other doctors had piled into the room and one unhelpful soul started ordering head and neck X-rays and an MRI scan of the victim's brain. Matt had looked at him incredulously. "Look at his abdomen," he had shouted, "he can't go anywhere until we stabilize him. His BP is in his boots and he's losing cardiac output. He's dying from his abdomen, not his head!"

All eyes had turned to look at the young man's abdomen and saw what Matt had been the first to spot. It was slowly but surely swelling. "He's bleeding out in there, we need to get him to theatre now," Matt had demanded. "Anaesthetist, you're going to have to intubate him without knowing if his neck is broken, okay?"

The Gemini Connection

Evie had wanted to say, "No, of course it's not bloody okay. I could be about to paralyse him for life doing that!" but had to concede that in the time it would take to get his neck X-rayed he would be dead anyway.

In the operating theatre the team had raced against the clock to save the young man's life. Evie didn't often pray but she had been praying hard as she pushed the anaesthetic tube down into his trachea, having to tilt his chin, and therefore move his neck, to do so. *Oh God, please let this be okay*, she had silently prayed over and over.

Matt was scrubbed and ready to go as soon as she was done and, grabbing a scalpel, made a deep incision into the abdomen. He would worry about tidying up the cut later, time was of the essence now. At first, he could see nothing as blood had poured out through the incision obscuring everything in sight.

"Suction," Matt ordered, "now."

Eventually the horrific scene cleared enough for Matt to assess the damage.

"Got it," he had declared.

"Ruptured spleen?" Evie had asked.

"No, massive tear in the liver but I can see it and get to it. How much blood has he had so far?"

"Six units," Evie had replied, "seventh going up and there's another ten on the way."

"Right, let's get him sorted," Matt had said through gritted teeth and then saved the young man's life.

As first dates went, theirs had been wonderful. Still basking in the glow of their theatre success (and Evie's relief that subsequent X-rays showed no fractures in the patient's neck, or indeed anywhere else, much to

The Gemini Connection

everybody's surprise) they had chatted away all night. First in the restaurant Matt had taken her to, then walking along the river and then, finding November in London really is too cold to stay outside for very long, they had talked into the small hours in one of London's 24-hour coffee bars.

Matt had showered her with love and attention those first months to the extent Evie had wondered if she was indeed falling in love with him. But this wonderful, shiny new relationship was starting to tarnish as Evie began to see another, less charming side to him she didn't like so much. Once they were back in London, she would have to initiate the 'We need to talk' conversation with him. She sighed and decided that, for now, all she wanted was to get back to the hotel and have a cool shower. Matt would be tied up until at least six o'clock so she might even have time for a little nap.

~~~~~

Back in London, Harry, awake and screen watching again, had eaten two bananas, three doughnuts, and was now keeping himself amused by cracking open pistachio nuts and throwing them up in the air before trying to catch them in his mouth. He missed more times than he succeeded and the floor around his chair was covered with discarded shells and lost pistachios. Stanners came back into the office to be greeted by the sight of Harry lounging back in his chair, feet up on his desk, with his mouth open trying to catch small flying objects.

"So where are we keeping them?" he asked Harry who looked back at him with a puzzled look on his face.

The Gemini Connection

"Keeping what Sir?"

"The chimpanzees I presume you just had over for tea looking at the mess!"

Harry peered around him. "Yeah, do we have a dustpan and brush anywhere boss?"

"How on earth do I know?" Stanners bellowed. "Do I look like the char lady?"

Harry was about to make what he perceived to be a witty reply about how fetching Stanners would look in a pinny and headscarf when his attention was caught by one of the computer images.

"Hey boss, look at this," he said instead to Stanners.

Stanners peered at the screen. "Isn't that the boyfriend? What's he playing at?"

"I can't believe what I'm seeing," Harry replied.

"Where's the girl at the moment?" Stanners wanted to know.

Harry flicked his attention to another screen. "Er, just about to walk back into the hotel!"

Stanners thought for a moment. "She's going to walk in on that isn't she?"

"Yep," Harry answered, "do you think she knows?"

"No idea. Get onto Jackson, I suspect she's about to pack her bags and leave. Get him to intercept her and you? You do whatever it is you do to make sure she can't get out of Paris tonight."

Stanners and Harry continued to stare in disbelief at the screen as Jackson was given a quick update.

"You've got to be kidding me," Jackson said, "but he's a surgeon, and supposedly a good one at that. How on earth can he be doing that?"

"Beats me," Harry replied. "Do you think Evie knows?"

"I doubt it," Jackson answered. "I suspect he has managed to keep her completely in the dark. But if she doesn't know, she certainly will in a few minutes!"

Chapter 12

Evie made her way down the corridor to their hotel room fumbling in her bag for the key card. It was so hot she could feel the sweat dripping down her back. Instead of cooling her, the hotel's air-conditioning was just making her feel clammy. Finally locating her key card, she slid it into the slot and walked into the room.

"Evie, what the…?" Matt shot to his feet off the bed, desperately trying to get the tourniquet off his arm and the needle out.

Evie stared at him in abject horror, totally speechless.

"It's not what it looks like, not really," Matt was now saying.

"I think it's exactly what it looks like," Evie said, finally finding her tongue. "What the hell Matt?"

"Come on, don't get uptight, we all need our little crutches."

"Little crutches?" Evie repeated his words back to him. "How long Matt?" she asked coldly. When Matt failed to answer, she screamed at him, "How long?"

"Two years…." Matt replied, his voice tailing away.

"How have you hidden this for so long? No, don't answer that, I don't want to know."

Evie looked at the ampoules, and needles and syringes on the bed. They were clearly all standard hospital supplies. How could she have been so stupid to not spot the signs? "You've been stealing it, haven't you?"

Matt did not answer but stared at his feet.

"How could you?" She clenched her fists as he remained silent. "Matt, answer me!"

Matt finally looked up. "Please Evie, don't say anything to anyone, please," he pleaded with her.

Evie looked at him aghast. "You are kidding me? Of course, I, WE," she corrected, "need to say something."

"You can't. It will be the end of my career, you know that. I'm not the only doctor who needs a bit of therapeutic help. Loads do it, you must realise that."

Evie was shaking her head in disbelief. "No Matt, they don't. You need help, you have to tell your bosses."

"Well, I'll take you down with me. I'll say you helped supply me, that you shoot up just as much as I do, everybody knows anaesthetists act fast and loose with the controlled drugs!" he exclaimed maliciously.

"You utter bastard," Evie screamed, "you're an addict, pure and simple. I'm out of here."

She grabbed her small suitcase and began to throw her things into it, as rapidly as she could.

"Evie, no," Matt shouted, "we have to talk about this."

"No, we don't," Evie countered.

Matt grabbed her by both arms. "Don't do this to me, don't you dare do this to me."

The Gemini Connection

"Matt, you're hurting me, let go," Evie cried.

"You're not going anywhere," Matt shouted and threw her back against the wall. Evie hit it with a bang and began to sink to the floor.

"Evie, I'm sorry, I'm so sorry," Matt said in horror, attempting to help her up.

"Don't Matt, just don't," Evie said but Matt had a firm grip on her arms again. In desperation, she drew up one of her legs as hard as she could and successfully kneed him full in the groin. As Matt staggered back in agony, Evie grabbed her bag and ran from the room as fast as she could.

~~~~~

Back in London, Harry let out a loud "Whoa!" followed by, "Go Evie."

Jackson, who by now was running in the direction of Evie's hotel, had been given a running commentary on the events.

"So, Matt's a junkie, didn't see that one coming," he panted.

"Yep, better than EastEnders this is, "Harry said, earning himself a withering look from Stanners. "Right, you're just two streets away and she's come out of the hotel, slow down. Next road on your left. No, not that left, the other left!"

"How can there be another left?" Jackson puffed in exasperation.

"Well, it's my left which makes it your right. Go right, now second left, your left, you're walking straight towards her," Harry paused before saying, "And bingo, over to you mate."

Jackson attempted to slow both his pace and his breathing and feign a nonchalant air as he walked down the street. He could see Evie coming towards him looking distressed and upset and moved across the pavement to ensure she would bang into him.

"Ouch, I'm so sorry," said Evie as she hurtled straight into Jackson. Looking up, she began to apologise again but then recognized him. "You again?" she exclaimed.

"Err, yes," Jackson replied, noticing her eyes were swollen from crying, "are you okay? I hope you don't mind me saying but you look a little upset."

"Bit of an understatement if you ask me mate," he could hear Harry saying in his ear. "She looks bloody awful!"

"I'm fine," Evie initially said, but then added, "Actually no, I'm not fine, I need to get back to London. I want to go home; I can't stay here." Her words now started to come out at speed and tears began to flow from her eyes. *Get a grip*, she told herself.

"Look," Jackson said kindly, "something has clearly happened. Let's go and sit down, get your breath back and we can try and find you a flight if you need to get home that quickly."

"Good luck with that one mate," he could hear Harry saying gleefully, "I've just marked every flight to London out of Paris as full for the next 24 hours. Couldn't book one even if she wanted to."

"Or maybe Eurostar," Jackson said, checking for Harry's sake rather than Evie's that he'd shut down that route too.

The Gemini Connection

"Ain't gonna work either mate. Signaling failure in the channel tunnel, I've just stuck all the lights on red."

Of course you have, Jackson thought to himself, making sure he wasn't smiling.

Evie allowed herself to be directed to a pavement café down a small side street. "I think we should sit inside," she said to Jackson, "Matt might come looking for me."

"Matt?" Jackson enquired as they sat down, realising that as far as she was concerned, he should know nothing about him.

"My boyfriend," she replied.

"Is he a doctor too?" Jackson asked, thinking that the more he could get her to tell him now, the less risk there was he would inadvertently let something slip out later he shouldn't know.

"Yes, a surgeon," Evie looked him directly, "and I just walked in on him injecting himself with heroin."

"What?" Jackson exclaimed. "For real?"

"Yes," Evie replied, "for real."

The waitress came over before she could say anymore, and Jackson ordered two coffees.

Evie was tapping rapidly on her phone. "I can't find any flights for this evening," she exclaimed. "There must be one seat, somewhere."

"Oh no there isn't," Jackson heard Harry chortling in his ear.

"Maybe try Eurostar?" Jackson said, pretending to be helpful. "They might have some seats."

"Oh, I don't believe it," Evie said in despair, "all the current trains are delayed, and it looks like they've cancelled the later ones."

"And I'll take my bow now," Harry's dulcet tones rang once again into Jackson's ear. "We're getting Vivian out of the apartment and home; the boss wants you to offer Evie a bed for the night. Nice one boss, subtle eh? You've still got the touch with the ladies then?"

Stanners muttered something to Harry and, whilst Jackson couldn't quite make out the words, the tone left him in no doubt it was something best not repeated.

Evie downed her coffee and without thinking said, "First that message and now this, I don't think this so-called long weekend can get much worse."

Three sets of ears went into high alert. "Message?" Jackson asked her as calmly as he could.

"Oh," Evie gathered herself together too quickly for their liking, "ignore me, I'm rambling."

"Ramble away," Jackson said but the moment was lost, Evie was now looking down into her empty coffee cup.

Looking up she said, "I guess I'll just go and wait at the Gare du Nord, there's bound to be a train at some point."

Here goes nothing, Jackson thought. "Look, I know you don't really know me, but you are very welcome to come and stay in the apartment I've rented here. It's better than a hard seat in a train station," he added sensing her hesitation.

"No, I'll try and find a hotel room, I couldn't possibly put you out like that," she exclaimed.

"Well, that might be difficult in August," Jackson replied, "so my offer still stands."

Evie looked around her, she suddenly felt utterly exhausted and drained of all her strength. "Okay, thanks, that would be great," she told him.

Jackson smiled at her, "You can trust me I promise" he said, thinking he had gained her trust.

"I hope so," Evie replied but a little bead of suspicion was already beginning to form in her mind.

Chapter 13

Back in the apartment, Vivian rushed round gathering up her things and throwing Jackson's belongings both onto the bed and around the bedroom to make it look as if he had been staying there alone. She gathered up two of his computers and pushed them under the bed knowing it would seem highly suspicious to Evie to see four different computers up and running. She was about to leave the apartment altogether when she remembered her lipstick in the bathroom and ran back in to get it. She was reminded of earlier times with the service when she and Stanners had had just six minutes to vacate their supposed safe house before it was stormed, and she shuddered. They had failed to clear it properly, had missed just one thing, and the results had been devastating. Vivian shook her head at the memory, now was not the time to revisit those events. She walked quickly away from the apartment and hailed a taxi to take her to the airport. Harry had, of course, booked her onto a late evening flight by kicking somebody else off it in order to get her home. *It was amazing what that boy could do,* she now reflected.

The Gemini Connection

~~~~~

"Sorry about all these stairs," Jackson said to Evie as they made their way up to the apartment.

"Oh, don't worry," she replied. "You should see the stairs I have to go up and down at work!"

"Yeah, I only saw the inside of lifts during my sojourn there," Jackson grinned as he opened the door to the apartment. "It's a bit small, I'm afraid…" he began.

"Oh, wow, look at that view!" Evie replied before he could get any further. She moved across to the window and stared out across the rooftops of Paris.

"I'm afraid there's only one bedroom," Jackson explained, "but obviously you can have it. I'll sleep on the couch," *again* he added in his head.

Evie turned round. "Oh no, I won't hear of it. I'll be fine on the couch, you're too tall for it anyway. You've already gone above and beyond in helping me. I can't believe how I keep bumping into you. I don't think I've ever done that before, not with a single patient, at least not that I can think of. It's really quite uncanny, isn't it?" She kept her tone gentle and innocent.

Jackson coughed slightly to buy himself some time. "Yes, just one of those strange co-incidences I suppose."

"Karma," he could hear Harry saying through the earpiece still in his ear, "tell her it's karma the way you two keep meeting up."

"It's not bloody karma, you fool," Stanners was now chiding him, "that's getting what you deserve. Like the smack around the head I'm about to give you!"

The Gemini Connection

"Well, what is it if it's not karma then?" He could hear Harry asking Stanners.

"Serendipity," Stanners replied.

"Serend-what? Never heard of that. Jackson, the boss says tell her it's serenpitery!" Harry instructed.

Jackson could not take it any longer. "Excuse me one minute," he said to Evie and dived into the small bathroom. He needed to remove his earpiece if he was going to stand any chance of their surveillance of Evie not descending into a complete farce. He fished around in his washbag for the tiny magnet that would extract it for him. He was using a state-of-the-art earpiece just 2mm in length, so tiny that it was impossible to extract it from the ear canal without the aid of the magnet. Once in, it was completely invisible to the naked eye. Too small even for a battery, it was powered by an electromagnetic field generated between the piece and the induction loop he was wearing under his clothing. Stanners and Harry would still be able to hear him, but he at least would be free of their banal chat.

"I'm switching you off," he hissed at Harry, "how can I make small talk and watch myself for slip ups when you two are bickering away in my ear all the time? I'm removing the earpiece now. If you need to talk to me urgently, text me!"

He splashed his face with some cold water and was about to go back to Evie when his phone pinged. It was Harry of course, messaging him with the Zany Face emoji and the message 'Ah, but you love me mate! And the boss says he'll detach your ears from your head next time he sees you if you don't put your earpiece back in!'

The Gemini Connection

Jackson sighed and shoved the phone into his back pocket, ignoring the comment from Stanners.

"So," he said as he returned to Evie, "do you want to freshen up? Get something to eat?"

"Err," Evie was unsure what to do, but the thought of a cool shower was very appealing. "Maybe a shower if that's okay? It's so hot."

"Sure, just through there, there's some clean towels on the shelf above the sink," Jackson replied, pointing in the direction of the bathroom whilst flinging the lounge windows open to try and get a breeze through.

"Thanks," Evie gathered up her bag and went into the small bathroom. She knew she was taking a gamble, coming here, and staying with this man she hardly knew, but she had decided to trust her gut instinct on this. And her gut instinct was telling her all was not what it seemed with Jackson Bridges. She reached over and locked the bathroom door as a precaution. Turning on the shower, she stripped off her sweaty clothes and stepped under the cool water. Looking around for shower gel she was surprised to see a distinctly female, flowery scented one on the side of the shower tray. Perhaps Jackson had a girlfriend hidden away somewhere. She looked around for any other telltale feminine items but could not see any at first glance. Maybe he had just bought it for himself, she reasoned, but then it did seem strange that there was a classic men's gel on the opposite side of the shower tray too.

When Evie padded out of the bathroom twenty minutes later, already fully dressed in fresh clothes, she found Jackson sitting at his computer. "Are you in Paris for work?" she asked him.

The Gemini Connection

"Yes," Jackson had his story ready. "Yes, I am. I've been checking cyber security for one of the banks here."

"Can't you do that from London?" Evie asked.

Good point, Jackson thought to himself, but he had it covered. "Yeah, actually I do a lot of it from the home office first but then I need to do a few things using their intranet networks, so I have to be here in person for that."

Evie was nodding, and Jackson was relieved that his explanation seemed to make sense to her.

"Do you want to get something to eat?" he asked, hoping his changing of the subject wasn't too obvious. He looked at his watch, "It's 8:30 now and I know I'm hungry."

"Okay," Evie shrugged her shoulders a little. "I'm not that hungry but you need to eat. Whatever suits you?" Her last sentence was more a question than a statement.

Fifteen minutes later, they were outside on the Boulevard Saint-Michel. It was still very warm despite being evening and, as they wandered up and down past various restaurants, everywhere seemed overwhelmingly hot and crowded. Evie let out a little sigh as they looked at another menu. Jackson looked down at her. "You know what? I think we need to do this differently."

"What do you mean?" she asked.

"Come with me," was all he gave by way of explanation, but she allowed herself to be led away from the crowded street as Jackson gently steered her by the arm Matt had so forcefully grabbed earlier.

Half an hour later they were sat on a stone bench under the Quai Saint-Michel by the river. The stone towers of Notre-Dame cathedral looked down upon them from the Île de la Cité just across the water, as imposing as ever despite the fire that had done so much damage in 2019. Jackson straddled the bench and placed a baguette and various cold meats and cheeses between them along with a bottle of red wine. He had taken them to the little minimarket Vivian had been using and bought them a picnic.

"This was a much better idea," Evie said as he poured the wine into two cardboard cups, grabbed from a takeaway coffee stall as they had made their way down to the river.

"Yeah," Jackson replied, "I didn't think a stuffy restaurant was conducive to trying to relax. Would Madame like to try the wine?"

Evie started to smile and then grimaced. "Can you believe Matt insisted on trying the wine on the plane and then he actually refused it?"

"Wow," Jackson said gently. "You can tell me to mind my own business but, what is going on with him? You really walked in on him injecting heroin?"

"Yep, well diamorphine to give it its correct medical name."

"But you said he's a surgeon, how can he possibly do his job if he's a junkie?" Jackson wanted to know.

Evie sighed. "Just google 'High Functioning Addicts'; I promise you'll be shocked. You're assuming that all addicts are the same – desperate; on the streets; stealing to pay for their next fix. Imagine having access to pure morphine, an ever-ready supply of sterile needles and syringes and being an expert in injection techniques. No risk of contaminated drugs; no risk of hepatitis or

HIV. Doctors can make surprisingly good addicts – if there is such a thing."

"But surely other staff would notice if drugs kept going missing?" Jackson asked.

"In theory, but in practice it's not hard to get hold of them, especially in operating theatres where we are not always as tight as we should be counting the vials in and out of the drug cupboards. Do you know he threatened to say I helped supply him?"

Jackson let out a low whistle, "Nice guy."

"I thought he was at first…" Evie's voice tailed off.

"But now?" Jackson prompted, topping up her wine.

"Oh, I think we're over don't you," she replied.

"So, what happens next?"

"I'll have to ring Noel, my boss, in the morning. Tell him what happened and then let the consultants handle it." Evie rubbed her forehead with her hand. "I still can't quite believe it myself though. If I hadn't seen him with my own eyes, with the needle in his arm…" she shuddered.

As they were speaking Jackson was aware of his phone, on silent but repeatedly vibrating in his pocket. "Excuse me a minute," he said as he pulled it out, "but this might be work."

"Of course," Evie said and began to eat some chunks of baguette and ham.

Jackson looked at his screen, there were multiple messages from Harry, all sent rapidly within minutes of each other. He quickly scanned down them.

'The boss says hurry up and get some more wine into her, it might make her talk.'

'Ask her what she meant by 'that message' earlier today…'

'The boss says he is going to kill you for taking your earpiece out.'

Jackson let out a louder sigh than he intended to, causing Evie to look up.

"Is everything alright?" she asked. "I completely understand if you need to go and get on with work."

"Oh no, it's fine," Jackson replied, as he topped up her wine again. "Just my colleague trying to fathom out a few phone tech issues."

Evie looked straight at him. "Do you work on mobile phone security too?" she asked.

Jackson nodded his head.

"Can I ask you something?"

"Of course," Jackson tried to keep his voice calm.

"Is it possible," Evie paused, "could a message be sent, from one person to another, but then be lost somehow, like a letter in the mail, and not get delivered? But then eventually make its way to the person it was meant for? Maybe weeks or months later?" Evie was now staring at him intently and he swallowed hard before replying.

"Well, in theory it shouldn't happen, but yes, you could get some glitches between phone masts and a message could go spinning round and round in the ether. So, it would be out there, but not delivered, then it suddenly hits the right mast at the right time and bingo, it gets delivered."

His phone buzzed again and glancing down he could see yet another message from Harry which said, simply,

'What a load of crap!' It didn't matter, Evie seemed to be buying it as an explanation.

"Why do you ask?" Jackson asked while he poured her a little more wine.

"Oh, it's probably nothing. It's just I received a message last Friday," Jackson held his breath as she continued, "but it made no sense."

Jackson released his breath slowly. "No sense? You mean it wasn't in English?"

"No, no, not in that way. I could understand it perfectly."

"I knew it!" shouted Stanners, slamming his hand down so hard on Harry's desk that he would probably have deafened Jackson had he been wearing his earpiece. "She understood it, it was a coded message and she understood it. We've got her."

"So why did it not make any sense? What do you mean?" Jackson wanted to know.

"Because the person it must have come from? Well, he couldn't have sent me a message four days ago. You see, he died, two years ago. He was killed in a terrorist attack."

As Evie's voice came across the speaker Stanners and Harry stared at each other in disbelief, both clearly thinking *What have we missed?* In Paris, Jackson was thinking exactly the same. Searching around in his head for the right thing to say to Evie, he was wondering where they had failed in their due diligence.

"I'm so sorry to hear that," he began, "was it someone close to you?"

The Gemini Connection

Evie's eyes had not left his face until he asked this question but now, she turned her head away. "No, just an acquaintance really."

She was lying of course, but she knew she'd said enough for now.

Chapter 14

Harry worked through the night trawling through everything they had found out about Evie but to no avail. He could find nobody in her past or present that linked into what she had said.

Stanners was pacing the floor; a cold and icy fear had taken hold of him. It simply wasn't plausible to do the kind of background searching they did and miss things like this. They should know who Evie was referring to; this person should have come up on their radar. Was this another example of him not being on top of his game; another episode where he would look an incompetent fool in front of his superiors as he presented intelligence he believed to be complete only to find it wasn't? He almost felt relieved when Harry came into the office in the early hours of the morning, bleary eyed and disheveled, and announced he still could not fathom who Evie was talking about.

"I don't know where else to look boss," Harry said. "I've crisscrossed back and forth between everyone this girl has ever known and all the terror attacks that happened in a timeframe of around two years ago. I've worked forwards and backwards starting with her name, starting with the victim's names. I can't find a common link, nada, nothing."

Stanners looked at Harry. "You look like shit boy," he said but then added, "I imagine I do too. I'll go and get us some coffee."

Harry couldn't hide the stunned look on his face. Stanners didn't 'get' coffee, at least not for other people. He was about to make a facetious comment along the lines of whether his boss needed GPS co-ordinates in order to locate the kettle but thought better of it. Stanners looked pretty wrecked so instead he simply said, "Thanks boss," and began to message Jackson.

~~~~

Jackson had also had a sleepless night. He had tried to find out more from Evie about the sender of the message but without success. After saying it came from an acquaintance, she said little else. They had spent the rest of the evening in relative silence, eating the food he had bought and watching the Bateaux Mouches go up and down the river.

In an attempt to make her lower her guard, Jackson kept offering her more wine but, instead of making her talk more freely, Evie seemed to become increasingly sleepy and less talkative. Time ticked on and it was becoming dark. There was no street lighting where they were sat as the road was up high above them but if Jackson had been paying a little more attention, he might have noticed that Evie was not imbibing as much alcohol as he thought and was instead surreptitiously pouring most of her wine away, very gently and very quietly, onto the ground.

When they got back to the apartment, Evie had certainly appeared to be drunk. She was slurring her speech and holding onto him as they ascended the stairs, appearing to stumble at least twice so that he had to catch her to stop her from falling.

"You are my knight in shining armoury, army, amour...what is that word I'm looking floor?" she had asked as he helped her to the sofa once they had finally made it into the apartment.

"Armour," Jackson replied.

"Yesh, that's the one, knight in shinning armour," and as she said this she had reached up and put her arms around his neck and began to kiss him.

No, thought Jackson, *this wasn't right, he couldn't do this.* He gently but firmly removed her arms and looked down at her. "I think you need to get some sleep Evangeline."

Evie nodded and mumbled "okay" and with that she slumped back onto the cushions and appeared to fall promptly asleep.

For the next few hours Jackson mirrored what Harry was doing in London and went back and forth through everything they had on Evie. At one point he had all four of his computers running different searches simultaneously whilst he and Harry passed information back and forth. He was concerned that Evie might wake and hear him but every time he went to check on her, she seemed dead to the world. By 6am he was exhausted. He didn't want to appear as if he had been up all night to

The Gemini Connection

Evie, so he jumped in the shower then went to get some coffee.

Once he was out on the street, he called Harry. "What have we missed?" he asked in exasperation. "With our resources, how can we not identify who she's talking about?"

"I've no idea mate, I can't find anything. Stanners is doing his nut over this. Can't you get her to talk more? She seemed like putty in your hands last night, where did it go wrong?"

"She bypassed being tipsy and went straight to full on drunk, I couldn't get any further without raising her suspicions."

"Well, Stanners wants me to keep her in Paris with you, spend the day together. 'Wine, dine and schmooze her' were his exact words." Harry was laughing as he spoke, but Jackson cut across him.

"She is never going to buy that idea, she's not an idiot."

"Well, she agreed to spend a night in Paris with you mate, she must be a bit soft in the head to say yes to that. Now if it was me in Paris of course...."

But Jackson wasn't in the mood. "Speak later mate," he said and hung up.

~~~~

Jackson was still ruminating over how to handle the day ahead as he returned to the apartment. He expected Evie might be a little worse for wear after the previous night and perhaps embarrassed by her attempts to kiss him. He reached the final stair and started down the corridor towards the apartment, hoping his offering of a freshly ground coffee would help mollify her. As he rounded the corner, he came to a shocked standstill – the apartment door was open, fully open. Putting the coffee down, he cautiously approached the door whilst quietly calling Evie by name. There was no reply, and he felt every muscle in his body tense up.

"Evie, are you there?" he called a little louder. He was at the door now and was able to glimpse directly into the lounge. He gasped. There on the small coffee table was a woman's shower gel; some previously scrunched up, and now flattened out, toilet tissue with the clear imprint of lipstick marks on it and all four of his computers. The computers were open, facing the door, their lock screens shining out at him.

"Evie, are you here? Are you okay?" he called out again.

Just then he felt something cold and hard press into his upper back, between his shoulder blades. Someone had come up behind him.

"I have a gun, I know how to use it and I want answers," Evie's voice rang out from behind him. "Let's start with this one, shall we? Just who exactly are you Jackson Bridges, assuming that's even your real name?"

Chapter 15

In London, Harry had heard it all. "Boss, you need to get over here." He replayed the dialogue on a separate headset for Stanners to hear.

"Pull up the visuals, quickly," he now ordered Harry.

"We don't have visuals," a perplexed Harry replied.

"Why the devil not?"

"Er, I didn't think to bug where Jackson and Vivian were staying. They're kind of on our side?"

Stanners rubbed his eyes, the exhaustion of pulling an all-nighter had not been cured by endless streams of coffee. He was still as tired as ever and now jittery as well thanks to all the caffeine. "No, course not. Just so used to having eyes and ears everywhere I forget where we are sometimes."

"Occupational hazard Sir," Harry replied.

"Has he got his earpiece back in? Can we communicate with him?"

Harry spoke into his microphone device, "Can you hear me Jackson? You know the routine." The routine was to use clicks of the tongue to communicate, one click to signify yes and two clicks for no, a tried and trusted way to answer closed questions under duress. Nothing. Harry looked up at Stanners. "That's a negative Sir, he can't hear us."

~~~~

Jackson swallowed hard. In his mind he was trying to rapidly calculate the odds of Evie actually having a gun in her possession. He didn't carry one, not that he would have left it lying around the apartment if he did. And if she did have one, then it begged the question as to how she had managed to get it through airport security without being detected. There was no way she could have bought one in Paris; they'd monitored her every move. He was cursing himself for not putting his earpiece back in, he could do with a bit of help here.

"Evie," he began slowly and quietly, "you say you want answers. If you shoot me, you won't get any."

"True," she replied, "if I shoot to kill. I know my anatomy remember; I know where to aim to incapacitate you without killing you."

Jackson let out a long and deliberate sigh to buy himself more time. "Assuming that is a gun," he said.

"Are you willing to take that chance?" Evie asked.

"Yes," he answered and in one quick move he spun round, grabbed Evie's arm, and swung it above both their heads. Looking up in horror he saw that she did indeed seem to be holding a small pistol. He twisted her arm violently, making her scream out in pain, but it had the desired effect and made her drop the gun. It clattered to the floor between them but before he could get to it

Evie, now facing him, repeated the move that had worked so successfully on Matt. She drew up her right leg and kneed him with all her strength in his groin. The loud groan and exclamation of "What the f...!" as Jackson fell to the ground had Harry and Stanners looking at each other in horror. What the hell was happening over there?

In the fallout from her actions Evie had grabbed the small gun again and now had it pointed at Jackson's head. "Don't move," she screamed at him.

Through the fog of his pain, *this was almost as bad as his appendix* he thought, Jackson began to focus on the weapon she was holding virtually in his face and a realisation dawned.

"Why? What are you going to do? Light me up and smoke me?" He could now see clearly what she was holding in her hand and he fixed her with a long, cold stare. "Evie, it's a cigarette lighter. You couldn't shoot me even if you wanted to!"

~~~~~

"So where did you get it from?" Jackson had recovered enough to get himself up off the floor and extract the replica gun from her hand. He was surprised Evie hadn't bolted from the apartment. Instead, she seemed to have frozen in front of him but, as he spoke, she came out of her trance and began to move slowly round the room, aiming for the open door behind her. Jackson dived for the door and slammed it shut before she could reach it, locked it, and put the key in his pocket. "Don't even think about it," he said with a grimace as his groin continued to throb, that girl could really pack a punch when she needed to.

Evie finally found her voice. "My question still stands, who are you?"

"I think I could ask the same of you," Jackson pointed at the coffee table, "what exactly were you looking for? And why did you feel the need to hold me at gunpoint? Sorry, cigarette lighter point," he added sarcastically.

"Don't you dare laugh at me, you have no idea what I've gone through these last few days." Evie was struggling not to break down.

Jackson tilted his head to one side and continued to look at her.

"Oh, but you do know, don't you?" she guessed correctly.

"Yes, of course I do. But I'm not here to harm you, I promise. You can trust me."

Evie burst out laughing. "Trust you? Trust you?? You have lied about everything, who you are, what you are, why you're here. I'd rather put my trust in a brood of vipers than trust you!"

Jackson shrugged his shoulders a little. "I think we both have questions of each other, don't you? Perhaps you would like to tell me why you're getting coded messages from a known terrorist hot spot?"

Quick as a flash Evie responded, "Messages? In the plural? I only received one."

Jackson winced; he was giving too much away, making stupid mistakes. Not trusting her to be out of his sight, he took her arm and propelled her into the bathroom. Once there he retrieved his earpiece and flicked it into his ear canal.

"I can hear you now," he directed at Stanners and Harry. "Give me an update from your end. Where do we go from here?"

"Blimey mate, what happened?" Harry wanted to know. "We thought she'd taken you out there for a moment."

"I'm fine, just a good job I don't want to be a father any time soon!"

Harry and Stanners looked at each other and winced in unison.

"Bring her in under the 2001 Anti-terrorism Act," Stanners said. "This young lady has a lot of questions to answer, starting with who sent those messages."

"I'm not sure using public transport is ideal Sir, I don't think I can trust her not to cause chaos on the way."

"I'll send a secure car, sit tight until then," Stanners ordered.

Jackson pulled Evie back into the lounge.

"What happens now?" she asked angrily.

"You have a lot of questions to answer," he said.

"And you don't?" Evie demanded to know.

"I'm not the one receiving suspicious messages," he replied.

"And I'm not the one stalking a woman through London and Paris!" was her quick response.

Jackson looked at her. "Okay, touché. We both have some explaining to do. But you're going first."

Evie sat down on the sofa. "Looks like you're in for a long wait then, because I'm not explaining anything until you do."

~~~~

The Gemini Connection

An hour later they were still sat staring at each other in silence and Jackson was beginning to realise they had under-estimated this girl. He was also increasingly concerned that any element of vulnerability in her he could capitalise on would soon be lost, replaced by the steely resolve that she clearly possessed. By the time he got her back to London it could prove impossible to extract any information from her and, contrary to the plot of many a B-rated movie, they wouldn't torture it out of her.

He leaned forward in his chair. "I'm going to make us some coffee. I would appreciate it if you didn't stab me, set fire to me, or otherwise incapacitate me as I do so. Agreed?"

Evie looked up at him, she didn't speak but gave a slight nod of her head. Even so he didn't take his eyes off her as he backed into the kitchenette area of the room and made a cafetière of coffee.

Handing her a mug, he said, "Okay, you get to ask questions first but on my terms. I'll only give you yes or no answers."

Evie took a sip of the hot coffee, she was tired, so very tired. It was an effort to keep up her act of cold calmness. She had put herself in work mode, but the reality was that inside her head she was running through a million scenarios. Who was this man? Would he help her or was he planning to kill her? And the messages, more than one, she now knew. How had he got them? And who was he talking to when he said, 'I can hear you now'. And what had happened to the woman who had clearly been here in this apartment until very recently given the lipstick smudged tissue in the bin? With horror another thought struck her, was he a psychopathic killer and she his next victim?

"Is Jackson Bridges your real name?" she now asked of him.

"Yes."

"Are you going to kill me?"

"No."

"Have you been following me?"

"Yes."

"Are you some sort of undercover guy?"

Jackson swallowed hard. "Yes."

"MI5?"

Jackson heard Stanners murmur through his earpiece, "She's already guessed, you might as well tell her."

"Yes."

"And they can hear this conversation?"

"Yes."

"Were there other messages meant for me that you somehow intercepted?"

"Yes."

"Are you going to show them to me?"

"Keep your powder dry on that one for now," Stanners instructed him.

"No."

Evie paused. "What do you want from me?" she finally asked.

"That's not a question I can answer with yes or no, is it?" Jackson replied.

Evie looked away and took another sip of her coffee. "I guess not."

"Okay, my turn now." Jackson said. "You received a text message on Friday night that shocked you, didn't you?"

"Yes."

"Do you know who sent it?"

Evie shrugged a little, "Yes."

"Did you understand it?"

"Yes."

"So, you know how to break its code?"

Evie turned her head back towards him and looked him fully in the face. "No."

"No?" Jackson repeated.

"No, next question?"

"Don't mess with me Evie, was the message written in code?"

"No!" she now said loudly.

Jackson sat back in his chair; he was baffled. "Evie, I've seen the message, it was indecipherable. I repeat, was it written in code?"

Evie looked down at her hands and was surprised to see they were not shaking despite the adrenaline coursing through her veins. She looked Jackson directly in the eye. "The message is not in code; it is in another language."

Jackson heard a "What the…" from Harry in his ear followed by, "No, it isn't. We ran it against every language and dialect known to man. What the hell is she talking about?"

"My colleagues want to know what the hell you are talking about. And so do I," Jackson now said to Evie.

"Cryptophasia," Evie answered.

"Sorry, crypto-what?" Jackson had never heard the term.

"I imagine your colleagues are already googling it."

Jackson could already hear the exclamations from Harry. "Mate, you're not going to believe this...."

As he heard Harry's explanation, Jackson looked at Evie with incredulity.

"The secret language of..." he began to say to her.

"Twins," Evie finished his sentence.

Chapter 16

Jackson stared at Evie in disbelief. "You don't have a twin."

Evie looked straight back at him. "I think I would know whether or not I had a twin brother, don't you?"

"Evie, we ran extensive background checks on you, you are an only child."

"For a service that has intelligence as its tagline, you don't seem to possess very much." Evie held his gaze, "How can you have missed something as fundamental as this?"

~~~~

In London, Stanners and Harry were asking each other the same question as Evie.

"How can we have missed something as basic as that Sir?" Harry exclaimed.

"You tell me, you two are the muppets who were meant to find out everything about her!"

The Gemini Connection

"Maybe she's lying," Harry replied, "she's clearly a bit nuts, she did threaten Jackson with a gun, even if it wasn't real."

"I don't know," Stanners looked thoughtful, "as lies goes it is a bizarre one, plus she would know we could easily disprove it. Something somewhere isn't sitting right about this. Do some digging."

~~~~~

Jackson was wishing he had had more than a few minutes of snatched sleep the night before. He was struggling to understand what Evie was telling him. Clearly, she had not fallen for his role of saviour; she had had him pegged as undercover all along. He wasn't a gambling man but if he was, he would have bet his money on the message sender being an ex-lover not a supposedly non-existent twin brother.

"Evie," he began again, "there is no twin brother. Please, stop lying."

Evie quickly opened her phone and thrust it in his face. "Then who is this?" she demanded furiously.

Jackson looked and saw a photo of Evie with a young man about her age. They were in a restaurant with a group of people, both smiling at the camera.

"Evie, with respect, that could be anyone, and we have already accessed all your photos, you must have only just put that one on. I don't recognise it."

"Oh, for pity's sake, look at me. I'm three years younger, my hair's a completely different length."

Jackson sighed. "That doesn't mean you haven't added it recently."

The Gemini Connection

"Well, I think the fact the photo is logged with a date is a bit of a giveaway, don't you?"

Jackson looked more closely; it was indeed dated three years ago.

He took her phone. "Can I look through your photos?"

"I thought you already had," Evie replied sarcastically.

"Well, yeah, we have but are there more with this guy in?"

"If you mean Michael, then yes. There are more photos of Michael, my twin brother."

Jackson winced as he scrolled through. Most of the photos he recognised from their files on Evie but there were a good handful he had never seen before. And they all had the man she had just named as Michael in them.

"It still could be anyone in these photos," he began.

Evie could feel the anger rising in her, she snatched back her phone and quickly pulled something else up on the screen. "Then read this and tell me I'm making all this up."

Jackson looked at what she was showing him. It was an online obituary for a Dr Michael Longshaw, son of Dr Edward and Professor Susan Longshaw, twin brother of Dr Evangeline Longshaw and alongside it a photograph of the family. There was no doubt that this was the same man as in Evie's photos. Jackson scanned the obituary, 'Dr Michael Longshaw was killed in 2020 in Kabul, Afghanistan, when militants attacked the university he was visiting as a guest lecturer.'

"He was training in orthopaedics; he was out there as part of an initiative by the Red Cross. A six-month voluntary role working alongside Afghan trauma surgeons. He was killed three days before he was due home…." Evie's voice was breaking, "it was in all the papers, I'm not lying Jackson."

"No," he conceded, "I don't think you are."

He went over to his computers and typed Michael's name into all of them. Nothing came up, no obituary, no press articles. This wasn't a simple case of shoddy work on their part, something sinister was going on and he started to panic. He pulled his audio device out from under his T-shirt and off his neck, dropped it on the floor and smashed it with his foot. He used the magnet to retrieve his earpiece and did the same with it, then turned to Evie.

"Come on."

She shook her head at first. "Where?"

"We need an internet café, let's go."

"I don't understand," Evie replied, "why?"

"I want to see what happens when I search on a public computer. I need a new phone too!"

Thirty minutes later Jackson had dumped his old phone, bought himself several cheap, new ones and found the internet café where he and Evie were now ensconced. He typed her brother's name in to the search engine and a flood of articles appeared.

"It's me," he was already talking to Harry using one of the new phones, "she's telling the truth. When I search on my computers, nothing. Use a public one, bingo. He exists, something or someone has been interfering with our searches."

"I know mate, Stanners has already had me ringing up half the Red Cross, the story checks out. But when I

The Gemini Connection

search for it on our systems? There's nothing. Oh, and the boss wants to know what that awful crunching noise was, I'm guessing you've ditched your audio? We lost you shortly after Evie said she wasn't lying."

"Yep, and my mobile. I don't know what the hell is going on here but I'm not bringing Evie back yet. I'll check in with you, but you'll have to wait for my calls. I have a bad feeling that this is an inside job."

"The boss agrees, wants me to go mole hunting! Mate, take care, okay?"

"Yeah, you too." And with this, Jackson pulled the SIM out of the burner phone and dropped it into the remnants of his coffee.

~~~~

Stanners was frantic. Harry's attempts to explain the how and why of what had happened only frustrated him further.

"You see boss, it looks like someone has been in our computer system and set up an entry in the access system to deny all traffic from certain IP sites, specifically to us. I'm just looking at the building configuration they used, and they've done all sorts to the fixed-up protocols and access lists. Then they've managed to reconfigure the pdm locations and the inside-outside interface, the static one of course…"

"Oh, of course," the sarcasm dripped out of Stanner's voice, "for the sake of my sanity can you please, just explain it in English and preferably using words of one syllable."

The Gemini Connection

Harry sighed. "Basically someone has got into our computer system and made sure that we'd never find Evie's brother. They've rerouted our searches so that whenever our online searches should have landed on something about him; a school record, a press article, or a social media account, they got there first and deleted it from our search findings. And it happened in nanoseconds, not real time, so we didn't notice anything."

Stanners looked bewildered as Harry continued. "Whoever did this knew it would be a gargantuan task to erase all on-line records of a Michael Longshaw to stop them appearing in searches, impossible in fact. So, they've focused on the searchers instead, us, and have been able to keep a step ahead of us."

Stanners still looked utterly confused.

"Right," Harry said, "imagine someone has decided they don't want you to know about the existence of coffee. It would be impossible to rid the world of its entire coffee supply to stop you finding out about it, but what if they could bug you so that they know whenever you are about to see some in a shop or a café?"

Stanners looked at him. "Why on earth would they want to do that?"

Harry clenched his teeth. "Sir, it's a metaphor."

"I'm surprised you know what a metaphor is."

"I'm not a complete idiot!" Harry exclaimed.

"Hmm, that's debatable at times."

Harry grimaced at him. "May I continue?"

Stanners nodded, "Okay, you don't want me to know about the existence of coffee. Continue."

The Gemini Connection

Harry let out an exasperated sigh. "Every time they know you are about to go into a shop or café where you'll see coffee, they get there first and remove it. Then they see you head to pick up a magazine with an advert for coffee in it, so they quickly rip the page out before you get a chance to see it. They are controlling what you see in those places; they're not doing anything about the actual existence of coffee. Whoever did this knew we would only do searches on Evie on our inhouse computers, not our private phones or home laptops, and they've been able to access them and control what we find. Whoever did this, it's someone who knows how we work."

Stanners was nodding slowly. "And this mysterious 'someone', can we find out who it is?"

"Yep, I can find who, when and where now I know what's happened."

"Well do it, now!" Stanners demanded impatiently.

"Okay, keep your hair on. I need to get into the configurations and..."

Stanners interrupted him before he could get any further in his explanation. "Spare me the jargon, just do it. And less of the rude comments. At least my hair has seen a comb, which is more than can be said for yours, you look like you've been through the proverbial hedge!"

Harry grinned up at him; his mop of blonde hair was tousled and sticking up from where he kept running his hands through it. "You know I did get pulled through a hedge backwards once Boss. Was at the after-after-party of my uni rugby club Christmas do and I'd been dared to leap over it, the hedge that is not the rugby club. I was blindfolded with a can of lager in each hand. Didn't get my launch right and ended up in the hedge rather than over it so Taylor and Phipps had to pull me out of it. Didn't let go of my lager though!"

"What on earth are you talking about?" Stanners was beginning to wonder if he was having some kind of psychedelic nightmare, in fact he rather hoped he was because then none of this would be real.

"How I got pulled through a hedge backwards, for real?" *Good grief,* thought Harry, *why were old people so dense?* Fortunately, he didn't have time to say this out loud because just then his computer began to churn out data.

"Right my lovely, let's see what you've got for me," Harry said to it.

"Are you actually talking to your computer now?" Stanners wanted to know.

"Yep," Harry's fingers were flying over the keyboard at lightning speed, "helps us communicate with each other."

Stanners stared at him in disbelief, then began pacing up and down just behind Harry's chair. "Come on, come on. Who's our mole? Who's done this?"

Knowing Stanners' penchant for paper copies of everything, Harry was jotting down information as he found it. Stanners could see that he had written down 'own home x 7, office x 19' and a series of dates. Harry wrote a large 'WHO?' on his note pad but then stopped, his pen hovering over the blank line where he should be writing the answer. He swivelled in his chair and turned to look up at Stanners who was leaning over him, desperation in his face.

The Gemini Connection

"Well? Do we know who it is?" he demanded of Harry.

"Er, yes Sir, we do."

"Well? Don't keep me in suspense boy. Who's our mole? Who's hacked into our computer system and done this?"

"Well, the thing is Sir," Harry couldn't stop a little gulp escaping before he continued. "The thing is Sir, apparently it's you!"

Chapter 17

"So, what happens next?" Evie asked Jackson.

They were still sat in the Parisian internet café and were on their second round of coffee.

"Honestly? I'm not sure. Someone worked damn hard to make sure we didn't find out you had a twin brother and until I know more, I'm not sure who we can trust."

"We?" Evie exclaimed. "I don't trust you let alone anyone else, there is no we!"

"Fair enough," Jackson replied, "but tell me, when did you have me pegged as undercover? And what was with all the 'I'm so drunk, I want to kiss you' routine last night?"

"I was testing you I guess." Evie broke off and looked into the distance. *Was it even worth trying to hide anything anymore?* she wondered. She shifted her gaze back to Jackson.

"Obviously your appendix was real, nobody could have faked that. And when you and your supposed mate, by the way I'm guessing that Harry is another MI5 guy?" Evie didn't wait for a reply. "Anyway, when you two were in the pub last Friday night that seemed plausible. I could even buy you being at the airport on Sunday as coincidence, but appearing outside my hotel after that episode with Matt? I mean, really?" She paused to laugh. "You might as well have been wearing a badge with 'I'm following you' written on it! And then I started to put two and two together. That message came through on Friday night in the pub, I go outside in a state and suddenly you and your friend appear. You were watching me, weren't you? You wanted to see what I would do when that message came through?"

Jackson winced at her accurate appraisal of all that had happened.

"I thought you guys were supposed to be the *crème de la crème* of the spy world," she continued, "did you really expect me to just fall into your arms as you plied me with wine and then tell you my life history? What kind of undercover agent are you? Other than a useless one, that much is obvious!" Evie finally paused for breath.

Jackson felt a fool for ever thinking she had fallen for their plan. "I usually work undercover in the cyber world," he began, "I can't tell you much more than that but yeah, I did tell my boss I didn't think I was the right man for the job!"

"Clearly," Evie replied sardonically.

Jackson ignored her acerbic comment and carried on. "But he figured I had the perfect route in thanks to you anaesthetising me. That was the one true coincidence, you'd come onto our radar just as I got sick."

The Gemini Connection

A thought suddenly struck Evie. "Matt's not in on this as well, is he? Was his drug taking just a ruse to make me walk out on him?"

Jackson shook his head. "Oh no, he managed that all on his own I'm afraid. We had cameras in your hotel room, Harry saw what he was doing. We just used it to our advantage."

Evie looked at him coldly. "You monsters," she finally said, "you just sat playing with our lives. What else have you sat and watched? No, don't answer that, I really don't want to know."

"We didn't have a camera in your bathroom for what it's worth."

If that was meant to appease Evie it didn't work. "Am I supposed to thank you for that?"

"Guess not...." Jackson's voice tailed off.

"The drunken routine?" he now remembered, "what was with that? Why didn't you just cut and run if you knew I wasn't who I said I was?"

"I wanted to know why you were trying to get me drunk. There's usually only one reason a man does that with a woman, but you dropped yourself right in it when you didn't return my kisses. If you weren't plying me with alcohol to try and get me into bed then you clearly had another motive, probably to get me to talk. Oh, and as we're in France, do you want to know what your *pièce de la rèsistance* was? Saying 'you need to get some sleep Evangeline.' I never use Evangeline; in fact, I hate it. I'm always Evie to everyone, so how could you know my full name?"

"Lucky guess?" Evie continued to stare at him without answering. "So, when you asked me if text messages could get lost, and then gave me that vague response to my question about who sent it," he said instead, "you were playing me all along, weren't you?"

"Of course I was. I knew there had to be a connection between you suddenly appearing everywhere and me receiving that message. Then when I saw you, up all night, bashing away on all those computers you just confirmed my suspicions."

"I was so convinced you were sound asleep; I must have checked at least half a dozen times."

"Jackson," Evie said his name slowly to imply she was clearly dealing with an idiot. "I put people to sleep for a living. Did you not think I might be capable of doing a remarkably good impression of being asleep myself?"

She held his gaze and Jackson had to admit to himself that she had done a far better job than he had when it came to fooling each other.

"So, who is she?" Evie asked.

"Sorry, what?" Jackson asked, genuinely not understanding.

"Girly shower gel, lipstick smudged tissue in the bin. There was clearly a woman in the apartment before you took me there, so who was she? And where is she now?"

"She's a colleague too, she was watching you on the plane over here."

"Not your lover then?"

Jackson burst out laughing. "She's nearly twice my age, so no!"

"And the fake gun?" he asked. "Where did you find that little gem?"

The Gemini Connection

"In a drawer in the kitchen when I was turning the place upside down whilst you were out," Evie replied. "I figured it would do the job."

"So why did you stay to confront me?" Jackson wanted to know. "You must have known you were taking a big risk there. Even if you are surprisingly good with your right knee!" he added.

Evie shrugged her shoulders. "I would say I'm sorry about that, but under the circumstances I'm not!"

"Don't worry, it's right up there with my burst appendix in the 'pain that will haunt me for the rest of my life' category. Anyway, answer my question, why did you stay?"

"Because I want to find my brother," Evie replied, "and from where I'm sitting, I think you are my only chance of doing that."

~~~~

In London Stanners was staring at Harry. "Given the rapidity with which you just told me I'm the culprit I'm guessing you realise it wasn't me, despite my home and office computers being implicated as the source."

"With respect boss, I'd be surprised if you can get a toaster to work let alone hack into a computer system. If this was you, you've done an incredible job of bluffing your supposed ignorance and I'm not buying it. Goodness knows who did this though, I bet it's one of our recent post grad intakes. They'll have been groomed at university, come in right under our noses and done this. This is the future boss; this is what we will be up against. But who are they? Oh, good grief boss, the list is endless, we haven't got a clue."

"Not necessarily," Stanners mused, "sometimes the answer lies in the past, not the future."

Harry was about to ask Stanners to explain himself but was distracted by Vivian coming into the office. "How was Paris Viv?" he asked.

"Bit hot and too short. Did you have to pull me out quite so suddenly?" she asked.

"I'm afraid so," Stanners replied.

"Why?"

Harry opened his mouth to start explaining but from the look on Stanners' face decided he should shut it again. For reasons he couldn't yet fathom, Stanners clearly wanted Vivian left out of the loop.

"There's been developments I'm not at liberty to discuss at present, Mr Rivers my office please."

Harry was confused, Stanners never used their surnames. In fact, he rarely used any names at all for him and Jackson other than 'idiot' and 'you, my office now' when he wanted their attention. Thrown by Stanners' formality he did as he was told and followed him into his office.

"I want you to get yourself to Paris, take false passports and documents for you, Jackson and the girl. Stay put until you hear from me. I need to sort this mess out before we do anything else."

"Sir," Harry began, "don't you think we should be running this past the big bosses? Going rogue when we don't know what we're dealing with doesn't sound like the best plan. What if this Evie has a whole terror

The Gemini Connection

network just waiting to greet us? They might be the ones who got into our computers pretending to be you."

"That's not what's happened," Stanners replied.

"You can't know that Sir. This is all a bit crazy; go and hide out in Paris; wait for my call. And how can you know what did and didn't happen?"

"Harry, just do it will you? I think I'd know if half of Al Qaeda had been traipsing through my house and using my computers. As your boss, I'm ordering you to do this. And I'm asking you to trust me. I will sort this."

Harry stared at Stanners, he looked utterly wretched, and Harry suspected it was not just from a lack of sleep. "You already know who did this, don't you?"

Stanners looked past Harry to the office beyond. "I will explain in time, but please don't ask me anymore."

Harry sighed. "I don't like this boss, but okay, I'm going. I'll go and get some passports sorted."

As soon as Harry had gone, Stanners went out into the office. "Vivian...."

Vivian looked up; she already knew what he was going to say. Her days of being the invisible one in the office were over.

"Oh Vivian, what have you done?" Stanners asked.

Chapter 18

"It didn't take you long to work it out William," Vivian said to Stanners, "but I suppose the moment you heard someone had accessed the servers from your own home there wasn't going to be a long list of suspects. I did think you might at least consider one of the boys as the culprit but obviously not."

Stanners looked at her with a mixture of both anger and pity. "It could only be you. Who else knows all my passwords and can pretend to be me at the drop of a hat? I'm guessing you are behind all the other things that have been happening. Disappearing e-mails, misplaced intelligence documents?"

Vivian looked at him. "Of course."

"Are you not going to deny anything?" Stanners asked.

"Would there be any point? It would only delay the inevitable," she replied.

"Which is what precisely?"

Vivian sighed. "My suspension and subsequent arrest of course."

"Oh Viv, why did you do this?"

The Gemini Connection

"Do you really need to ask? You know why, you ruined my life. I wanted you to finish your career known only as the pathetic man who screwed up his final years in the job because he refused to move with the times. I wanted you named and shamed, remembered only for your ineptitude."

"You still hate me that much? After all these years? You hid it so well." Stanners shook his head in bewilderment.

"The fact you didn't want to see it helped enormously but then, you never wanted to face anything connected to what happened to David, least of all the fact that you killed him."

"I didn't kill him! How can you think that? He was killed by the lowlife scum who found that photo."

"The photo you should have found when you swept the room," Vivian cried.

"The photo that should never have been there in the first place," Stanners replied softly.

~~~~

"Viv, we need to get out, our cover's been blown!" Vivian could still remember the panic in Stanners' voice when he ran into their hotel room in Cairo.

It was 2005 and, in the aftermath of the London bombings, Vivian and Stanners were two of a small number of agents tasked with infiltrating the social lives of a group of overseas businessmen based in the capital and suspected of being the financial support behind the attacks. Posing as man and wife they had been successful, thanks in no small part to Vivian's skill at

The Gemini Connection

befriending the wives of the group. With an English father and a Jordanian mother, Vivian was able to move easily between western and middle eastern cultures, an asset not lost on MI5 when they first recruited her. Together, she and Stanners were so successful making inroads into the group that in November of that year they were invited to join two of the couples on a trip to Egypt.

Staying in one of the most luxurious hotels Cairo had to offer, Stanners and Vivian had kept up their persona of a married couple in private as well as in public, despite the fact Vivian was engaged. Her fiancé was a university lecturer and blissfully unaware of the true nature of her job. He knew she worked within MI5; indeed, he had been vetted by them when Vivian first began dating him as all partners were, but he had accepted her story of working purely in administration at face value. It was perfectly plausible, and he had no reason to doubt it. When she was in Egypt, he believed her to be in Edinburgh at a conference with colleagues. *If only she had been,* Vivian had thought a million times since his death.

In Cairo a dangerous game had unfolded. Stanners was no longer sure if they were the hunter or the hunted as a terrifying game of bluff and double bluff unfolded. As he tried to find out more about the financial transactions of the two men, they in turn offered him a chance to join them in an undisclosed venture they promised would make him rich. Tensions rose as both parties tried to ascertain where the others' loyalties lay until that fateful day when Stanners' phone pinged with the message from HQ. What would appear to others to be an innocuous message from a friend, 'How's Cairo?

Bet it's very hot there!' was the pre-arranged signal to get out fast.

When Stanners ran into the room shouting at Vivian to get out, they had just minutes to remove everything important and disappear.

"You do the bathroom and sitting area, I'll do the bedroom," Stanners ordered.

Less than ten minutes later two armed men arrived in the room, but Stanners and Vivian had gone. Even so the men turned the room upside down, right down to ripping the sheets off the bed and pulling the mattress off the bed frame.

As they were driven away at high speed to a military airfield, Vivian turned to Stanners. "Can I have my photo?"

Stanners looked at her blankly. "What photo?"

Cold fear swept through Vivian. "The photo from under the mattress, the photo of me and David."

Stanners shook his head very slowly. "We don't bring personal things. Viv, please tell me you didn't."

Tears began to run down Vivian's cheeks, she could only nod in reply.

"It will be fine," Stanners tried to reassure her, his arm round her shoulders. "Even if our cover is blown, they won't be interested in him."

But even as he said it, he felt a deep feeling of unease spreading up from the pit of his stomach. A feeling of unease that was justified when just three days later David McDonald, Vivian's fiancé, was shot dead outside his home by a masked gunman. The photo had been placed in his jacket pocket by the assailant. The official story released to the press was that David was killed when he disturbed burglars as he returned home. Behind closed doors they knew he had been deliberately targeted, as Vivian's fiancé, to send a message. Stanners and Vivian had operated with fake identities and documents but that didn't extend to the people connected to them in real life. The line between their real and false lives was meant to remain strong and unbroken. There was never any overlap between your two lives unless you caused one, say by carrying a photo from your real life into your false one affording others an opportunity to wreak revenge.

"You killed him!" Vivian was now screaming at Stanners in the office. "When you left that photo behind, you signed his death warrant. You destroyed my life and I'll never forgive you."

"Vivian, why did you take the photo with you? Why? Yes, I should have checked under the mattress, but I had no reason to. There isn't a day goes by I don't think about it, I'll never forgive myself."

Vivian sobbed uncontrollably, "I still miss him William, I miss him every single day. I hate you; I have to hate you. It's the only way I can cope."

"But you haven't coped, have you?" Stanners gently chided, "not at all. And I didn't even notice. I'm so sorry Viv, so very, very sorry."

Vivian collapsed onto the floor sobbing violently. Stanners dropped to the floor beside her and gathered her into his arms.

"I hate you, I hate you," Vivian kept saying over and over, but she allowed herself to be held as Stanners rocked her back and forth in his arms, soothing her with gentle shooshes as if she were a small child, until her crying eventually abated and her emotions were finally spent.

Chapter 19

When Stanners told Jackson he was sending a secure car to Paris to bring him and Evie back to London he hadn't intended for Harry to be the driver but, after the revelations about a resurrected twin brother, not to mention the computer sabotage and Vivian's role in it all, he needed to buy himself some time. He decided it was better to keep things between him and the two lads for now at least; going to his superiors would set off a chain of events where Vivian was concerned that he wasn't sure he wanted to start.

"How did you do it Viv?" he asked her when a degree of calm had finally fallen on them both. "I didn't understand a word of what Harry said you'd done to the computers. Mind you I never understand a word he says at the best of times!" he added in an attempt at a little humour.

Vivian looked at him and managed a weak smile. "It took me a long time to assimilate everything I needed to know but, between night classes in computing, YouTube and watching over the boys' shoulders, I got there. Getting to grips with coding was the hardest part." She paused, it was almost a relief to be telling him, she didn't care anymore how much he knew. "I'd already tried to do it a couple of times before. Tried to make it look like you fouled things up, but I never succeeded until now. Then I did," she said simply.

"Then you did," Stanners repeated her words. "Were you acting alone Vivian? I need to know. I've got two of my men caught up in this and a girl who may, or may not, be a terrorist holed up in Paris with one of them. I'm sure neither of us want Jackson or Harry to become the next David, killed to send us a message." Stanners didn't say this with malice; he was taking a gamble that Vivian's affection for the pair was genuine and would make her tell him the truth.

"No," she replied, "of course there's nobody else. This was personal, not political. I was going to sit back and watch you fall as everybody blamed you for not finding vital information. I thought it would give me closure. But now…." She shrugged her shoulders as she spoke, "but now I'm wondering if it was really worth it."

The pair of them were still sat on his office floor, her head resting on his shoulder with his arms wrapped around her, when Stanners heard Harry coming back into the main office. "Stay here," he said to Vivian as he got up and went out to talk with him. *How on earth was he going to clear this up?* he wondered, as he began to give Harry a list of instructions.

~~~~

In Paris, Jackson was trying to decide if it was wise to go back to the apartment. It was probably safer to lie low, at least until he had spoken to Harry again. He looked across at Evie who was getting her phone out of her bag. He reached across and took it from her, switching it off in the process.

"What are you doing?" she cried. "I need to phone my boss, have you forgotten what happened with Matt? I must speak to Noel. What if Matt tries to spin his own version of events and implicates me?"

"Evie, you have bigger problems than that at the moment. Work will have to wait. You can't use your phone, not for now at least. We might not have been the only ones monitoring it."

"I just want to go home, preferably today."

"You can't, not yet. And certainly not on your own."

"I'm more than capable of getting a flight or train home, I don't need you to hold my hand!" she retorted.

Jackson sighed. "Evie, let me be a little bit clearer. Right now? You are a terror suspect, not a tourist. You're not going anywhere without me, and you'll go back to London when I say, in handcuffs if necessary."

Evie stared at him then buried her head in her hands. "I'm not a terrorist, my brother is not a terrorist. For pity's sake he was killed by terrorists."

"But apparently he's not dead, is he?" Jackson replied. "He, or someone pretending to be him, is running around sending you messages in some bizarre language that apparently only you and him understand. It's not looking great from my end Evie."

Evie looked up at him, she was exhausted to the point of not knowing what day it was anymore. "Less than a week ago I was just living my life," she began. "I've spent two years grieving my brother, my twin, my soul mate. Then suddenly I get a text message, apparently from him, saying he wants to come home, back from the dead. Oh, and then my wastrel boyfriend turns out to have a drug problem I hadn't even noticed. And you? Under your guise of pretending to help me, you turn out to be a complete psycho who is in fact stalking me. Can you even begin to comprehend what I'm going through right now? Why I just want to go home and pretend none of this is happening?" She choked back a sob and dropped her head back into her hands.

"Evie," Jackson said more gently, leaning in towards her. "Everything you just said is true. Well, not the part about me being a psycho. Yes, I lied but think about it. If I was intending to harm you, I would have done it by now, I've had ample opportunity. But you do have a heck of a lot of questions to answer and it may not seem it right now, but I'm one of the good guys. If you are as innocent as you claim, then there is nothing to be gained from holding back."

Evie looked up at him again and Jackson could tell she was weighing up what he had just said. "You might want to consider the fact that if we have been able to find you and follow you because of those messages, so might other people," he ventured. "And they won't be the good guys," he finished.

Evie nodded her head a little, she could see some sense in what he said.

"Come on, let's go for a walk, clear our heads. I need to call Harry again and I don't want to do that here."

"Okay," Evie acquiesced and followed him out onto the pavement. It was now gone ten in the morning and the day was heating up fast. Jackson guided them through the tourist crowds and back down towards the river, close to where they had been sat just the night before. He fished out another of the new phones and dialled Harry's number.

"Yo, hello."

Jackson felt strangely comforted by Harry's familiar tone as he answered his phone. "Hi, what's happening? The boss said he was sending a car to collect us."

"Mais oui, c'est moi," Harry replied, with a hint of glee. "I'm driving to the tunnel as we speak, just on the outskirts of Folkestone."

"What? What do you mean it's you?"

"I've really no idea what's going on mate. The mole? Who erased all existence of this twin brother? Supposedly it was Stanners who got into the computers but honestly, the man can barely boil a kettle, there's no way on earth it was him. But I reckon he knows who it was, told me to stop asking questions and that he would sort it, whatever that means. Oh, and something is really up with Vivian, when I went back into the office she was sat on the floor in his office!"

None of this made much sense to Jackson.

"Anyway," Harry was still talking, "the boss wants you to use different passports and stuff for now. Got them with me. Should be with you in about three to four hours; where shall I meet you? Somewhere I can easily find you I reckon, how about by the Eiffel Tower?"

"Oh yeah," Jackson replied sarcastically, "that fits well with keeping out of public places and not drawing attention to ourselves. Why don't I just go up it and fly a banner from the top with 'Welcome to Paris Harry' on it whilst I'm at it?"

"Well, give me a road name or something smart arse," Harry quipped.

"I can't at the moment, I don't have a map to hand."

"How about Disneyland then?" asked Harry.

In Jackson's mind the thought of Harry let loose in Disneyland was only marginally less frightening than unearthing a terrorist cell.

"I take it you're joking?" he asked.

"Of course I am! Look ring me in three hours on the number I'm about to give you, I'm ditching my phone before I leave England. Find a place in Paris and tell me where to rendezvous. Hey, see what I did there? Not even using Google translate for that one, I'm nearly fluent!"

"Yeah, keep telling yourself that, you idiot," Jackson was smiling as he pulled a pen from his jeans pocket and wrote the number down on his forearm. "Just behave yourself when you get here."

"Hey, I'm not the one with a pretty girl on his arm," was the quick reply.

Jackson looked over to where Evie was standing, just out of earshot. She suddenly looked very vulnerable to him and a world apart from the feisty young woman who had cornered him in the apartment just a few hours ago.

"Frankly Harry," he now said, "I was right all along when I told Stanners to send someone else. So far, I think all I've managed to do is completely alienate her."

"Want me to work my charms on her when I get there?" Harry asked.

"Absolutely not and if you value your manhood, you won't even think about it. She has a mean knee kick, trust me on that one!"

The Gemini Connection

Harry winced. "Understood. Right, I'm at the tunnel check-in. But one last thing, Jackson?"

"Yes?"

"Are you sure we can't fit in a little detour? I'd love to meet Mickey Mouse!"

Jackson groaned, "Well he probably doesn't want to meet you, you lunatic!" he declared down the phone and hung up without waiting for an answer.

Seeing him end the call, Evie walked back up to him. "What now?" she asked.

"We sit tight and wait for our ride. Are you hungry?"

Evie shook her head. "Not really."

"You ought to have something. Come on, let's grab a croissant or something and then we need to talk. You can explain this secret language thing to me but before that I need to know exactly what that message said. You must see that by not telling me I must assume you have things to hide?"

Evie had already reached her decision; she had watched Jackson on the phone with Harry and gone over the last few days in her head. She had contemplated trying to run off, but she doubted she could outrun him. Even if she did, it would only be a matter of time before he caught up with her again, either here or in London. She was going to have to trust him; she couldn't see any other viable options.

She looked up at him. "The message said 'Hello Evie, it's me. I'm alive and I want to come home. This message will start to make it happen. I love you, Michael.'"

The Gemini Connection

Chapter 20

"This message will start to make it happen?" Jackson repeated back to her. "Are you sure he said that?"

Evie nodded. "I'm positive. I think he knew his message would be intercepted. In fact, I think that's exactly what he wanted." She paused. "I want to find my brother Jackson and you've already admitted there was more than one message from him. I need to see the rest; I can't help him, and I can't help you, if you don't let me see them. You keep telling me to trust you, but what about you? I had your life literally in my hands a few weeks ago; I think it's time for you to trust me again, don't you?"

Jackson sighed. "The thing is Evie, if I show you the other messages, I only have your word for it that you are telling me the truth about what they say. I have no other way of checking them which makes it a very high-risk strategy."

They were making their way down the street to where Jackson had spied a large map of the city on a the side of a bus shelter. He needed to find somewhere, ideally to the north of the city, to meet up with Harry.

"True I guess," Evie replied, "but what would I gain from hiding the truth?"

"Well, you tell me. Let's say you are part of some terrorist cell, and the messages are instructions about a pending attack in the UK. You would hardly spell that out to me, would you?"

Now it was Evie's turn to sigh. "Think about it. If that really was the case, why am I still here with you? I'd hardly have to rely on some bargain basement version of James Bond to get messages to and from my supposed terror group. Believe me, if I could think of a way to contact my brother without your help, you wouldn't see me for the dust."

Jackson stopped walking and turned to face her. "Bargain basement James Bond? Not quite the image I was hoping to cultivate." Placing a hand on each of her shoulders he looked down at her. "So, what is it going to take to call a truce between us?"

Evie shrugged, in part to dislodge his hands. "Well, you could let me phone my boss for starters. I shall have no job to go back to at this rate thanks to Matt. And you." she added.

"Hey, don't lump me in with him," Jackson exclaimed. "He deceived you for months and months."

"Oh, and you only deceived me for a few days. Is that supposed to be better?"

"Well, I at least was doing it for a higher cause, it's my job."

Evie burst out laughing. "A higher cause? Which movie did you pinch that line from?"

"None that I know of, I just thought it sounded good." He paused before adding, "That's the first time I've seen you laugh since Friday night, it suits you."

Evie's face instantly clouded over. "I was laughing at you, not with you. If you didn't realise that then you're a bigger idiot than I thought."

Jackson wasn't going to rise to the bait. "If you think I'm an idiot just wait until Harry gets here!"

Evie rolled her eyes heavenwards. "Can't wait," she said through gritted teeth.

~~~~

Stanners had made his decision, turning Vivian over to the relevant authorities was not an option for him. They would have to go down together but he was going to do his level best to make it as painless as possible. He would need to throw away the rule book and simultaneously keep them just the right side of the law, not an easy combination.

He knew he had the reputation for being completely clueless on anything and everything computer related, a reputation that was also well deserved. He needed to use this now, to somehow convince his superiors that in trying to do clever things outside of his expertise, he had managed to accidentally mess up their entire computer system and then present them with the evidence to back that up. Unfortunately, he had no possible chance of doing that alone. He didn't know how to access the system in the first place, let alone get into it to lay a breadcrumb trail that would make him look like a stupid, but innocent, idiot rather than a traitor. Vivian on the other hand, she had done it once, he was sure she could do it again.

~~~~~

"That's a good rendezvous point," Jackson said, pointing to a spot on the large map of Paris. "The Bichat-Claude Bernard hospital in the 18th arrondissement."

"Why a hospital?" Evie asked.

"Easy for Harry to find, lots of people and vehicles coming and going. It's about four miles from here, bit of a long walk but we haven't got much else to do."

They set off in silence until Jackson said, "Tell me more about this crypto thing, the secret language you claim to speak."

"I don't claim to speak it, Michael and I do speak it. And it's cryptophasia, from the Greek."

"Sorry, ancient Greek isn't my thing," Jackson replied.

"Crypto means secret and phasia means speech, so literally secret speech. It's something a lot of twins do but Michael and I took it to a whole new level."

"In what way?" Jackson asked.

"Most twins who do this just have a unique spoken language that's quite basic and they grow out of it. Our language? It grew with us, becoming ever more complicated. Then we composed a written version which we invented from scratch. So, our names for example. Michael became "Clocal" and written as "Clcl". Evie became "Leenie" but written as "Ln". We took the vowels out of the nicknames we had called each other from our early days."

"Why those names?"

"I called him Clocal from the "col" sound at the end of Michael. And neither of us were ever going to be able to say Evangeline for a long time, his first name for me was Leenie. Then we just took it further and further, inventing our own words for things. Cat became nud, dog became stan, but we took the vowels out when we wrote them down."

Jackson was visualising the first message in his mind; he remembered it ending Clcl and having Ln near the beginning. "How on earth did you manage to form an entire language though?"

"Oh, mixture of parental neglect, a series of nannies and two very precocious children I suppose," Evie sighed. "We rarely saw our parents which, where my father was concerned, was a good thing."

Jackson refrained from asking her what she meant by her last comment, fearing that if he interrupted her, she might shut down and so he continued to listen in silence.

"First and foremost, they were married to their jobs," Evie was saying. "The nannies never lasted long I'm afraid because we refused to have anything to do with them. We weren't naughty as such, just locked in our own little world that nobody else was allowed to enter. I think we bored our nannies into leaving. I remember on one occasion, nanny number three or four took us to the zoo. Michael and I spent the whole time gabbling away in our language, completely ignoring her. When we got to the lion pen, I was genuinely captivated by them and for just one moment I let my guard down and said how incredible they were in normal English. The nanny was so overjoyed, I think she thought it was a breakthrough moment between her and us, but it wasn't of course."

Evie broke off and paused. "If only we'd realised," she finally said.

"Realised what?" Jackson asked.

"Realised that, if only we had let them, the nannies might have given us some of the love we were so desperate for from our parents. I can't even remember the name of the one who took us to the zoo."

"So, you didn't see much of your mother and father growing up?"

"Not really, even on family holidays nanny went too. Do you know when we flew, my parents would book themselves into business class and we would be in economy with whoever the current nanny was. They didn't even want us with them on the flight."

Jackson couldn't help smiling. "Sounds a bit like my flight here on Sunday. My boss would happily have strapped me to the plane's undercarriage to save money if he thought he could get away with it."

Evie let out a little laugh. "I'd have paid good money to see that!"

"So, did you and Michael remain close?"

"Oh of course, but my parents became increasingly frustrated with us and before we knew it, we were packed off to separate boarding schools. We were only seven years old."

"You went to Roedean," Jackson remembered.

"How do you…" Evie began to ask, "oh, of course you know which school I went to. But it's okay, you were only 'doing your job' and after all, it is for a 'higher cause'." She mimicked his earlier words but this time with a hint of a smile on her face.

Jackson gave a little shrug. "Would it help if I said sorry?" Without waiting for a reply, he continued. "I don't know where your brother went though, in fact I know very little about him."

"Oundle, he went to Oundle school. But those were our secondary schools, our parents sent us off to two different primary boarding schools in Sussex first. I don't think we ever forgave them."

"That's tough, really tough."

"Yep, but that was when our secret language came into its own. We used to write to each other all the time, good old-fashioned pen and paper letters, and we kept adding more and more words, challenging each other as to who could come up with the most bizarre. The irony is they separated us to stop us using our language and it made us more reliant on it than ever."

"We figured all the vowels had been removed when we first got the messages," Jackson said. "No wonder we couldn't work out the original words though, they don't exist."

"Correction," Evie said, "they do exist, but only in my world."

"But what about the numbers? They all had various numbers in them."

"Nothing more than punctuation marks. When we were writing letters, we had to have ways of breaking up words and sentences so we would just insert any number at random. Sometimes a five, other times, oh I don't know, 347. No rhyme or reason, there's no hidden meaning to the numbers."

The Gemini Connection

"Clever," Jackson said. "It certainly had us foxed. So, when you received that first message, you knew instantly who had written it."

"It was from Clcl, Clocal. Except he died two years ago Jackson. That's why I fell apart in the pub on Friday night."

"And why, when I said 'You look like you've seen a ghost', you said 'I think I have'," Jackson now realised.

"I just can't get my head round any of this but please, show me his other messages," Evie pleaded.

Jackson nodded slowly. "I need to check in with my boss first. I hope you can understand that. Harry is bringing a bunch of new phones and laptops with him but, until then, we need to wait. I haven't got a clue what is going on back in the office. I can't risk contacting anyone there until I know more, Harry will bring me up to speed. Talking of whom, time to tell him where to pick us up from," said Jackson as he pulled out yet another phone and dialled the new number Harry had given him.

~~~~

An hour later Harry pulled up outside the outpatient department of the Parisian hospital where Jackson and Evie were waiting.

"Come on," Jackson said to her, "he's here."

Evie was taken aback. "Not exactly an Aston Martin, is it?" she said looking at the ordinary family car that had pulled up.

Jackson laughed. "Only in Bond films I'm afraid. In real life we prefer to try and blend in." He opened the front passenger door, in theory for Evie to get in, but seeing the debris scattered over the seat he thought better of it. "You might prefer to sit in the back," he said turning to Evie.

Peering over his shoulder she could see a young man she recognised from the previous Friday. "Hiya," he said, "I'm Harry and absolutely nothing he's told you about me is true!"

Evie managed a small smile. "Well, I would say 'Hi, I'm Evie' but you already know that."

"Yeah, true. Hi mate," he now directed at Jackson, "are you getting in or not?"

"Not until I clear this lot!" was the exasperated reply as Jackson swept away coffee cups, chocolate wrappers, empty crisp packets, and various discarded bits of food. "Feel free to use a bin once in a while, they're an amazing invention, been around for some time now."

"Had to eat on the hoof mate," Harry said cheerily "haven't had a decent meal since I don't know when. Too busy running around saving your hide. Haven't slept much either," he continued and deliberately swerved the car a little as he set off as proof, "but reckon I'm safe to drive."

"Behave yourself!" Jackson chided him. "So, what about our stuff in the apartment? My computers are still in there."

"Stanners gave me a list of instructions as long as your arm, the first of which was not to go back there. We're sending the cleaners in."

In the back of the car Evie let out a little gasp. "Is someone dead in there?"

Harry and Jackson looked at each other in bewilderment.

The Gemini Connection

"I might not speak spy, but I know 'the cleaners' means people who go into places after murders to dispose of the bodies and erase any evidence," she cried.

"Err, no. In this case I literally mean cleaners," Harry explained. "Two women supplied courtesy of our French colleagues who will go in with buckets and mops under the pretence of cleaning and get your stuff out. We'll be able to grab it back later. Mind you, from what I heard, they might find a bit of Jacky-boy's anatomy on the floor too!" He chuckled, referring to the kick in the groin she had given Jackson earlier. "How are you feeling now mate? Voice still stuck at soprano level?"

Jackson looked at him. "Really? You're going to do this now? Just get us home."

"We're not going home," Harry said.

"What?" said Jackson and Evie virtually in unison.

"Second order from the boss, don't come back until he says so. We're disappearing into the abyss for a while, perhaps never to return." Harry gave a sinister laugh for added effect.

Evie, uninitiated in Harry's humour, was terrified. "Stop the car, I'm not going anywhere with you two."

When Harry made no attempt to slow down her panic only grew. "STOP THE CAR!" She was screaming now and tugging at the door handle.

Harry pulled over into a lay-by concerned that Evie was about to throw herself from a moving car. As soon as he had done so she flew out of the car. Jackson, who had exited the car just as quickly, caught up with her and grabbed her by both arms.

"Evie, calm down. For heaven's sake, why are you screaming? What's the matter?"

The Gemini Connection

"You're going to kill me, aren't you? We're not going home, talking about cleaners, the abyss…all this 'you can trust me' … it's all an act, isn't it? Let me go!"

Evie struggled to free herself, but Jackson was not going to risk any more injuries to himself. He pulled her tightly into him to limit the amount of room she had to manoeuvre.

"Nobody is going to kill you Evie, I promise. Harry just has a rather unique sense of humour at times."

Evie was sobbing now, long hard sobs she had been trying to keep in for days. The combination of sleep deprivation, stress and lack of food were taking their toll. Jackson's face started to swim before her eyes as everything in her field of vision began to go black. "I'm going to faint," she managed to whisper before slumping down.

Jackson swiftly lifted her up and bundled her back into the car, getting in beside her this time. He cradled her head in his lap and stroked her hair, pulling it back off her face as she started to come round.

"Bit hysterical, isn't she? Is she always like this?" Harry queried.

"Just tone the humour down a bit mate, she's been through a lot these last few days. She's allowed to be on edge."

As Harry started the car again and headed back onto the main road he glanced at Jackson in the rear-view mirror. Was it his imagination or was Jackson being just a little over-attentive? Evie was starting to sit up but still looked dazed and afraid.

The Gemini Connection

"It's okay," Jackson said to her, "I promise it's all going to be okay." He kept his arm around her shoulders, expecting her to shrug it off but she didn't.

"So, where are we going?" Jackson now asked Harry.

"To the mountains. Stanners has a place in the French Alps. Who knew eh? Says he never goes there; can't say I'm surprised. Could you imagine him skiing? Bellowing every time he fell over; his voice alone could set off an avalanche. Anyway, Les Contamines is the village, going to be a long drive I'm afraid. He wants us to hole up there, get Evie to read all the messages and then report back to him. Sorry if I frightened you Evie, I'll try and tone down the humour a bit."

"I'll believe that when I see it!" Jackson retorted. "So, you'll get your wish," he looked at Evie. "You can read all the messages."

"And you will help me find him?" Evie asked.

Jackson nodded. "We all want to find him."

Harry glanced at them in the rear-view mirror. As soon as he was able, he would need to tell Jackson that they did indeed need to find Michael, but there would be no welcome home party for him, no loving reunion with his sister. Because Harry had done a lot of digging that morning and, if Michael turned out to be who he thought he was, it would probably be best for everybody if he came home in a body bag.

Chapter 21

The sound of Harry's gentle snores filled the car as they drove on through the night. Jackson, now the one behind the wheel, was grateful for the quiet after what had already proved to be a trying journey. They had nearly 400 miles to cover from Paris to Les Contamines, a tiny hamlet in the French Alps, and he wanted to get them there as soon as possible.

They were now in a French car after a carefully co-ordinated swap en-route 100 miles south of Paris. Harry had detoured down a country road where a French colleague was waiting for them with both their new car and Jackson's and Evie's belongings from the Paris apartment. The car Harry had arrived in would be taken back to England that night along with three passengers, two men and a woman, carrying passports in Jackson's, Evie's and Harry's names. With a link now established between Evie and the messages, and too many unanswered questions, Stanners wanted a false trail laid. It also bought him some time to deal with the fallout from Vivian's actions without Jackson and Harry noticing something was amiss.

The Gemini Connection

Jackson had a sense of foreboding about the next few days, fuelled in part by the feeling Evie was going to prove tricky to handle. Harry had not helped the situation having managed to antagonise her further with his joking. During the car swap, Evie had asked again to phone her boss, Noel, back in London. This time Jackson relented and handed her a burner phone.

"Don't say you are still in France," he instructed her. "Say you are on your way home but need some time off after everything that happened in Paris."

"It's not as simple as that," Evie replied, "he's bound to want to see me, in person, to talk about Matt. I'm not supposed to be back in work until Saturday but if he thinks I'm back in London he'll want to see me sooner than that."

"Well, do your best. Say you've gone to stay with a friend or something."

Evie moved away from the two men to make the call and was taken aback to see them follow her. "Can I at least have some privacy?" she asked.

"Sorry," Jackson replied, "but we need to hear everything you say. Officially you are still a terrorist suspect, we can't let you go wandering off into the woods to make phone calls."

"Urgh, fine," said Evie in exasperation, "this is like living in a police state."

Jackson stared at her. he didn't need to say anything, his expression alone said, *you can argue all you like but you're playing by my rules.* Evie turned her back on the pair of them to show her annoyance.

"Does she think we can't hear her if she has her back to us?" Harry asked Jackson with a quizzical look.

The Gemini Connection

Hearing him, Evie slowly turned back round and glared at him. She realised she didn't know Noel's number by heart, who needed to remember numbers when they were all stored on your phone? She said as much to Jackson, but he refused to hand her own phone back to her. "Do you know the main hospital number?" he asked her.

Evie nodded.

"Contact him via the hospital switchboard then, I'm sure that's possible."

She sighed, gave them both another glare and dialled the hospital. When finally connected and able to talk to Noel, Evie was horrified by what she heard. As the two men heard her side of the conversation, it was crystal clear that Matt had framed her as the drug addict who had been stealing supplies from the hospital to feed her habit.

"Suspended? Noel, you know me, you know I would never do that," Evie was crying, "I walked in on him injecting, he begged me to keep it quiet, then attacked me. I ended up on my own in Paris..." As she said this Jackson shot her a warning look, a look which clearly said, *don't say too much.*

"I can't come in," she continued, "I'm not in London. I'm with a friend in Manchester for a few days. I needed space to clear my head away from Matt. So, what happens now?" Listening in silence the colour drained out of Evie's face. "Okay," she finally said, "until then. Bye."

She ended the call and unleashed her anger on the two men. "I've been suspended. Did you hear that? Suspended! If you," she jabbed a finger at Jackson, "had let me phone this morning, when I wanted to, this might not have happened. But now," she flung her arms up in the air, "Matt got there first. And now he's portraying me as the addict, and he's flounced in to work today looking as right as rain whilst I'm missing in action. Which makes me look even more guilty! What gives you the right to mess with my life like this?"

"Uh oh, she's getting hysterical again," Harry muttered to Jackson. "Watch out for fainting episode number two any moment now."

"Why don't you just shut up, you stupid little man," Evie shouted at Harry. "You're just as bad as him!" She pointed at Jackson.

"Hey, I'm not little," Harry defended himself. "I might not be as tall as giant Jackson here, but I've got a few good inches on you Miss."

Jackson stared at Harry in disbelief. "Really? You have a problem with the 'little' but not the 'stupid'?"

"I was building up to that," Harry retorted, but now he couldn't think of anything to say. Instead, he resorted to sticking his tongue out at Evie.

"How old are you?" she cried. "Six? Is sticking your tongue out part of MI5 training? I bet you terrify our enemies with that. Good grief, if the safety of our country is in your hands, kill me now."

"Oh, believe me, that can be arranged," Harry shot back. "How would you like to be dispatched? Shot? Poisoned? We have 24-hour access to 'Assassins-Are-Us-Dot-Com', all it takes is one call!"

"And exactly where did MI5 dredge you up from? 'Rent a Spy'?" Evie threw back at him.

The Gemini Connection

"Enough!" Jackson's roar stopped them both in their tracks.

"Evie, I'm sorry about your job but there's nothing we can do about it right now. And you," he said to Harry, "grow up! We're all tired, we're all hungry and like it or not we're all stuck with each other for the foreseeable future. Now get in the car, the pair of you. And give me the keys, I'm driving!"

They made their way back to the car in silence although Evie was sure she heard Harry mutter 'she started it!' under his breath. They had driven for another hour or so in silence before finally stopping at a motorway service area to eat. Harry was in heaven as he loaded up his tray with two main courses (unable to decide between a chicken dish and a burger with frites, he decided to have both) and various desserts.

"Is he really going to eat all that?" Evie enquired of Jackson.

"Oh yes," Jackson replied, "and knowing him, he'll probably go back for more."

"I never leave the table wanting," Harry interjected hearing their comments.

"True," retorted Jackson, "and even then, you go back on the off chance there's anything left! I dread to think of the carnage you could cause at an 'All You Can Eat Buffet', bankrupt the restaurant probably."

Evie let out a small laugh; her own tray only had a small salad on it.

"May I suggest you eat a bit more than that?" said Jackson, proffering a generously filled baguette to her. "I think you need a proper meal."

She shrugged her shoulders. "Who made you the doctor?" she asked, but she took the baguette from him and threw in a small apple tart for good measure.

"Happy now?" she enquired in a sweetly sarcastic voice.

"Indeed, I am," Jackson agreed, pleased to see her at least smiling a little.

Harry watched this little scene with amusement. Other than Vivian, Harry couldn't recall the last time he had seen Jackson talking with a woman and it was quite a revelation to him.

Once seated together at a table in the corner, Evie was warned not to talk about anything connected to Michael or his messages in such a public place.

"We still operate a 'the walls have ears' policy," Jackson told her.

"Daft expression though," Harry said with a grin. "Imagine a wall with ears all over it, weird! And if it didn't have mouths to repeat what it heard it wouldn't matter anyway! So, we should say 'we operate the walls have ears and a mouth policy' if you think about it."

Evie looked at Jackson. "Is he always like this?"

Jackson nodded. "I'm afraid so."

And he was right, Harry was only just warming to his topic. "And imagine if they had eyes as well! Walls with ears, eyes, and mouths. Now that would be very creepy...."

He had to pause to take another mouthful of food and Jackson used the brief interlude to tell Evie, "Harry here is quite a clever chap though I admit he disguises it well. I think of him as a pet, if I make sure he's fed and watered at least twice a day and gets plenty of exercise, he's pretty easy to look after!"

Evie laughed. "I'll take your word for it on that one."

Harry grinned at them both. "Ah, but you love me mate!"

"And you'll hear that a lot too," Jackson warned Evie jokingly.

~~~~

Driving through the night, calm had descended after the frayed nerves of earlier. Evie was asleep in the passenger seat, her jacket bunched up to make a pillow and wedged behind her head. Harry, still snoring away, was lolling in the back seat.

Jackson knew Harry came across as an idiot, but he hoped Evie would realise his buffoonery hid a solid heart. When Jackson was jilted, it had been Harry who had propped him up, listening to him and drinking beer with him for four nights in a row as the shock washed over Jackson again and again. With the honeymoon cancelled, Harry booked them a five-day break in Benidorm instead, (Benidorm – Jackson had been horrified!) but to his surprise, they had had a good time. Even if Harry did manage to fall into the hotel swimming pool fully clothed late one night after too many tequila shots. Jackson had had to fish him out, not because he was drowning but because he refused to get out.

"It's lovely in here mate, very refreshing," he had kept calling at the top of his voice whilst the occupants of at least three nearby rooms shouted at him to shut up.

The Gemini Connection

Despite the fact Harry's behaviour could be irrepressible at times he had kept Jackson sane when Claire jilted him, something Jackson would never forget.

~~~~~

When Evie woke up the next day, she couldn't remember where she was initially. They had arrived at the chalet in Les Contamines in the early hours of Wednesday morning and, after some difficulty locating the key (Stanners had told Harry the cleaning lady in the village still went in weekly and would have one, which she did, although she was not best pleased to be woken at 3am by him hammering her door down to collect it) the three of them had fallen into their respective beds.

Evie glanced at her watch; it was already nearly 10am. She was still in the same clothes she had arrived in but at least she had her small suitcase again. Hopefully she could shower and change later but all she wanted for now was to see the rest of Michael's messages. She made her way down to the kitchen to find Jackson already there, seated at the table, a computer open in front of him.

"Morning," he said, looking up and leaning back in his chair. "There's coffee in the pot and I've got us some supplies. Croissant?"

Evie took one off the plate he offered her and poured herself a mug of coffee. She sat down opposite Jackson and only then did she realise how spectacular the view through the window behind him was.

"Wow, the mountains," she exclaimed.

The Gemini Connection

Jackson looked over his right shoulder. "I know, beautiful view." He turned back to face Evie and a look of horror swept over his face. "Which is more than can be said for that!"

Evie turned and followed his gaze to see Harry, stark naked, wandering into the kitchen.

"Morning," he said, seemingly unaware of their stares.

"There are no words," Evie groaned.

"Mate, clothes? Clothes would be useful here!" Jackson admonished him.

Harry looked down at himself. "Oh yeah, right. Let me just get some coffee first."

Jackson grabbed a tea towel lying on the table and threw it at Harry. "For pity's sake, at least cover your crown jewels!"

Harry deftly caught the small towel. "Not sure this will be big enough, but I'll do my best."

"Harry?" Evie directed her gaze at him and said sweetly, "I'm a doctor, I've seen it all. Trust me, in your case that towel is more than big enough."

Jackson nearly choked on his mouthful of coffee. *Touché* he thought, *had Harry finally met his match?* Harry just grinned and, deeming himself to now be 'dressed', came and joined them at the table.

"Sorry Evie," Jackson said, "nobody needs to see that first thing in the morning."

Evie grimaced and wrinkled her nose. "Just remind me not to use that towel on any dishes!" She now looked directly at Jackson. "Can I see my messages? You promised."

Jackson nodded slowly, "I know."

The Gemini Connection

He turned his computer round to face Evie, *here goes nothing,* he thought to himself.

Evie looked at the screen and blanched. There were two messages, both longer than the first. And both clearly from Michael. She read them, quickly at first and then again more slowly but struggled to fully understand them. She had promised Jackson she would not lie about their contents but, now she had seen them, the time had come to decide, was she going to keep that promise?

Chapter 22

Evie rested her forehead against the wall as the hot water from the shower streamed over her head and down her body. She had managed to persuade Jackson and Harry to let her get her head together before fully translating the messages into English for them and wished the tension in her body could drain away as easily as the water. She had not understood parts of the messages, but she was sure neither of them had believed her when she had said as much. But she had been telling the truth, she needed to remember how she and Michael had invented new words during their school days of letter writing before she could make proper sense of the messages.

"I'm not sure about some of the words in them," she had told them. "The gist of this one is saying he wants to come home, a bit like the first one, and wants to see me. The second one..." Evie paused. "I think he might be saying where he is but I'm not sure."

Jackson had been studying her carefully. "That is probably the most critical part of all three messages – where he is – yet you can't read it, that's a bit of a coincidence isn't it? Don't even think about trying to go alone on this."

Evie glared at him. "I'm telling the truth; I can't unpick some of the words."

Jackson's gut instinct was that she was being honest, at least for now. "So how did you invent new words?" he asked her instead.

"When we wrote our letters to each other, we needed to be able to invent more and more words. Not seeing each other face to face meant we couldn't just keep making them up the way we had at home. So, it was something like we changed each letter of the original word to the following fifth one in the alphabet if we were writing on a Monday but the twelfth if it was Tuesday. And it varied with the month too." She looked up to find Jackson and Harry staring at her blankly.

"Good grief, couldn't you have just used Egyptian hieroglyphics or ancient Sanskrit instead?" Jackson asked. "You know, something really simple!"

Evie pulled a face at him. "Of course not, then others could have deciphered it."

"Err, I was being sarcastic," he replied.

"I know," Evie quipped, "so was I, two can play at that game!"

Now, alone with her thoughts in the shower, Evie wondered how it was even remotely possible that her beloved twin brother, who she had always thought she knew better than herself, could have done this. Why had he covered up his own death and put her through so much pain in the process?

Down in the kitchen Jackson was admonishing Harry for his behaviour.

"Are you deliberately trying to antagonise Evie?" he asked him.

"I don't follow," Harry replied.

"Waltzing in here in your birthday suit? At best she'll think you're an exhibitionist, at worst some sort of sleazy sexual predator!"

"I thought she'd still be asleep," was the only excuse Harry could come up with. "Anyway, I do it all the time at home."

"Yeah? Well, you're not at home now are you mate? We're holed up with a somewhat vulnerable young woman, halfway up a mountain in France, and none of us have a clue what is going on. I, no we," Jackson corrected himself, "need her to be calm and cooperative and for both of those things to happen she needs to trust us and feel at ease with us. If you keep making jibes about 'Assassins-Are-Us-Dot-Com' and sauntering around naked in front of her neither of those things are going to happen."

"Is it me or are you falling for this girl?" Harry asked. "Is she going to be the one to finally thaw that frozen heart Claire left you with?"

"What the hell are you talking about?" Jackson responded angrily. "This is work and Evie is our asset. My only interest in her is professional."

"Fair enough," Harry replied, not overly convinced by Jackson's reply. "Anyway, I must fill you in on everything we now know about her brother, there's loads to tell you. I can't do it within earshot of Evie though."

The Gemini Connection

"Fine, but for the love of all that is sane go and get dressed first!" Jackson retorted.

Harry reappeared ten minutes later more suitably attired in shorts and a T-shirt rather than a tea towel and, with Evie still in the shower, the two men sat out on the balcony of the chalet to talk quietly.

"So," Harry began, "before I set off yesterday morning the boss gave me a couple of names in MI6 to contact. And guess what? Apparently, they have been working on a theory that someone from our side, either the UK or the US, has gone rogue overseas and," Harry paused for emphasis, "and that 'someone' is probably a medic."

"How come?" Jackson asked.

"Well, as you and I both know, there are loads of places overseas where supposedly we are not operational on the ground, but that's just the official line. Special forces were tasked with rounding up and capturing certain targets in one of these areas of interest and, as per usual, most of the men they caught were sporting various injuries, occupational hazard of being a terrorist I guess, but normally they are badly patched up, medically speaking. Then something changed, our guys started noticing that injuries were being dealt with more expertly. One bloke, so called Jihadi Joe, had previously lost half his lower leg and a hand months before they lifted him in a night operation. The Americans took him and the first thing they noticed was that he'd had expert amputations done. They compared notes with our side, same thing. The Brits have lifted a couple of assets with professionally treated war wounds."

"But surely they could have their own medics amongst their groups patching them up?" Jackson asked.

"Yes, but their local intelligence informants are as certain as they can be that it isn't one of their own doing this, something to do with the surgical techniques used apparently. Whoever was tending to these injuries was more of an expert than anything they'd seen before. Probably an orthopaedic trained specialist…"

"Like Evie's brother…" Jackson interjected.

"Like Evie's brother," Harry confirmed. "Anyway, MI6 and the CIA have been scrutinising all their 'missing in action', looking for any army or forces medics who could have been captured, or turned, to work within the terrorist groups. But they've drawn a complete blank."

"When and where did they start noticing this?" Jackson wanted to know.

"Are you ready for this?" Harry looked at him intently. "Initially in Afghanistan about 18 months ago and then a few months ago they started picking up the same thing in Syria."

Jackson stared at him. "So, the places and the timings fit with what we currently know about Michael."

Harry nodded. "And nobody had made a connection because a) he's not in the military and b) he was supposed to have been killed in Afghanistan."

Jackson let out a low whistle. "If, and it's a big if, this supposed terrorist surgeon and Michael are the same person, why is he getting in touch with Evie now? Why not 18 months or a year ago?"

Harry shrugged. "Can't answer that one yet mate."

"Maybe he has been forced to do this?" Jackson conjectured. "Held against his will, made to operate on the injured, only been able to access a mobile phone more recently?"

"That's exactly what I thought," Harry replied, "until I called in a favour from Ham the Spam, remember him?"

"Oh yeah, Spammy," Jackson laughed, "our American pal. Poor guy, seconded to MI5 for a year and hounded mercilessly because he thought spam fritters were the best thing going. He made your food choices look positively gourmet!"

"Well, who calls their son Hammond in the first place? Didn't help his cause with a name like that!" Harry countered. "Anyway, I had an interesting chat with him whilst I was driving to Paris. He had a little dig for me in their CIA files and this bomb blast that supposedly killed Evie's brother? All is not what it seems."

"How so?" Jackson asked.

"Well, there was an attack on the university, and the list of the presumed dead did include a Michael Longshaw."

"Why do I feel a 'but' coming on?" Jackson wanted to know.

"The truth about that attack was kept out of the press. The university was owned and operated by the Americans; it had long been a target for the Taliban. Anyway, Michael was giving the lecture that day, he was at the front of the lecture hall, talking about administering first aid on the frontline. But here's the rub, the students that day were not the usual university ones, they were volunteers from the allied troops who were training to be first responders, people who intervene in the field until the qualified medics take over."

"So, they were the target then," Jackson said, "wiped out in a single stroke."

"Yeah, and I'm afraid it gets worse," Harry answered. "According to Spammy, the epicentre of the explosion was by the lectern, the one Michael would have been using and leaning on as he was talking."

"He wouldn't have stood a chance," Jackson said and then a realisation dawned on him. "Unless…."

He looked at Harry who was slowly nodding. "Unless…. unless he knew a bomb was about to go off and cleared out. Jackson, if Michael really is alive then he didn't have a lucky escape. He must have known the bomb was there in the first place. He might even have planted it."

"Shit!" Jackson stared across the valley at the mountains beyond, it all seemed so peaceful and in sharp contrast to what he had just heard. "What on earth do we say to Evie?"

"Nothing for the moment," Harry replied. "Stanners said to keep schtum on all of this where she's concerned but use her to find him. Once we determine exactly where he is, then MI6 will go in."

"To lift him?" Jackson asked.

"No mate, given the fact he's officially dead, he's going to stay dead. As soon as they find him, I think they intend to kill him."

The Gemini Connection

Chapter 23

By mid-afternoon Evie was close to deciphering Michael's third message. She was sat out on the balcony surrounded by sheets of paper on which she had had been scribbling different ways of adjusting Michael's words as she searched her memory again and again trying to remember how they had devised new words as children. Jackson was sat across from her, watching her out of the corner of his eye and reading her different interpretations as she jotted them down.

Harry in the meantime was laid out at the far end of the balcony, sound asleep on a blanket. "May as well get some rays and zeds," he had announced after they had all had some lunch.

"Sorry, what?" Evie asked, thinking this was yet another MI5 phrase she didn't understand.

"Bit of sunbathing and a nap," he replied with a cheery smile. "I can't do much more until you've got those messages done."

Evie shook her head at him. "Well don't think I'm going to treat your sunburn when you've frazzled yourself half to death!"

Harry shrugged his shoulders. "I'll take my chances."

"Idiot," Evie muttered under her breath.

"Yep, that's me," was the reply as Harry nonchalantly strutted off down the balcony.

An hour later, Harry was still lying there in the full sun.

"He's going to give himself sunstroke," Evie said to Jackson, nodding towards Harry.

"At least he's dressed," Jackson replied, "could have been a lot worse!"

"Oh don't," Evie laughed. "Tell me, was his flashing this morning a deliberate provocation? Or is he genuinely the class clown?"

"Oh, definitely the clown. He might operate on a slightly different plane to the rest of us but he's harmless, he really is."

"And you? Are you harmless?" Evie stared hard at Jackson.

Those eyes, he thought yet again as he met her stare.

"Well?" Evie was now saying, "Are you?"

"Am I what?" he berated himself for allowing himself to be distracted.

"I asked you if you were harmless too?"

"I could point out that I should be asking you that question. You're the one who threatened me with a supposed gun and then almost turned me into a eunuch!"

Evie smirked. "Sorry, well not overly sorry if I'm honest," she reflected. "I was scared, I still am."

"I know, you've had a lot to process in the last week."

"That's an understatement," Evie said. "My dead brother appears to not be dead, and he may or may not be involved with terrorists so therefore you think I am too. My boyfriend – ex-boyfriend –" she corrected herself, "turns out to be a drug addict but somehow has managed to get me suspended at work rather than himself. And now I'm stuck up a mountain somewhere in France with two men who I don't trust an inch, but don't seem to have any choice but to be with." Evie sat back as she paused for breath. "And who know virtually everything there is to know about me yet have told me nothing about themselves," she finished.

"Well, you have put me to sleep and seen my appendix being removed," Jackson suggested. "That's a pretty unique thing to know about me."

"Yeah, well with hindsight I should have sent you off to sleep permanently," Evie said, but with a small smile.

"Oh no, think about it," Jackson laughed. "If you'd done that it might have just been Harry here with you now!"

Evie raised her eyebrows in mock horror. "Good point! I'd probably have killed him by now!"

As she said this, Harry sat up on his blanket. "Oi, I heard that!"

As he walked towards them, both Jackson and Evie burst out laughing. As Evie had predicted, he had managed to thoroughly burn himself in the sun and, when he removed his sunglasses, he looked like a reverse human panda with a face like a beetroot save for two large white circles around his eyes.

"That is really going to hurt later," Evie warned, pointing at his face but Harry just shrugged.

"I'll be fine, I can handle pain," he claimed as he sauntered back into the chalet.

The Gemini Connection

Two hours later Evie announced she had cracked the messages although Harry didn't hear her at first, primarily because he was screaming about the agony he was in and how he had never known pain like it.

"You need paracetamol, loads of water and slosh some moisturiser on your face," Evie instructed him absentmindedly as she looked up. "I think I've got it; Michael wants to meet me. He's told me where he is and there's a number, another phone number. That's why it was so hard to decipher, he's had to write the number as words because we use numbers as punctuation."

"And you called me an idiot," Harry moaned. "At least I communicate in English, an internationally recognised and understood language. Oh, the pain…"

"Jackson, put a towel under the cold tap and get it very wet. Then slap him round the face with it. That one will do the job nicely." She pointed to the infamous tea towel Harry had used on his nether regions earlier in the day.

Jackson duly complied and, having dropped the drenched towel somewhat unsympathetically onto Harry's face, he sat down next to Evie. "What does he say?"

"I said I'm in pain," Harry began.

"Not you, you fool. Try having a burst appendix if you want real pain. Michael, what does Michael say?"

"He is saying he wants to come home in all three messages. In the second one he says he will need me with him if he is to come home. I'm not sure why he says that though, he doesn't explain himself. In the third message he starts by saying he's going to tell me where he is and that I need to go there. Once I'm there, I'm to ring the number he has given me."

She paused; Jackson looked at her. "Where is he Evie?" He could see the conflict in her face.

"Promise me you'll help me find him." Seeing him hesitate she pleaded, "Please, help him come home."

Jackson winced and hoped she didn't notice. He didn't want to lie to Evie, but neither could he tell her the truth. Eventually he settled for a half truth. "I promise you we will do all we can to find him."

Evie sighed, her options were limited, and she couldn't do this alone. "Gaziantep," she said. "He says to meet him in a place called Gaziantep, but I don't know where that is. Do you?"

Jackson was nodding slowly; his worst fears were being realised. "Yes," he said, "I know it." He looked at Harry who was suddenly alert and seemed to have forgotten about the pain from his sunburn. "We both know it well. It's in southern Turkey. Evie, it's a town we watch closely."

"Why?"

"Because it's about 35 miles from the Syrian border and it's one of the most porous parts of the Syria-Turkey border."

"So?" Evie still didn't understand.

"So, it's the last stop for most would be Jihadi brides before they cross over into Syria and disappear forever."

The Gemini Connection

Al Bab, Syria

Michael stood outside the ruined building they were currently using as their field hospital and checked his phone yet again. The sun beat down on his head and the acrid smell of burning, both of buildings and human flesh, filled his nostrils. It was four weeks since he had sent his final message to Evie but still there was no hint of a reply from her. He knew there could be a myriad of reasons why; she may have a different phone number to the one he remembered; she may be choosing not to reply; or perhaps she was not being allowed to reply.

He had reassured Boran that the use of their secret twin language would ensure no one else would understand it. It would prove to Evie that he was alive whilst simultaneously ensuring the intelligence agencies would be unable to analyse it. He was fully aware of the fact his messages would be intercepted. Boran had told him that every message, every communication, was vulnerable to listening ears and watching eyes in the West.

It was always going to be hard to reach her, but Michael was utterly convinced that Evie would reply if she could. Whether his conviction about this was based on his twin-twin intuition, or a reflection of Boran's belief rubbing off on him, he couldn't decide.

"Michael," he heard Boran's voice as he came up behind him. "You are needed in there for another casualty. You are checking your phone again I see brother."

"Yes," Michael replied, "but still nothing."

The Gemini Connection

"Do not worry. She will be here soon, I know it." As he said this, Boran clapped Michael on the back. "She will be here, God Himself wills it, and all will be well. You will have your sister; we will have our lady doctor and I will have my wife."

Chapter 24

"What the hell have you done to your face?" the voice bellowed into the chalet. Stanners was staring incredulously through the computer screen at Harry.

"Nothing boss, just a bit of sunburn," Harry winced as he touched his face without thinking.

"Well, you look like a racoon!" Stanners said.

"Thanks boss," Harry replied as Jackson simply rolled his eyes heavenwards.

With the messages now translated by Evie the two younger men were relaying their content to Stanners. Evie had wanted to join them for the call, but Jackson had made it abundantly clear that was not going to happen. When he had told her she must sit outside, within sight of them but out of earshot, she had begun to argue with him.

"This is my brother we are talking about. Without me you wouldn't be any further forward. How can you make any decisions about Michael without involving me?"

"This isn't a friendly zoom call with the boss Evie, we are dealing with highly sensitive information that we need to be very careful with," Jackson told her.

The Gemini Connection

"But I already know what it's all about, I get that it's sensitive, but I know as much as you do so why shut me out?"

Oh, if only that was true, Jackson thought to himself, given what Harry had told him about Michael earlier in the day.

"Evie, I don't have time to argue. You wouldn't let people just come and sit in your operating theatre whilst you were working, would you?"

"Well, I would actually, if I thought that person might have useful skills or information to bring," she retorted.

Jackson sighed. "We don't have time for this, so I'll give you a choice. You either sit there," he pointed to a grassy area that dropped away from the chalet balcony, "or I'll have to lock you in the bathroom. You decide."

"Fine," Evie knew she was not going to persuade him. "But next time you burst your appendix I'm going to let them remove it without any anaesthetic!"

"Good job we only have one then, isn't it?" Jackson taunted her.

Evie admitted defeat; the truth was she was growing tired of fighting with him, and her head was beginning to hurt. "Unlike panda eyes over there," she pointed in Harry's direction, "I'll sit in the shade."

And so, she had flung a blanket in the place Jackson had indicated and thrown herself down upon it. The early evening sun was still very warm and, despite her best efforts to hear what was being said in the chalet, she began to doze off instead.

Up in the chalet Stanners was pondering everything he had just been told.

The Gemini Connection

"How much can I tell Evie?" Jackson wanted to know.

"I think you need to start laying the groundwork that this isn't a family reunion we are arranging. But she must believe we are all working together to bring him home, despite what MI6 is telling us. It goes without saying that you don't tell her anything about our real intentions where her brother is concerned, just say we are working with colleagues to find him, words to that effect." Stanners paused for a moment before continuing. "Has she not said anything about how and why her brother has turned up like this? She must have questions of her own."

"I think she's still processing it all Sir," Jackson replied. "At the moment all she is focused on is finding him and bringing him home. I don't think the implications of exactly what he's been up to for the last two years have hit her yet. I suspect she thinks he is being held against his will and we're going to go in and rescue him."

"He may be being held against his will," Stanners mused, "but I doubt it. For now, at least, we must assume he is playing her and has ulterior motives. We also must assume she is implicated in some way and could even be playing us!"

"Somehow I doubt that," Jackson replied, "I think her bewilderment at his reappearance is genuine."

"So do I," Harry chipped in. "She's a right mess if you ask me. She keeps having the hysterics and attacking us!"

Jackson stared at him. "She does not 'keep having hysterics.' You managed to freak her out within an hour of meeting her by talking about her disappearing into the ether never to be seen again!"

Harry pouted. "Well, she did nearly castrate you; you can't deny that!"

"Because she was terrified you moron," Jackson threw back at him.

Harry was staring quizzically at him.

"Now what? Why are you looking at me like that?" Jackson demanded to know.

"I think you doth protest too much," Harry winked at him. "I think you have a touch of the hotties for our Evie!"

Before Jackson could furnish himself with a reply, Stanners' voice cut through the air again. "If I had wanted to know about your love lives, I would have asked. But a word of warning, you view this woman only as an asset, a very valuable one but an asset no more and no less. Keep her safe, keep her alive and use her to locate this bloody brother."

"Yes sir," Jackson and Harry muttered in unison.

"Right, this is what is going to happen," Stanners began. "You're to get yourselves to Gaziantep, establish contact with Michael and then MI6 will take over. You two are not trained for lifting someone so you get the hell out of it. When MI6 tell you to jump you don't even ask 'How high?' You go. Understand?"

"But what happens to Evie?" Jackson asked.

"After Gaziantep, she's not your problem anymore."

Jackson swallowed hard, he wanted to argue with Stanners but thought better of it. Instead of saying he could not, and would not, abandon her he heard himself say, "Okay Sir."

The Gemini Connection

~~~~

Later that evening, with the call to Stanners finished, the three of them were sat at the chalet's kitchen table whilst Jackson, as per Stanners' instructions, relayed a somewhat fabricated version of what was going to happen next. When he had explained more about the concerns they had about the final endpoint for young women travelling to Gaziantep, Evie was incredulous.

"Are you completely insane?" she asked. "Do I look like a runaway jihadi bride?" She didn't wait for an answer. "And even if I was, why the hell would I go through such a convoluted route to be one? A route that was bound to attract the attention of you and your cronies."

"Of course I don't think you are Evie," Jackson replied. "I'm just explaining why we know all about Gaziantep, that's all."

"Mind you, if you do want to get married, I reckon me and Jacky-boy would make great bridesmaids, we'd look good in pink," Harry interjected, earning himself a withering look from Evie.

"Yeah, it would match your sunburn!" Jackson laughed.

"So, what happens now?" Evie was not in the mood for jokes. "We go to Gaziantep, yes? Find Michael, bring him home?"

"Hold your horses there, Miss," Harry answered. "The boss wants us to tread carefully, this is bigger than the three of us."

The Gemini Connection

"But I thought the whole point of you stalking me across two countries was to help me get my brother home?" Evie looked enquiringly at them both.

"Err, no," Jackson began, "we were just the guys analysing the messages. We have my appendix to thank for our paths crossing, something our boss was keen to exploit. You weren't supposed to end up in Paris two days after we let you receive the first message; it left us with no choice but to run with it."

"But you are coming to Gaziantep, with me?"

Jackson looked at her. With her long, curly hair scraped back off her face into a ponytail and no make-up on she looked younger than her 28 years, young and vulnerable.

"Yes, we are, we leave in the morning," he replied but inwardly he was full of foreboding. *And heaven help us when we get there,* he thought to himself.

Chapter 25

At 7am the following morning, the three of them were at Geneva airport waiting for their flight to Istanbul. After the tensions of the previous days, a gentle truce had settled over the trio the night before as Harry had entertained them with his stories about his forlorn love life. The wine had flowed and, unlike in Paris, Evie had drunk some of it this time.

"I just don't know how a woman's mind works Evie," Harry had moaned. "It all seems to start so well and then, whoosh," he did a downwards motion with his hand, "it's downhill all the way!"

"Yeah, I notice you're leaving out some of the finer detail," Jackson interjected. "Like the time you accidentally arranged two dates at once, in the same place and at the same time!"

"Yeah, I got a bit carried away with all the swipe left or right malarky," Harry sighed. "That was quite an evening. I turned up and there were two beautiful women, waiting just for me!"

"In your dreams," Jackson muttered.

"What did you do?" Despite herself, Evie wanted to know more.

The Gemini Connection

"Yeah, well I tried to make it work. Sat with the first one, Veronica she was called, for fifteen minutes; got her a drink; schmoozed her. Then excused myself and shot over to the other one, did the same with her, can't remember her name. Went back to Veronica, said I'd got a bit of a gippy stomach and that's why I'd been gone a while. Almost got away with it too but by the third or fourth round of drinks I muddled them up, got their names wrong, then they spotted each other. And the bartender, the swine, cottoned on and told them both what I was doing. I mean, why did he do that? Where was the male solidarity eh?"

Evie laughed. "So, what happened next?"

Harry shuffled uncomfortably in his seat.

"Go on mate," Jackson grinned, "tell her what happened next!"

"They both chucked their drinks over me, and Veronica hit me! Then three other women who I didn't even know started having a go at me. It was carnage, I ended up locking myself in the loos until they'd all gone!"

"Serves you right you idiot," Evie said gleefully. "You deserved everything you got!"

"I was just looking for love," Harry said wistfully. "I wasn't expecting to get punched for my trouble. Still, I reckon they should be grateful to me, they became best friends apparently. Last I heard they went to Tenerife together."

"How on earth could you know that?" Evie asked.

"I still go to that pub, and they sent me a postcard via the barman!"

"And he doesn't even hang his head in shame!" Jackson laughed.

"Your turn," Harry said, looking at Evie.

"Well, I can't really judge," Evie began. "As you are both well aware, my boyfriend turned out to be a rather undesirable specimen." As she spoke, memories of Matt and the scene in their Paris hotel room came flooding back. She buried her face in her hands and groaned. "I might not even have a job to go back to thanks to him."

"Oh, you will, no problem," Harry said. "We have the footage of him shooting up, you walking in on him and then him attacking you. All you'll have to do is show that to your bosses and case closed."

"How on earth do I explain how I got the footage though?" Evie asked. "I can't say 'the thing is Noel, unbeknownst to me two MI5 agents had bugged my hotel room because they were tracking me because my dead brother isn't dead so here's the proof, I'm telling the truth….'" her voice trailed off.

"Ce n'est pas un problème," Harry replied. "I'll send the footage to your phone. Just tell your boss you were suspicious and left your phone recording Matt whilst you went out and voilà, there is the proof."

"You can do that?" Evie asked.

"Hey, you're looking at the guy who successfully bugged the staff room at his school aged fifteen, of course I can!"

Jackson looked at him. "You bugged the staff room?"

"Yeah, and the girls' showers!"

Evie was staring at him open mouthed. "Please tell me you were caught!"

The Gemini Connection

"Nope, but the showers were refurbished only a few weeks later so all that effort went to waste!" Harry pulled a sad face.

"Serves you right you pervert!" Jackson exclaimed.

"It was only for sound, no pictures involved. Got a lot of useful intel from the staff room though."

Shaking her head at him Evie turned to Jackson. "So, what about you?"

"Me? I never bugged anything in my school, I promise."

"No, not that. your love life. Harry and I have laid it all out on the table, what about you? Have you got a woman in your life? Or maybe a man?" she added.

Jackson's face clouded over. Harry held his breath, Jackson never discussed Claire and their doomed relationship was one of the very few topics Harry didn't joke about. Evie realised instantly she had touched a very raw nerve.

"I'm sorry," she began, "none of my business…"

"No, it's a fair question," Jackson answered, "after all we've delved in to every aspect of your life. I have been single ever since my fiancée ditched me, three days before our wedding."

"Oh Jackson, I'm so sorry, that's awful."

"Yeah, well it is what it is," Jackson shrugged his shoulders. "I guess she did me a favour in the long run, at least I didn't have to shell out for a divorce as well as a wedding."

His attempt at humour didn't fool Evie. "How long ago was this?" she asked gently.

"Two years ago, as of July."

The Gemini Connection

"About the time we lost Michael. Correction – thought we lost Michael," Evie said. "Seems like we both went through emotional hell two years ago."

Jackson nodded, grateful that she wasn't probing further.

"Two years ago? Now I think that was when I was seeing Judith, and she took me to meet her parents and things got very awkward at their house I can tell you." Harry frowned as he recalled the incident.

"Let me guess," Evie said. "Her mother made a pass at you?"

"Nah, not her mum," Harry explained cheerily.

Evie sat back in her chair. "Well, that's a relief."

"It was her dad!"

Jackson and Evie stared at him. "Oh, shut up Harry," they exclaimed in unison.

~~~~

Waiting for the flight to Istanbul, Evie felt tense and scared. The relaxed humour of the previous evening felt like a distant memory. She had so many questions that only Michael could supply answers to, but she was apprehensive about what those answers would be. She had been so caught up with the revelation her brother was still alive that, in her desperation to see him again, she had not paused to think through the implications of his reappearance. Where had he been the last two years? And why had he waited so long to contact her?

Evie looked across at Jackson and Harry, sitting several rows away in the departure lounge and studiously ignoring her. They were all booked onto the flight under false names, and she was to give the impression she was travelling alone. She wouldn't have been able to do this on her own and their presence gave her some assurance. She hadn't realised that she had started to feel safe with them around her until now. She sighed and tried to read the magazine she had on her knee, but she just kept reading the same sentence again and again.

~~~~~

"She looks scared," Jackson said, as he and Harry observed her from a distance.

Evie was biting down on her lower lip, something Jackson had realised she always did when she was feeling scared or vulnerable. He was dreading the next 24 hours and would gladly have sold one of his limbs to the lowest bidder if it meant he could scoop Evie up and return to the relative safety of London with her. But Stanners had been clear. They would fly via Istanbul to Gaziantep where the local security service would be waiting to drive them to a safe house used jointly by Turkish and British operatives. Evie was not to phone the number her brother had given her until they were behind closed doors at the house. She would be guided on what to say in the hope Michael would agree to meeting with her, at which point MI6 would take custody of her and Jackson and Harry were expected to get themselves on the next flight home. Jackson didn't like the plan; he felt the margin for error was too wide, but Stanners was having none of it when he suggested he stay until Michael was found and subsequently removed.

"You're not trained for this," Stanners had told him. "You'll be a hindrance, not a help. You and Harry have your orders, follow them. Your MI6 contact is a chap called McAllister; he's based in Turkey. He'll take things from there."

Jackson couldn't reconcile his conscience with the fact that they were using Evie under the guise of helping her. He remembered her face as she had asked him several times if he would help her find Michael. He had always said 'yes' and she had begun to trust him, he was sure of it. Now that trust was going to be destroyed with no hope of him ever being able to redeem himself.

~~~~

Al Bab, Syria

"Good news Michael," Boran was shouting excitedly. "Your sister has boarded a plane for Gaziantep, she is coming!"

Michael could hardly believe what he was hearing. "You are sure?"

"Yes, she is travelling under a different name, but it is her. Our contact has confirmed it. It is wonderful news, no?"

Michael swallowed hard and nodded his head, his mind was in too much turmoil to speak. Everything now hinged on what had happened when Evie had received his messages. When Boran had told him all their communications were intercepted, Michael had spotted an opportunity. He had spent many months convincing Boran that his sister would be keen to join them if only he could contact her. Eventually Boran had been persuaded and declared that God Himself must be the orchestrator in bringing first Michael, and now Evie, to him.

He had warned Michael that only one message could be sent to her. "We know how our enemy works, one message they cannot decipher will eventually be dismissed by them. But more than one could draw too much attention to your sister and, by default, to you. We don't want that."

But Michael had disobeyed Boran. He had sent three messages to Evie and was fervently hoping that he had indeed drawn attention to her, in fact he was counting on it.

"So, we will go and meet her at the airport?" he now asked Boran.

Boran laughed. "My friend, you are still so naïve. She is travelling under a false name; she will not be alone."

"I don't understand," Michael said apprehensively, "how are the two linked? Perhaps she booked her flight under a different name because she didn't want anyone to know where she was going."

"Michael, Michael, think about it. Her passport, her travel documents, they are all in the name of Stephanie Peters. How could she forge a passport?"

Michael stared blankly at him. "She had help?"

"Exactly," Boran replied, "most likely from your MI5. There will be at least one agent on that plane with her and more waiting for her in Gaziantep. We can be sure of it."

The Gemini Connection

"So, what do we do?"

Boran's face took on a sinister look. "They always underestimate us. I have already sent three of my best men to bring her here. They will take care of everything; your sister will soon be safely with us."

"But what about anyone travelling with her?"

Boran shrugged his shoulders. "My men will deal with them. They will be dead by sundown."

Chapter 26

The black SUV pulled into the parking bay at Gaziantep airport. The driver remained in the car as the other two passengers quickly got out and entered the terminal building. The men, dressed in business suits and carrying briefcases, blended into the airport surroundings as they made their way to the arrivals hall. The flight from Istanbul had just landed as they weaved their way through the crowds until they spotted their first target. They stationed themselves either side of the man who was there to meet Evie and swiftly dealt with him. Now all they had to do was wait.

~~~~

Evie didn't think she had ever felt as scared as she did now. As the plane came into land at Gaziantep, she wanted to be anywhere but there. Any initial excitement at the thought of being reunited with Michael had dissipated over the last 24 hours.

She had been unable to sleep the night before despite the convivial evening with Jackson and Harry. Eventually she had given up trying and had gone downstairs in the chalet. Jackson, who had also been tossing and turning, found her there when he too had given up on the hope of ever falling asleep. In the half shadow he didn't initially see her as he went into the kitchen area and turned on the tap to get a glass of water. Only when he was heading back for the stairs did he catch sight of her, sat on the settee with her legs drawn up to her chest and her arms wrapped around them.

"Can't sleep?" he had asked.

Evie shook her head in reply.

Jackson moved towards her. "Want some company?"

She looked up and nodded at him.

As he sat down next to her Evie had turned and looked at him. "I'm scared Jackson."

"I know."

"This is just too overwhelming; I don't know what I want any more. I thought I would be so pleased to be finally finding Michael but what if he's changed? What if I barely recognise him now? What kind of brother lets you think he is dead for two years? God forgive me but part of me is wishing he had died; does that make any sense?"

"Yes, perfectly."

"I've already gone through losing him, I've done so much grieving but at least it was for a brother who had remained unblemished. Now? The brother I knew might still be gone, replaced by who knows what?"

Evie started to cry as she spoke. Jackson moved closer and wrapped his arms around her. She didn't resist but allowed herself to be hugged, tight, into his chest.

"I'll be there with you," he promised, "every step of the way."

The Gemini Connection

And sod my orders, he thought to himself.

~~~~~

Evie made her way hesitantly into the arrivals hall. She had been told to look for a card with 'Hotel Delphinium' on it and soon saw it. Going up to the man holding it she looked enquiringly into his face.

"Evie?" he asked.

She only nodded in reply.

"Please, come this way." The man pointed in the direction of the exit.

In the hustle and bustle of the airport, Evie didn't notice the kerfuffle going on in one corner. Paramedics were administering first aid to someone they assumed was a collapsed passenger with badly controlled diabetes given how low his blood sugar reading was on their glucose monitor. However, they were wrong; the passenger in question was not diabetic. In fact, he was not even a passenger; he was the Turkish operative who was supposed to meet Evie and take her safely to the rendezvous with MI6. But, whilst waiting to meet her, two men had sidled up to him and, before he knew what was happening, one of them had injected him with a lethal dose of insulin.

~~~~~

"I don't like this one bit," Jackson muttered to Harry as they emerged into the arrivals hall. "She's too vulnerable for this."

The Gemini Connection

"Don't really have a choice though mate," Harry replied. "This is being dictated by those above."

They could see Evie ahead of them and watched as she was approached by a swarthy, dark-haired man holding a sign with the agreed details on it.

"That's our guy." Harry nodded towards someone else holding a sign with a fabricated business name on it and they walked briskly towards him.

"Hi, I'm Yusuf, this way please. We have a car waiting for you. My colleague will already have met the girl."

The heat of the full sun hit them as they left the terminal. Jackson scanned the horizon but couldn't see any sign of Evie. He had given her her phone back at Geneva airport with strict instructions. "Keep it switched on but don't use it, not for anything. It's a way for me to track you. And here," he had given her another slimmer and smaller phone, "hide this in your clothing, it's a backup in case you lose the first one."

"Why would I lose it?" Evie had asked.

"Just covering all bases, that's all."

Now in the passenger seat next to Yusef, Jackson started trying to track Evie's phone, but it was still showing as being at the airport.

"According to this, she hasn't left yet?" he said.

"She should have," Yusuf countered, "don't worry, we were told she was to be handled carefully. Ahmet will take good care of her," Yusuf chuckled, "although she may have been surprised to be greeted by a blue-eyed, fair-haired Turkish man."

Jackson stared at him in disbelief. "What did you just say?"

The Gemini Connection

"Ahmet, he looks like him," Yusuf indicated Harry with a backwards nod of his head.

"But we saw Evie leaving the airport and the man taking her was dark; dark skin, dark hair."

Harry and Jackson stared at each other.

"Shit," Jackson cried, "she's been grabbed!"

He looked in desperation at the tracking symbol on his phone, Evie was still supposedly in the airport. *The other phone* he thought, and quickly called up its location. It was already five miles away.

"She's there!" He waved the phone in Yusuf's face.

Yusuf did a sharp U-turn in the road whilst calling his colleagues waiting at the safe house and barking orders at them in Turkish.

Harry meanwhile was already talking to Stanners back in London. "Boss, we've been tricked. Evie's been lifted by persons unknown."

~~~~

Evie quickly realised something was wrong when her phone was taken off her and thrown into a bush as they left the airport building.

"Hey," she started to say but got no further as she was manhandled into the back of a large SUV.

The man who had met her got in beside her and the car made off at speed. The front seat passenger turned to Evie. "You are safe with us. We take you to your brother, Michael. He waits for you."

"I don't understand," she began but then decided it might be safer to keep quiet. She could feel the phone, the second one Jackson had given her, digging into the small of her back. She had hidden it as Jackson had said and could only hope and pray that it hadn't been accidentally switched off by the sudden jolting movements of the car.

The car twisted and turned round the airport roads but before long they were driving on isolated, dusty roads. Evie saw a dilapidated signpost but could not understand what was written on it. Had she been able to, she would have been horrified to know they were heading for the Syrian border.

Half an hour later the car screeched to a halt in what appeared to be the middle of nowhere. There was a small river ahead of them spanned by a footbridge. The man next to Evie pulled her from the car and began to walk towards the bridge with her. Evie could make out two people standing on the other side and as she got closer, she recognised him.

"Michael!" she cried out and began to run towards him.

At that moment another car skidded to a halt next to the SUV. She heard her name being called and looked over her shoulder to see Jackson, already out of the car and running towards her.

"Evie, stop, don't go any further!"

Evie stopped, she was halfway between her brother and Jackson. She turned fully to face Jackson and saw that Harry was also out of the car and running up behind him.

"Kill them!" the man standing next to Michael shouted to his men in Arabic.

The man who had met her in the airport pulled a gun out from underneath his jacket and pointed it at Jackson.

"No!" screamed Evie as a shot rang out, quickly followed by another one. She watched in horror as both Jackson and Harry fell to the ground and then ran over to them to find Harry, bleeding heavily, lying on top of Jackson who was otherwise unhurt. Harry had seen the gun before Jackson did and had pushed him out of the way. Both bullets had hit Harry, one in the shoulder and one in the thigh.

Evie flung herself down on the ground. "Harry, Harry, stay with us," she cried.

She pulled the thin scarf from around her neck and pushed it hard against the torrent of blood emerging from his thigh but, before she could do anything else, she was pulled roughly away by one of the assailants.

"We don't need them, only you," he was saying.

"Keep pressing on that wound," Evie shouted at Jackson as she was dragged away.

The other men from the SUV were advancing towards them.

They're both going to be killed, she realised but then, as if in slow motion, she found herself able to think clearly; there was only one course of action she could take. She lunged for the gun she could see in the waistband of one of the approaching men and pulled it out cleanly into her own hand. Knocking off the safety catch, she pointed it towards the sky and fired a shot.

"Let them go!" she screamed.

A stunned silence descended as she slowly put the gun to her own head and backed away until everybody was in her field of vision and there was nothing but scrubland behind her.

"No, Evie!" She could hear Jackson shouting her name.

"If it's just me you want, you will let them go. But if they die, I die. Your choice." She looked squarely towards where Michael was waiting and said something indecipherable to all but him. Michael paled and turned to the man standing next to him.

"She means it Boran," he said, "she will kill herself."

Boran raised his arm and signalled his men to lower their guns.

"Evie, no." She heard Jackson's voice call out again.

"Jackson, get Harry out of here," Evie pleaded with him. "He will die if you don't, please."

Harry was moaning as he lay in Jackson's arms. "Mate, it hurts…" was all he managed to say.

"Go," Evie was pleading again. "You must see this is the only way. You can't die because of me, please don't put that on my conscience."

Oh God, forgive me! Jackson prayed to a deity he wasn't sure he believed in as he hoisted Harry up off the ground and stumbled back to the car with him. He looked back at Evie, still holding the gun to her head, and hung his own head in shame but he did as she asked. He pushed Harry into the car and threw himself in after him. Yusuf didn't wait for Jackson to change his mind; he slammed the car's accelerator to the floor and sped towards the open road.

Jackson turned in the back seat to look out the rear window and could only watch as Evie continued to hold the gun to her head. As they drove to safety, he cursed himself, Stanners, the Service, and the whole world. He had failed her, completely and utterly failed her. He turned his attention to Harry and continued to press down hard on his thigh, alarmed by the volume of blood that was flowing from the wound.

"Don't you dare die on me," he admonished him. "I swear I'll kill you if you die on me."

"I knew you loved me mate," was the weak reply before Harry finally slipped into unconsciousness.

Chapter 27

"What a complete and utter shitstorm," Stanners kicked the bin by his feet across the room in frustration. "One operative dead, another critically injured, our asset who knows where. Heads will roll for this, mine first I expect." He went over to the window and leaned first his arm, then his head, against it.

Jackson looked up but said nothing. It was 24 hours since the shooting; Harry was back in the operating theatre where surgeons were battling to save his leg after complications had developed after his first operation. The Turkish operative intercepted by Boran's men in the airport had died and they had lost the signal to the spare phone Jackson had given Evie.

When Stanners heard what had happened in Turkey, he had flown out on the next available flight to Istanbul cursing the fact that there were no direct flights from London to Gaziantep. After losing his patience (and his temper) several times in Istanbul airport when staff kept telling him there were no seats available on flights to Gaziantep for at least 24 hours, he flew instead to Diyarbakir where he then hired a car and drove the final

190 miles to Gaziantep. He had abandoned the car outside the hospital entrance in the 'Strictly No Parking' zone, not caring in the least that it would soon be towed away, and run into the hospital to find his men.

He and Jackson were now sat in Harry's hospital room, an aching space in the bed where Harry should have been. The surgeon had told Jackson he had saved Harry's life by following Evie's instructions and keeping up the pressure on the wound in Harry's thigh. The bullet had fractured his femur which in turn had severed his femoral vein but miraculously not the artery. In comparison Harry's shoulder wound was relatively minor, the bullet had passed straight through causing some soft tissue damage but little else.

"That vein can drain out your entire blood supply in minutes," the surgeon had explained, "but you bought him that time before the paramedics took over. Just a millimetre or two to the left though and it could have been his artery, and we would have lost him."

Initial surgery to pin and plate the bone and repair the vein had seemed successful but in the early hours of the morning it became clear that the muscles in Harry's lower leg had been compromised by the large amount of blood that had pooled in them when first Jackson, and then the ambulance crew, had been compressing his thigh wound. They had stopped Harry from bleeding out but had also stopped the blood circulating properly in his lower leg. As Harry's leg began to swell at an alarming pace, he had been whisked off back to theatre.

"He might lose his leg I'm afraid; those muscles are dying," the surgeon had told Jackson. "It can happen after the sort of trauma he suffered. We need to relieve the pressure before it gets any worse, but I can't promise we can save the leg." Seeing the anguish on Jackson's face he added, "I promise we'll do our best."

Stanners had arrived to find Jackson sitting alone in an empty room and initially assumed the worst. He almost felt relief to hear that Harry might only lose his leg having thought just moments before that he had died.

"Did they say how long before we know what's happening?" he asked Jackson.

Jackson shook his head. "As long as it takes, I guess."

"Was he able to talk to you yesterday?"

"He lost consciousness in the car, but he was kind of awake after his first operation. He wasn't making much sense though, rambling on nonsensically."

"Oh, so pretty much back to normal then." Stanners made an attempt at humour, but Jackson could see from his face that he was in mental torment.

"What were we doing here Sir?" he asked. "We should never have come to Gaziantep with Evie; you know we should have all come back to London. We weren't trained for this, a fact you pointed out to us several times. We weren't even armed for pity's sake; we couldn't protect her."

Stanners let out a large sigh and shook his head but said nothing.

Jackson was becoming increasingly frustrated. "I'll ask you again. Why were we here Sir?" He emphasised the 'Sir' loudly. "I promised Evie I would keep her safe, that I wouldn't let her out of my sight."

Stanners moved over to where Jackson was sitting and placed a hand on his shoulder. "You cannot make promises like that, not in our work," he said, but then he

The Gemini Connection

thought of Vivian and his empty promises to her about David all those years ago, "but I understand, more than you realise." His words were greeted with stony silence.

"This is all my fault," he continued. "I wanted all three of you back in London, not for this shambolic farce to happen. But I was over-ruled, I'd burnt my bridges. My esteemed colleagues in MI6 told me in no uncertain terms that given how much I'd already ballsed everything up, they would set the rules this time."

"I don't follow," Jackson replied. "Aren't we supposed to work together?"

Stanners paused and sighed. "Not when I had made a mess of things from the get-go."

Jackson stared at him in confusion.

"Harry told you that someone had messed with our computer systems and deleted all record of Evie's brother. Well, it was me, I was trying to be clever, but I messed up. I put the whole operation back weeks with my interfering." Stanners could tell from the look on Jackson's face that he didn't believe him.

After the fall out from Vivian's confession, that she had sabotaged their investigative searches, Stanners could not bring himself to turn her in. Instead, Vivian was now officially on compassionate leave for a 'private matter', but this would lead to her eventual resignation. He had asked her to explain to him again and again every detail of what she had done on his computers until he could repeat it word for word. Then he had handed her his computer and told her to make other, more clunky, errors on it as if he had tried to cover up his own ineptitude after realising what he had supposedly done. Initially Vivian had refused; she was shocked that

The Gemini Connection

Stanners was prepared to take the fall for her and had told him she alone would face the consequences of her actions. However, the prospect of jail was not appealing and eventually he had managed to convince her that quietly retiring was both a viable and far better option for them both.

Just hours after the existence of Evie's brother had emerged, Stanners had gone to his superiors and taken responsibility for Vivian's actions. "I was trying to prove to the youngsters that I was a match for them," he had said to them, "but I messed up. I was too clever for my own good. I thought I had set up a sweeping search for people related to Evie, but I'd done the opposite. I'd directed everything away from us into the computer's bin instead." He began to explain more, using the carefully rehearsed words he had practised with Vivian, and they seemed to have the desired effect.

One good thing about being considered a complete buffoon where modern technology was concerned was that they seemed to believe him. They clearly thought he was stupid enough to have done what he was claiming. However, he was not off the hook. Once this operation was over, he was politely told he should consider the tenability of remaining in his position with the service.

"Leave before I'm pushed," he said out loud without thinking.

"What?" Jackson's voice brought Stanners back into the present.

"Oh, my superiors are furious with me. I was heading towards retirement anyway, but I reckon when all this is over, I'll be gone, one way or another. What I did was inexcusable."

"I don't believe you."

"Sorry, what?"

"I said, I don't believe you," Jackson repeated.

"Why not?"

"I know you; Harry knows you. You are not computer savvy enough to even begin to start the process that would end up in such a disaster. So, I'm going to ask you a simple question and I want a simple answer. Who are you covering for?"

Stanners winced at the lad's pinpoint accuracy of events. "Nobody...." he began but then thought better of trying to spin yet another lie. "You don't need to know," he said instead.

"Oh, I think I bloody do," Jackson retorted, his anger building. "My partner was nearly killed yesterday and even now may end up in a wheelchair for the rest of his life; we used an innocent girl for our own gain without even thinking about the ramifications and she ended up risking her own life to save ours. We have no idea what's happened to her, she might even be dead by now. And all of this could have been avoided if we'd known from the start that Evie had a twin brother. We'd have been onto him sooner and this destructive, stupid, suicidal dash across Europe would never have happened."

Jackson leapt up from his chair and stared Stanners directly in the face, just inches away from him. "I'm going to ask you again and I want the truth. Who really did this?"

Stanners swallowed hard. "Vivian, I was covering for Vivian."

The Gemini Connection

Jackson was speechless for a minute; he took an involuntary step backwards. "Vivian?" he finally said incredulously, "our Vivian?"

Stanners nodded. "She never forgave me for the death of her fiancé. We were once field operatives together, but our cover was blown, and her fiancé was murdered as a result. She blamed me and this was her payback, it was a long time coming but please don't blame her. Her actions were aimed at me, not you or Harry or Evie."

Jackson looked at him in disgust. "Well, I do blame her, I blame both of you. Whatever happened between you, it had nothing, NOTHING," he shouted, "to do with Evie. If she dies, if Harry loses his leg, this is on your shoulders. You and Vivian. You make me sick; I can't even look at you."

As Jackson stormed from the room, Stanners flopped down into the empty chair utterly exhausted. He dropped his head into his hands and, not for the first time over the last 24 hours, wished he could turn back the clock and do things differently.

~~~~

Jackson stumbled down the hospital corridors until he finally found the main entrance and made his way out into the fresh air. He found a bench in a secluded area and sat down with a heavy sigh. He had not slept since they'd arrived in Turkey and images of Evie holding the gun to her head, and Harry lying wounded in his arms, danced around in his head, tormenting him. He groaned as his mind conjured up different scenarios Evie may now be in, none of them good, and then he suddenly had a vision of her lying dead on the ground, a bullet wound to her head. He couldn't take anymore; Jackson dropped his head into his hands and sobbed, his whole body shaking with emotion. He wasn't sure how long he cried for, but the tears were still running down his face when a plastic cup of coffee was gently thrust into his face.

"You look like you need this," he heard Stanners say. "And this." He looked up to see a chocolate bar in Stanners' other hand.

"May I sit?"

Jackson nodded and pushed the back of his hand across his nose and eyes trying, and failing, to disguise the wetness on his face.

"You're right to be angry lad, I would be in your shoes. If it helps, I'm angry enough at myself for both of us."

"No, that doesn't really help, but thanks for saying it."

Jackson took a sip of the coffee; it was disgusting but he didn't really care. "How did this go so wrong?"

Stanners rubbed his forehead; he had a thumping headache. "We underestimated 'them', whoever 'they' are. It's clear now that they knew Evie was on that plane. They probably knew you were too."

Stanners paused whilst Jackson unwrapped the chocolate and started munching. "The Turkish chap who drove you? Yusuf? He managed to get a couple of photos of the men waiting for Evie on the other side of the river. That river is the border between here and Syria by the way."

"I guessed as much."

The Gemini Connection

"Anyway, one of the men? It was definitely Michael Longshaw. They're still trying to identify the others, in particular the man next to him who gave the order to kill you. He's not coming up on any of the Turkish data bases though which seems odd, they have pretty comprehensive intelligence on most terrorists still using Syria as a hiding place. Doesn't look like he's a remnant of IS or anything of that ilk."

"So, what do they want with Evie? Yesterday one of them clearly said 'It's you we want' to her."

Stanners shrugged his shoulders. "I'm afraid we don't know yet."

Just then Jackson's phone began to ring, he looked at the screen and quickly answered. He spoke briefly with someone then stood up. "That was the ward, Harry's out of theatre. We need to go."

~~~~

"Didn't they say anything about his leg?" Stanners puffed as they raced back to Harry.

"No, it was the ward clerk, I don't think she knew."

Jackson hurtled down the corridor, eventually leaving Stanners behind, and slammed straight into the surgeon who was just coming out of Harry's ward. He was relieved to see that the surgeon had a broad smile on his face, surely it was good news.

"Well?" he gasped.

"It went well, very well. We made multiple deep incisions in his lower leg to relieve the pressure and then I managed to use this experimental new technique to split open some smaller veins and stitch them to each other to increase their calibre..."

In his enthusiasm for how well it had all gone, it took a minute or two for the surgeon to register that Jackson was beginning to look pale with a hint of green; perhaps a detailed surgical explanation was not warranted. "He still has his leg," he concluded, "it will be very painful, he'll have a lot of scars, he's going to need intensive physiotherapy, but he still has his leg."

"Thank you," Jackson grasped his hand. "Can I see him? Is he awake?"

"Oh yes, but I should warn you, he's had a lot of analgesia. He's a little, er...."

No further explanation was needed. As Jackson pushed open the door to the ward, he could hear someone singing. Someone singing very badly, completely off key and slurring at least half of the words.

"Show me the way to go home, I'm tired and I want to go to bed...." rang out down the ward.

Jackson walked down into Harry's room to find him now declaring undying love to the exasperated nurse trying to check his assorted wound dressings. "You're lovely. If I don't marry a pineapple, I want to marry you," Harry told her before resuming his singing.

"Show me the way to go.... Jacky boy, you're here." Harry's face lit up as he saw him. "This is my bestest mate ever," Harry insisted on telling the bemused nurse. "Why do you look so miserable mate? Sing with me, that'll cheer you up. 'Show me the way....' oh, hang on a minute. You're much posher than me, you need the posh version. After three; 1, 2, 4 and sing."

Harry began singing hopelessly out of tune again. "Indicate the way to my abode, I'm fatigued, and I wish to retire…"

Jackson just smiled. *And he's back,* he thought.

Chapter 28

24 hours earlier

Think Evie, think! Evie admonished herself as she kept the gun to her head and watched the car with Jackson and Harry in disappear down the dirt track and towards safety. Whatever happened, she knew she needed to avoid crossing the bridge that stood between her and Michael. Like Jackson, she had correctly guessed that the river was also the border with Syria, and she knew her chances of escape would be higher if she stayed this side of it.

Think Evie... she had had to do it so many times with critically ill patients; stay calm, look for the obvious first, break the problem down into chunks.

She heard her name being called and turned slowly to see Michael and Boran advancing towards her across the bridge. The familiarity of Michael hit her so hard in the chest she felt physically winded. She wanted to run onto the bridge to him, but she knew it would be a mistake – the situation must remain balanced in her favour.

"Evie, drop the gun," Michael was imploring her. His voice jolted her racing brain into action.

"Stop," she shouted. "I won't drop it until my brother, just my brother, is by my side. I will shoot myself if you don't do as I ask."

Michael turned to Boran. "She will be okay once I'm with her, but believe me, she is stubborn enough, and strong enough, to carry out her threat."

"Michael, you said she would want to join us. I am not pleased with this, not pleased at all. Bring her here to me, now," Boran's tone was threatening, "or you can both face the consequences."

Michael blanched; he was acutely aware that they were surrounded by Boran's armed men who wouldn't hesitate to shoot if ordered to do so.

Boran fixed him with a hard stare that chilled him despite the heat of the burning sun. "I said, go and get her!"

Michael nodded and began to advance on his own towards Evie.

Stay calm and look for the obvious first, Evie kept repeating her mantra over and over in her head. She scanned the area around her. The bridge was only a foot bridge, the car on the other side of it, that presumably had brought Michael and Boran, could not cross it. On her side there was still the SUV that had brought her from the airport. The men from the SUV had abandoned it when all hell had broken loose with Jackson and Harry and were now further away from it than she was. Evie edged slightly to her left, the gun still in her hand, its metal tip pressed into her temple. She reached a point where she could glance sideways for a fleeting moment

The Gemini Connection

and see the steering column of the car. *Look for the obvious first* – the keys were still in the ignition.

She stopped moving and called out to Michael who was now just a few feet away from her. "Clocal, wij jaf; mo gaw laish, wij jaf."

The language was their own, and only Michael understood her. He reached her side, and she repeated the words. "Clocal, wij jaf; mo gaw laish, wij jaf – *Michael, dad's car; we were twelve, dad's car.*"

Michael looked at her and gave a virtually imperceptible nod of his head. "Jaf, geg!" he said to her. *"Car, now."*

The men nearest to them were looking at each other, baffled by what they were hearing, but their momentary confusion bought Evie and Michael a few precious seconds. They both ran to the car; Michael sprinted around to the driver's side and had the engine started as Evie threw herself into the passenger seat. He spun the car around and was speeding off before she had even closed her door. Boran's men were too slow to react. They ran after the car shooting aimlessly down the track but to no avail; one bullet hit the rear of the car, but all the others fell wide of their target. Boran was furious, he had realised before his men had that they were going to make a run for the car but had not been close enough to stop them.

As the cloud of dust caused by the departing car settled, he noticed the sun reflecting off a small object on the ground. It was the second phone Jackson had given Evie; it had been dislodged and fallen from her when she had raced to the car. Boran's face turned crimson as he realised what had happened. He poured out curses on them both, so that was how the English men had found her so quickly.

"I will find you," he screamed into the empty air as he smashed the phone with his booted foot. "I will find you both and I will kill you!"

~~~~

"Wij jaf, you remembered?" Evie looked at Michael.

"Of course I did, I thought dad was going to kill us that day!"

One summer, sixteen years ago, their father had left his car on the drive with the engine running whilst he raced back into the house for some forgotten item. Evie and Michael were bored, school holidays always saw them left to their own devices by their parents. They had run out of ideas on how to entertain themselves until Michael had spied an opportunity.

"Come on," he had told Evie grabbing her hand and, before she knew quite what was happening, they were in their father's car. Michael, always a keen observer of all that went on around him, knew what to do. He had managed to dip the clutch, get the car into first gear and begun to lurch the car forward before their furious father caught up with them.

"What the hell do you think you are doing?" he had bellowed as he yanked Michael from the car. As the twins both began to laugh, their father struck first Michael, then Evie, hard across their faces. So forceful were his blows, Evie was knocked sideways into a bush. Their father's persona as the caring family GP rarely extended to his own family. After that they had been made to stay in their separate rooms for the next two days, but this only made them more determined than ever to remain united. Michael's door had a lock, his father took advantage of this and made him a prisoner in his own room. Evie's room however did not. The twins had spent the time scribbling endless notes to each other in their secret language and Evie would dash out onto the landing to post them back and forth under Michael's door whenever the coast was clear, which was quite frequent. Their parents employed a live-in housekeeper, but she refused to act as jailer to the twins and turned a blind eye when she heard Evie's door opening and closing upstairs and the sound of her running up and down the corridor. She hadn't particularly warmed to the twins, finding them rather aloof and elusive, but any sympathy she felt was with them not their parents.

"I thought if I just said 'car' it wouldn't be enough. I needed you to know the keys were still in it," Evie was explaining.

"Oh, I understood," Michael said, "but we need to ditch this car as soon as possible; it has tracking devices in it, and they will be onto us. It's good to see you by the way."

Evie's mouth fell open. "Good to see me? Good to see me?? I thought you were dead Michael; we had a memorial service for you. I wrote a eulogy for you and broke down reading it. And all that time, you were alive?" Evie shook her head, she had so many questions but did not know where to start.

"I promise I'll explain everything, but right now we need to focus. And the first thing to do is ditch this car."

"Stay calm and look for the obvious," Evie recited.

"Sorry, what?"

"It's what my boss always says. 'At critical moments in theatre, look for the obvious first. Don't panic and pump your patient full of drugs if their oxygen levels are falling; first check the oxygen tubing hasn't disconnected.' The obvious thing here is we need to get back to Gaziantep. If we abandon the car in the middle of nowhere, how are we going to get back into the city? I need to contact Jackson, he will know what to do." She reached for the phone that should have been tucked into the back waistband of her jeans, but realised in dismay that it was gone. "I've lost my other phone; I must have dropped it. They won't know where I am."

She looked at Michael in bewilderment. "What are we going to do?"

"Hide in plain sight," he replied. "I know Gaziantep a little, we'll leave the car at the bus station in the hope they'll think we've left. Do you have any money on you?"

Evie shook her head. "My bag's still in this car but I don't have any Turkish money, just credit cards."

"We can't use cards; they'll be traced in an instant. I have some Turkish lira, not much but enough for a day or two."

"Enough for bus or train fares?" Evie asked.

"We can't get on any public transport Evie; they'll quickly pick us up on the security cameras. Can't risk a taxi either, they might spot us."

"Who are 'they' Michael? What are you caught up in? Jackson said you were a terrorist, but I didn't want to believe him."

"Which one was Jackson?" Michael asked.

"The one who wasn't left fighting for his life after your newfound friends shot them," she replied angrily. "Harry was haemorrhaging like crazy from his groin, he might not have made it." Evie's eyes started to prick with tears.

"They're MI6 yeah?"

Evie didn't correct him. "I'm not telling you anything else about them. I can't trust you right now."

She stared out the car window; they were racing down an open road, and she could see the city's buildings ahead of them. "Harry will have been taken to a hospital; we could go there. Try and find them."

Michael shook his head. "Way too many cameras, we'll be seen. And if he is there, he'll be heavily guarded. We'd never get to him."

He turned sharply off the main road and started going through a maze of back streets before finally stopping the car. "We'll abandon it here, we're a couple of roads away from the bus terminal."

"Leave the keys in the ignition," Evie said. "With a bit of luck, it will be stolen and send your friends on even more of a wild goose chase as they look for us."

Michael smiled at her as he pulled her travel bag from the car boot. "You always were the clever one, I've missed you so much."

"Don't, just don't," Evie replied in dismay. "At least you've had the luxury of missing me knowing I was alive; a comfort you didn't think to grant me."

Michael knew there was nothing he could say to counter this, she was right. "Come on," he said instead. "We need to get away from here, Boran won't be far behind us."

"So, that bastard who ordered the shooting has a name does he?"

Michael grimaced. "Yes, and there was a time when I trusted him."

"How can you trust a man like that?" Evie asked in bewilderment.

"I don't anymore Evie, but I owe him; he is the reason I didn't die in Kabul."

Chapter 29

It had taken several hours for Harry's euphoric state to subside. He continued to sing, loudly, for so long that Jackson began to wonder how ethical it might be to seal his mouth shut with some of the micropore tape left on the side table by the nurse. Harry eventually fell asleep until late afternoon when the excruciating pain in his leg woke him from a vivid dream in which he was being shot.

"Are you okay mate?" Jackson had been dozing in the chair beside his bed and was roused by Harry's moans.

"My leg's killing me!" Harry scanned the room. "And where on earth are we?"

Jackson pushed the call button on the bedside table. "I'll get them to give you more painkillers. You're in hospital, you were shot, remember?"

Harry frowned; the pain made thinking almost impossible. "Vaguely, there were men everywhere. Men with guns...." He was struggling to concentrate.

"Yeah, you saw them before I did. I was racing towards Evie, you pushed me out of the way and took both bullets."

"Did I? I don't remember, does that make me your hero?" Harry started to joke as the nurse came in and busied herself giving an injection of analgesia directly into Harry's intravenous line.

"Will he start singing again?" Jackson asked her.

She smiled. "Probably not, but I can't promise."

"I hope you have a lot of sedatives on the ward then," Jackson replied.

"Oh no, we wouldn't want to sedate him again," she explained.

"Not for him, for me, if he starts serenading me again!"

She laughed, shaking her head at him. "You crazy English," she said as she left the room.

As Harry took in his surroundings, he realised someone was missing. "Jackson, where's Evie?"

Jackson looked at him. "We don't know," he replied eventually. "Do you remember what she did?"

Harry shook his head.

"She grabbed a gun and threatened to kill herself if they didn't let us go. She held it to her own head, she said if they killed us, she would kill herself. She told me to get you to safety, we would both be dead if she hadn't done that. She saved our lives, and I had to leave her behind…" Jackson's voice cracked under the strain of his emotion.

"Shit," Harry said slowly, "that's brave. I don't remember that."

"She was just standing there, still holding that gun, as we sped off. I can't get the image out of my head. I'll never, NEVER, forgive myself if she dies."

"You really care about her, don't you?" For once Harry's tone was serious.

Jackson could only nod his head in reply.

"Can we still track her?"

Jackson coughed and tried to regain his composure. "No, the signal from the back up phone disappeared around the time of the shooting. We don't know where she is, we don't know who the men were who took her. Well, apart from her brother; Stanners says they have positively identified one of the men as Michael."

"He is her brother Jackson." Harry tried to offer some comfort. "I doubt very much he wants to see her harmed. Whatever his motives, he surely wants to keep his twin sister safe."

"Yeah, but what if she shot herself anyway after we left? What if she felt so trapped it seemed the only way out?"

Harry could only look at him, there was nothing he could say to refute the possibility of what Jackson had just said.

~~~~~

When Evie woke up the next morning, Michael was sitting on the edge of the bed holding a cup of coffee for her.

"Hey, sleepyhead, rise and shine."

"Thanks," she said, pushing herself up against the pillows and taking the coffee.

The Gemini Connection

"I thought I should let you sleep as long as possible, but we need to get moving soon."

Evie yawned; she was exhausted. They had talked long into the night, and she hadn't fallen asleep until after 4am.

After they had abandoned the car the previous day, Michael led them through part of the old town until he found a small and shabby guest house tucked away down a side street. Paying with cash, he booked them a room for the night. "We should be safe here, no cameras," he told Evie.

"Why are you so obsessed with cameras?" Evie asked but Michael had not replied.

Once they were in the room, Michael locked the door and closed the curtains. He turned round to face Evie who threw herself into his arms. She sobbed and sobbed, repeatedly saying, "I thought you were dead; I've missed you so much."

Michael simply held her; her face was buried into his chest, and he stroked the back of her head in an attempt to soothe her. When her tears were finally spent, she stood back from him, searching his face for answers. As Michael remained silent, her emotions changed to anger. She raised her hand and slapped him, hard, across the face.

"How could you do that to me?" she cried. "We were a pair, remember? We promised each other that we would always be there for each other, but you let me believe you were dead for two years. Two years Michael, two years!" She was shouting now.

"Shush, people may hear," Michael began to say but Evie cut him off.

"So what? What's the worst that can happen now Michael? Are you going to die again? Do you want me to die with you this time? I didn't ask for any of this, so start explaining, now."

"I thought you were going to die when you held that gun to your head. Jackson and the other man, do they really mean that much to you?"

"Yes," Evie said evenly.

"When you called out to me in our language the first time, you said 'I really care about him Michael. I mean it, I will do it.' That's when I told Boran you would shoot yourself, I knew you meant it. Which one Evie? Which man did you mean?"

Evie stared at him. "I am not telling you anything more. It's you that needs to explain."

Michael sighed. "I don't know where to begin, it's all such a mess."

"Well, I suggest you start with the bomb in Kabul you so miraculously survived."

"I wasn't in the room when it detonated, that's how."

Evie continued to fix him in her gaze but said nothing; Michael knew that look. She'd always had the ability to communicate just with her eyes and she was doing it now.

He continued. "But it all began earlier than that. Those six months in Kabul; I saw things Evie that I will never unsee. Such atrocities: sex workers raped then beaten to death; young Afghan men rounded up and mercilessly shot; girls and women living in fear every day of their lives."

"Everybody knows the Taliban are ruthless Michael."

The Gemini Connection

Michael looked at her. "But this wasn't the Taliban Evie, or any extremist group. It was done by *us* Evie, the people who were supposedly there to help maintain law and order and rebuild the country. I saw people being lauded in media interviews for their 'fantastic work' in Afghanistan who spent their nights roaming the streets looking for their next hit of opium or the next girl to rape."

Evie swallowed. "Go on."

"I tried to do something Evie, I really did. I went to senior people, very senior people, but everything fell on deaf ears. I was told, I was ordered, to turn a blind eye. Told I was simply witnessing the collateral damage of any war. But we weren't at war and even if we had been, it was no more justified."

"So, you what? Swapped sides? Joined a different set of killers?" Evie's tone remained unforgiving.

"No, I didn't, well not really, not exactly."

Evie raised her eyebrows at him but said nothing.

"The day of the bomb, that was the turning point. Security at the university was tight, really tight. My bag was sent through the x-ray machine as usual but then I was taken aside for a random pat down check. I didn't know it at the time, but I was given back a different bag, it looked identical to mine, but this one had the device in it. I went into the lecture theatre; I was supposed to be teaching trauma aid to a group of allied personnel. Before I had even had time to open the bag, there was a knock on the door, and I was asked to go to reception to take an urgent phone call. Well, I did just that. I went, I picked up the phone and a man's voice said, 'Michael, stay where you are.' Before I had time to ask who it was and what he meant, the explosion happened. I was far enough away to not be caught up in it. The next thing I knew, there was a hand on my shoulder, and I was guided out through all the mayhem and bundled into a car. The man who helped me? It was Boran."

Evie was confused. "But how did he know you had the bomb? How did he even know your name? How on earth did he get a bomb into the university in the first place?" Evie's questions came tumbling out. "And why did he decide to spare you?"

"Boran already knew someone at the university had tried to blow the whistle on the abuse against the local population, but he only heard at the last minute it was me. That's when he decided to recruit me. He didn't have to get anything into the university Evie; not himself, not the device. He built the bomb right there under their noses and orchestrated my bag swap. He already worked there; he's a highly accomplished engineer. But the moment I got in that car with him, I was trapped. Not only was my life in his hands, but now my death was too. And he decreed I had died."

Chapter 30

"Jackson, wake up, I think I'm hallucinating!"

Jackson's eyes sprang open as Harry kept nudging his arm. "I can see the boss standing at the end of my bed!"

"That's because I am standing at the end of your bed, you twit!" Stanners' voice filled the room.

Harry looked at Jackson. "And now he's talking to me!"

"I can see him too mate, doubt we're both hallucinating."

Harry gulped. "Boss? What are you doing here?"

"Sorting you out for starters!" was the gruff reply.

It was late evening and Harry had been sleeping fitfully again. Stanners had just returned from a meeting with an attachment of MI6 and Turkish security operatives. Jackson had tried to insist he go too but Stanners had refused. He could see the exhaustion and turmoil in Jackson and didn't want him present if any graphic images of Evie lying dead emerged.

"Stay with him," he had told Jackson nodding in Harry's direction. "I don't want him on his own."

Jackson had acquiesced but his heart began to race when he saw Stanners enter the room looking grim.

"Any news Sir?"

"They've been trying to find satellite images from yesterday of the area where you were shot. The trouble is the main images are in the hands of our American friends and they are proving reluctant to hand anything over. Probably because they've got people and operations on the ground there they would prefer us not to know about."

"Ring Spammy, you know, Ham the Spam, he might be able to help," Harry began but was quickly interrupted by an exasperated Stanners.

"What with? A pizza order? I need information from the CIA not recommendations for a takeaway!"

"He's our CIA contact," Jackson explained. "Ham the Spam is just his nickname."

"I don't care if he's called Ham, Bacon, or the whole Full English, we can't put him in the position of leaking info to us. Not when we are already hounding them through the official channels."

"He's done it before," Harry chipped in but when he saw the look on Stanners' face, he began to wish he hadn't.

"I'm going to pretend I didn't hear that!"

"So, what happens next? I can't just sit here, bored stiff and doing nothing. No offence," Jackson added looking at Harry.

"None taken," Harry replied and winced as he went to shrug his shoulders. "Keep forgetting I was shot there too."

The Gemini Connection

"Well, this one is going to be medevacked back to London as soon as the surgeon gives the okay for him to fly," Stanners said pointing at Harry. "They tell me you are going to need a lot of intensive rehab on that leg of yours. I pity the physios who'll have to work with you day in and day out. They'll be committing hara kiri by the time they've finished with you."

"Nah boss, they'll love me," Harry said with a wink.

Stanners rolled his eyes in reply. "Right, I'm going to phone my opposite number in MI6 again, see if we've made any progress." He made to leave the room but then turned back and looked at Harry. "I gather you pushed Jackson out of the way, stopped him from being shot. That showed some courage."

"He'd have done the same for me," Harry replied.

Stanners nodded and allowed a smile to break out on his face. "Well at least I only need to convince the finance department to cough up the money to get one injured operative home rather than two after your 'Gunfight at the O.K. Corral' antics."

"Gee boss, you're all heart," Harry said.

"Yep, that I am." Stanners paused and coughed awkwardly. "But I'm glad to see you safe Mr Rivers, very glad to see you safe." And with that he left the room leaving the two younger men staring at each other with open mouths.

~~~~~

Evie rummaged through her bag looking for some painkillers. She had the mother of all headaches, no doubt brought on by the combination of poor sleep, little food, and high levels of anxiety. Ironically the very thing Stanners and Jackson were hoping for, that their movements would be picked up by covert monitoring, was the thing Michael was avoiding at all costs. He had moved them to another cheap hotel, still in the old town where he knew the crowded and narrow streets made any kind of video surveillance difficult.

"We need to keep moving," he had told Evie. "We shouldn't stay in the same place for too long."

"Do you have any kind of plan?" Evie demanded to know when he had again locked the door and closed the curtains in their latest room. "What exactly did you hope would happen when I showed up here?"

"Well, not this," Michael admitted. "I don't know, I thought I would be on MI6's radar and that when I met you here, they'd pick me up and take me back to England. I was counting on you not coming alone. I was only supposed to send you one message, Boran said any more than that would ring alarm bells. As soon as I knew that, well I wanted those bells to ring. In my head I thought, 'She's bound to be followed when she comes to Gaziantep, they'll arrest me of course as soon as I appear but at least I'll be back in the hands of the British.'"

"If you were so keen to leave, why didn't you just do it? Why go through this tangled web of deceit when you could have just walked away?"

Michael let out a hollow laugh. "You don't walk away from people like Boran. I saw what he did to the few who tried. And besides, I had no passport, very little money, I wouldn't have got far alone. I would never have made it out."

"Which is where we have found ourselves anyway," Evie grimaced at him. "And also with no means of getting out." She moved over to the window and pulled one of the curtains back by a tiny fraction, the light momentarily blinding her.

"Why did those men say 'It's you we want' to me? Why did Boran say 'Get her now'? What exactly had you said Michael? Who are these people?"

Michael swallowed; he had hoped to avoid that question. "I don't know what to tell you Evie. They are not terrorists as such, not in the conventional way at least."

"Oh, I'm sorry, I didn't realise there were conventional and non-conventional terrorists." Evie's voice dripped with sarcasm.

Michael winced. "What I mean is they are a group, predominantly men, who see their role as righting the wrongs they witness, whatever the side. In the same way they planned the Kabul bomb, they've also taken out huge chunks of ISIS. In a way, they're vigilantes."

"Vigilantes? Vigilantes?" Evie shook with anger. "They shot my friends in cold blood. They killed innocent people in Kabul. Why do they get to decide who lives and who dies? I don't care if they also target extremists. Who gave them the right to play God?"

"Boran believes God has told him to do this."

Evie spun round. "What?"

"Boran, he believes God has appointed him to mete out justice. He said he had a vision where God told him to do this."

Evie could not believe what she was hearing. "So basically, he is a religious fanatic as well as a homicidal maniac. And you fell for this? Michael, you always ribbed me mercilessly when I said I prayed. You don't even believe in God, you said anyone who did was insane and yet you were blindsided by a man like that?"

"It didn't seem like that at first. Boran was so articulate, intelligent, charismatic even. The night before I first met him, I had been patching up two young women who had been raped and beaten senseless by a gang of western workers. They had been left for dead, the only reason they survived was because some British soldiers pulled off the attackers and got them to hospital."

"So, they were saved by the same people Boran wanted dead. Surely you have just defeated your own argument?"

"It wouldn't have happened in the first place though Evie, if senior people weren't turning a blind eye to what their subordinates got up to in the towns and villages. I know you're going to say two wrongs don't make a right but when Boran said sometimes a wrong can right a wrong, well it kind of made sense to me."

"Could you have left Michael? At the very start, did you choose to stay?"

"Boran said he would give me 24 hours to decide but if I chose to leave there was the small matter of the fallout from the bomb to deal with. A bomb that had been carried into that lecture theatre in my bag. I was already a marked man for whistleblowing in the first place. If I went back, I would have been arrested."

"But you could have told the truth, explained that your bag was switched. That you had nothing to do with it."

"Do you really think they would have believed me? Boran said they most likely wanted me out of the picture anyway and I had just given them the perfect reason to lock me up and throw away the key. Or worse."

"So, you stayed with Boran."

"Yes, I did. He has gradually recruited so many people Evie. Engineers, computer experts, physicists…"

"Doctors," Evie finished for him.

"I was his first medic. At the start, I honestly thought I could finally make a difference. Let's face it, I'd tried through all the proper channels and got nowhere. I liked the idea of fighting for the underdog, protecting the defenceless, meting out justice for the vulnerable."

"Even when it meant killing?" Michael didn't answer her, and his silence infuriated her.

"So, what changed Michael? When did the scales finally begin to fall off your eyes?"

"About a year in. We had been travelling around for so long. We couldn't stay in Kabul, Boran knew the bomb would be traced back to him. One of his men had sabotaged some of the university security cameras to play the same loop over and over in the evenings. It fooled the security guards into thinking no one was there when he was assembling the bomb. But he had to use components from the engineering department, once it had detonated there was no going back for him either."

"Am I supposed to feel sorry for him?" Evie asked in disbelief.

"No, of course not, that's not why I'm telling you this. We then spent a year going through various countries. There were six of us to begin with, all drawn to Boran's idea we were on a mission to see justice done."

"I still can't believe you went along with this Michael; you must have seen that he was a monster."

"Not initially, his arguments were very persuasive. Boran is very good at reading people. He can spot the issue you are struggling with and home in on it. With me, he reminded me daily of what I had witnessed in Afghanistan. He recruited a brilliant computer guy in Pakistan by playing on his hatred of what extremists had done to his family; he worked his magic on several people in Iraq by reminding them of what we and the Americans had done when we invaded. When people are carrying deep wounds, and someone comes along offering a possible solution, well sometimes they listen. Boran knew within half an hour of talking to a man if he was ripe for recruitment. What I didn't know at the time was the true scale of his intentions. By the time we arrived in Syria he had gathered over 40 men, plus some women because a few of the men were married. Once we were there, he said God wanted him to exact revenge on all the perpetrators, irrespective of allegiance or side, that had wreaked so much devastation in the country. He began drawing others into the group that were happy to fight for any cause if they were paid enough. When he started ordering death after death, I knew then I was dealing with someone who was completely delusional. He was creating a cult with him as its supreme leader, and I hadn't even realised. I began to plot how to escape, and I managed to convince him of something so well he began to believe it. He allowed me to message you because he thought, he believed…" Michael couldn't go on.

"What did you convince him of Michael? What did you promise him?"

Michael looked at her pleadingly. "I, I, I said…" he struggled to speak. "I told him that if you knew I was alive and what I was doing you would want to join us and…" Michael paused.

"And?" Evie's eyes tore into him.

"And that you would want to become his wife."

Evie stared at her brother, a mixture of horror and disgust on her face. "You said what? You bartered with my life like that? How could you?"

"Evie, please, I was desperate. I needed to do something radical that would sway him. He controls everything, I couldn't get access to phones without his say so. I couldn't jump on a computer and e-mail you. I knew his one Achilles heel was that he wanted a wife; not a passing woman; not a one-night stand; a wife. I exploited that and it very nearly worked but clearly, I hadn't done enough to convince him you would come alone, that I could waltz off on my own to meet you at an airport. Please say you forgive me."

Evie continued to stare at him but said nothing.

"Evie, please."

Eventually she spoke, "I don't know you any more Michael. Our bond, our shared life, our love? You've destroyed it. I wish you had died in that bomb attack. I really do because then at least I would have lost the brother I loved." She began to sob. "Now I've found a brother who is unrecognisable from the one I grew up with. I can't stay here with you; I'm going to find a way out of here by myself."

"Evie, it's not safe. You must stay with me!" Michael exclaimed.

"I'll take my chances," Evie cried grabbing her handbag and shoving a few items from her travel bag into it. "I'll find Jackson, he won't have left me here. I know he will still be in the city somewhere."

"Evie, you can't…" but Michael's words fell onto deaf ears.

Evie had already unlocked the door and was halfway down the stairs. She ran out into the street with little idea of where to go.

In the shadows a man watched her go and began dialling a number on his mobile phone. It was answered within two rings. "I've found her," he told the person at the other end. "Tell Boran I've found her."

The Gemini Connection

Chapter 31

Evie ran through the streets of the old town trying to formulate a plan in her head. She knew Michael would be following her and dived haphazardly down different streets in the hope of losing him. His confession about what he had said to Boran about her had rocked her to the core. Michael alone knew the extent of the abuse Evie had suffered in her teenage years at the hands of their father and for him to use her as bait with his vile promise to Boran was the ultimate betrayal.

She turned another corner and found herself in a larger square. Although it was evening, many of the shops were still open and her attention was drawn to the clothes shops selling the abayas, hijabs and niqabs some of the women wore. She entered one of the busier shops but was clueless as to what to ask for. She was grateful for her dark eyes and hair – at least she blended in with the other women in the shop. She looked around her at the array of clothing and then approached one of the older assistants hoping that she would take pity on her.

"Hello, do you speak English?" she asked.

The Gemini Connection

"I do, how can I help you?" The woman looked her up and down and Evie realised she must look utterly dishevelled and unkempt.

"I have come from England to see my grandfather. He's very ill, in hospital. My mother told me to get here as quickly as possible. He is very conservative; I can't go and see him in my western clothes. I need to buy some very modest items. Can you help me?"

Evie held her breath, but the assistant seemed to believe her story.

"I'm so very sorry, you don't have anything with you?"

"No," Evie lied, "I didn't have time to pack. When my mother rang, I just booked a flight and came."

"Can you not borrow clothing from your mother?" the assistant asked kindly.

Shoot, thought Evie, *that would have been the obvious thing to do, if I was telling the truth.*

"I think it best I buy my own things," she said instead to the assistant. "My mother isn't at my grandfather's home, she's at his bedside, so I didn't want to rifle through her things."

The assistant reached out and took Evie's hands. "Beautiful girl, so thoughtful. Let's get you clothed appropriately to go to your grandfather. I suggest darker colours in the circumstances."

Twenty minutes later Evie was unrecognisable from the girl who had entered the shop. Swathed in dark blue and grey from head to toe she already felt safer. She told the woman she wanted to wear the clothes immediately and it was only when the assistant was totting up the cost of the clothing on the till Evie remembered she had no

The Gemini Connection

Turkish money. She had her credit card but Michael's warnings about everything being traceable made her reluctant to use it.

"Er, I don't have any Turkish lira." Evie looked imploringly at the assistant. She was bound to say she could use a credit card.

"You can pay in Euros; do you have those?"

Relief flooded through Evie; she had taken some out from an ATM in Paris. She nodded as she fished her purse out from her bag, she had enough to pay with some to spare.

"You will find many places are happy to take Euros. I will pray for your grandfather Kiz," the assistant said using the Turkish word for daughter. "I hope he recovers."

"Thank you." Evie began to leave then turned back as a thought struck her. "He was in a terrible car accident, on the road that goes from the airport towards the east. He was taken to that big hospital, the one that deals with major trauma, oh I can't remember its name."

"Ah, I imagine that will be our main City Hospital, it is the closest to where you say his accident happened. I'm sure it will be that one, it is an excellent hospital; your grandfather will be in good hands."

Evie nodded. "Yes, that's the one." She was tempted to ask for directions but felt it would stretch the credibility of her fabricated story too far for her to appear to have no idea how to get to the hospital her supposed grandfather was in. Instead, she said, "May I use your phone to ring the hospital? My mobile phone has run out of charge, I'd like to tell my mother I'm on my way."

"Of course, do you know the number?"

The Gemini Connection

Evie shook her head.

"No problem, I will find it."

As the woman quickly looked up the number for the hospital, Evie was hoping and praying that if Harry had survived, he would be in this hospital. And where Harry was, there was a very good chance Jackson would be also.

"Here you are Kiz," the assistant was handing her the shop phone. "I have already dialled the number for you."

~~~~

Michael hesitated at the door of the hotel. Peering out into the street he saw the man Evie hadn't noticed and watched him make a call on his mobile phone. Judging by the nodding of his head he was being given instructions. When he set off, clearly trailing Evie, Michael's heart sank. You could not live alongside Boran for two years and not understand what had just happened. This man could have been tasked with killing him, it was obvious he would be in the same building Evie had just emerged from, but finding Evie was clearly Boran's priority, killing Michael could wait. Michael watched until the man was nearly out of view then slunk out from the hotel and followed him.

~~~~

Boran's man cursed as he saw Evie disappear into the clothing shop. He could not enter too; it was strictly women only. He tried to peer through the windows but to no avail. There were no direct views into the shop. All he could do was lurk in the shadows and wait. He guessed correctly that Evie was buying clothing to act as a disguise, but as similarly clad women milled up and down the pavement in front of the shop it would be much harder to spot her leave. He positioned himself a few metres down from the shop entrance where he could more easily scrutinise the women walking past. If she had a face veil on too it would be virtually impossible to spot her, but he hoped her telltale footwear of bright blue canvas shoes would give her away.

He didn't have to wait long. As several women emerged from the shop, they were closely followed by another. She gave the impression of being with them as they went down the street but as they turned left, she turned right instead, and he caught a glimpse of the blue shoes. Smiling to himself he set off after her but he forgot to pay attention to his surroundings. He did not notice the man coming up behind him, a man with a knife in his hand who pulled him into a side alley at the first opportunity and did not hesitate to plunge it between his ribs. The last thing the man saw was Michael's face.

"Nobody hurts my sister," he hissed as the man's life ebbed from him.

~~~~

"Jackson, I need a word, now!"

Stanners put his head round the door of Harry's hospital room and beckoned him out.

"There's been a call to this hospital, somebody calling herself Leenie asked for you and Harry by name."

"That was Evie," Jackson cried. "Did she say where she was? We need to find her."

"Just wait a moment, we need to be careful. She did give a location but why use the wrong name if it is Evie?"

"Because Leenie was the nickname Michael gave her, only Evie would know that. It's her way of proving it's her. Come on, we need to go."

Stanners put his hand on Jackson's shoulder to hold him back. "I've already relayed her message to our MI6 colleagues; they'll go with some of the Turkish guys to pick her up. We have no idea if her brother is with her or not and we can't rule out the possibility she made the call under duress. Better for the experts to do it."

Jackson looked fit to explode. "What, the same experts who couldn't even protect her at the airport? Give me the address."

Stanners sighed. "Leave it to the others..." he began to say.

"No!" Jackson voice was rising. "This girl risked her life to save mine and Harry's. We owe her. She won't know who to trust if a bunch of strangers try and lift her. She knows me, she trusts me. I'm the one who has been with her 24 hours a day for the past week. I need to be there and right now we're wasting precious time arguing about it."

Stanners looked at Jackson, the clenched jaw and steely eyes staring back at him told him there was no point arguing with him. And the lad had a point, Jackson was probably the only person in Turkey Evie would trust right now. "Fine," he said at last, "but I doubt they'll furnish us with a lift, we'll have to grab a taxi."

~~~~~

After Evie had made her call to the hospital, she had hurried away from the shop pulling her flowing garments around her. She had told the switchboard operator the name of the shop she was in. "Tell Jackson Bridges this is where I am, Leenie is near this shop." She spoke as quietly as she could, mindful that she could be overheard.

"We have no Jackson Bridges in the hospital," came the reply.

"Yes, you do, he's British and with Harry Rivers. They were shot."

There was such a long delay before anybody replied that Evie had begun to wonder if she had been disconnected but then she heard a distinct click on the line and another voice began speaking to her.

"Hi Evie, my name is McAllister, I'm relieved to hear your voice. We've been very worried about you," a British voice told her. "Where are you?"

Evie gave the shop name again and listened carefully as she was told to make her way to a coffee shop a few streets away.

"Sit at a table just inside the entrance, order a coffee and wait. We will come and get you."

Her heart was pounding as she recited the instructions again and again in her head. Turn right, then second left, through the next small square, down the road to the left and into the first café she saw.

Evie had managed all of this and was now sat at a table in the café turning a coffee cup round and round in her hands. Her stomach was churning too much to be able to drink any of it and its contents kept spilling out onto the table. She looked up expectantly every time the bell over the cafe door rang. Half an hour or so had passed before a man clad in dark clothing, a baseball cap pulled down low to partially obscure his features, approached her, and grabbed her arm without speaking.

"Hey!" Evie tried to break free from the tight grip as she was pulled up from her seat. She looked up into the face of the man who was handling her so roughly and an icy fear gripped her. She gasped in horror; she had only seen the man who had ordered the shooting of Jackson and Harry fleetingly, but his face would forever be imprinted on her memory. It was the man now pulling her silently out of the coffee shop, it was Boran.

Chapter 32

"Here," Stanners and Jackson were in a taxi racing into the city centre. "Take this. I presume you remember how to use it."

Jackson looked down and saw Stanners was surreptitiously passing him something out of the eye line of the driver. It was a small handgun. When they had hailed the cab at the hospital Jackson had started towards the front passenger door, but Stanners had insisted they both get in the back. Now he knew why.

"Yep, course I do," he said quietly. "Did the MI6 guys give you them?"

"Good grief no!" Stanners exclaimed. "They wouldn't sign off on as much as a cup of tea to us let alone a couple of firearms. Our Turkish friends were a lot more amenable though. I picked these up this morning, as a precaution."

Jackson raised his eyebrows at this comment but chose to remain silent. It had been a while since he'd handled a gun but, rather like riding the proverbial bike, the feel of it in his hand triggered his muscle memory and it quickly felt familiar. He hated guns but hoped his accuracy was still up to scratch because, if it came to it, he wouldn't hesitate to shoot anyone standing in the way of getting Evie to safety.

He leaned forward to speak to the driver. "Can you drive any faster?"

~~~~

"Get off me!" Evie was screaming as Boran pulled her from the coffee shop. She tried in vain to kick him and free herself from the vice-like grip he had on her arm. Why wasn't anyone coming to her aid? Surely, they could see she was being dragged away against her will. Several bystanders were indeed witnessing what was happening, but they had also spotted the gun Boran held in his free hand. Their desire to help Evie, a complete stranger, was outweighed by their desire to stay alive. No-one came to her aid.

As Boran man-handled her across the street Evie could see an area of dimly lit waste land between two buildings ahead of them. As she was dragged onto it, she could just make out a car, its headlights still on, on the other side of it and realised Boran was heading for that car.

"No," she screamed again, "I'm not going with you, NO!"

Boran had not uttered a word since grabbing her and, even now, he responded by simply pulling her even further into his side and increasing his hold on her right arm. When she went to scream again, he spun her round to face him and hit her hard, across the face, with the back of his free hand. Pain exploded over the right side

The Gemini Connection

of Evie's face, and she would have fallen to the ground had he not effectively been holding her up. Instead, despite her knees buckling under her, she was still being pulled towards that car. She could feel something trickling down her face and realised she must be bleeding from the blow to her face.

"Evie!" she heard a voice she recognised calling her name. "Evie!" it called again.

"Jackson, help me," she shouted as loud as she could before Boran shoved his hand across her mouth to muffle her.

~~~~

Ironically, Stanners and Jackson had reached Evie before any of the other operatives despite relying on a taxi to get them there. Their driver had proven his worth when asked to step on it and had darted round several back streets and then down the pedestrianised zone after Jackson said "Police" to him and then flashed what was, in reality, his driving licence at him. He and Stanners had leapt from the car as soon as they spied the café Evie should have been in only to quickly realise, she wasn't there. Jackson cursed his complete lack of Turkish as he tried to ask people if they had seen a young English woman. Nobody seemed to understand him and just as he thought he might explode in exasperation he felt someone tugging on his sleeve.

"There, she go there," a young woman was pointing in the direction Evie and Boran had gone. "She go there, I think with a bad man. She was not happy, the bad man had gun."

"Boss!" Jackson shouted over her head to Stanners. "This way!" He nodded his head at the woman by way of thanks and ran in the direction she had indicated. He struggled to see anything ahead, and despair was rising in him at the hopelessness of the situation, when he heard a scream, a distinct scream, coming from somewhere in front of him. He ran towards it and heard another scream, louder this time but followed by a hollow cracking sound. He knew that sound, it was the sound of someone being hit, hard.

"Evie!" he screamed her name and was terrified when no reply came again. He called again and this time, he heard her.

"Jackson, help me."

Jackson sprinted towards Evie's voice, the gun Stanners had given him in his hand, and then he saw them, two figures in the shadows in front of him. It took him a moment to realise it was Evie because of how she was dressed. His plan, if it could be called that, was to try and circle round them and somehow surprise the man with Evie but he was too slow. They both stopped just a few yards in front of him and Boran slowly turned to face him, spinning Evie round with him in the process.

"Let her go," Jackson bellowed pointing his gun at Boran's chest. But Boran didn't even flinch. Instead, with a menacing smile, he pulled Evie in front of him and put his gun to her head.

"I don't think so." Boran spoke for the first time. "You now have a choice Jackson Bridges. That is your name is it not?"

Jackson flinched but tried to keep his voice steady. "Yes."

"You see," Boran continued, "I know everything. I see everything. I hear everything. I have already anticipated your every thought and move. You cannot shoot me without shooting her. If you want her to live, then you put down your gun and she leaves with me. If you want me dead, well you will have to shoot me through her and kill us both, so I win either way. I will be united with Evie in this life or in the next. I don't care which."

"You're insane," Evie hissed at him, but Boran simply shrugged his shoulders. "Jackson, just shoot him," she cried out.

"Be quiet." Boran shook her violently and tightened the arm he now had around her neck and shoulders. "Jackson, make your choice!"

Jackson was rooted to the spot, his gun still pointed at Boran. Where the hell was Stanners? Or any form of back up for that matter.

"I'm getting tired of waiting, so I'll make it easier for you, shall I?" Boran's voice was edged with impatience. "If you don't put your gun on the ground, I will shoot her myself. That should speed up your decision making." As he said it, Boran clicked the safety catch off his gun and pushed it harder into Evie's temple.

"No, I'm putting it down, now!" Jackson knew he was trapped and Boran would shoot him the moment he was unarmed but if Evie's life was spared then there was no other way. He slowly lowered his arm until his gun was hanging limply by his side. He looked at Evie's face and her eyes seemed to be saying, *it's alright, I understand.*

The Gemini Connection

"On the ground, put the gun on the ground and kick it towards me," Boran was ordering him.

Slowly Jackson complied but he never took his eyes off Evie. If he was about to die, her face was the last one he wanted to see, not this madman's.

He heard a diabolical laugh as Boran reached out with his foot and flicked Jackson's gun away from where they were standing.

"You see? Was that so hard? I knew you would do the honourable thing; you would not see her harmed, so you sacrifice yourself. Didn't I say that I know everything?" Boran took a step forward releasing his grip on Evie a little as he moved her back to his side. He pointed his gun in Jackson's face. "Time to say goodbye Jackson Bridges."

A shot rang out and Evie screamed as she felt herself falling to the ground. Jackson, convinced he had just been shot, couldn't understand for a few seconds why he felt no pain. Then, realising he was unharmed, he looked towards Evie assuming the worst.

Boran however could only look in astonishment at the face of the man who had just mortally wounded him. The man he had not seen hidden behind Jackson. The man who had bided his time, knowing from experience that a moment would come when Boran's arrogance would be his downfall and he would lower his guard. Boran realised too late that moving Evie away from his chest to advance towards Jackson was his fatal error as the quickly spreading dark red wetness on his T-shirt confirmed.

The Gemini Connection

"Turns out he doesn't quite see or hear everything after all," Stanners remarked to Jackson as Boran slumped to the ground at his feet.

Chapter 33

Stanners wasted no time. As Boran had fallen, he had taken Evie with him, and she was now trapped underneath him. Jackson began to run towards her, but Stanners stopped him.

"Wait!" he barked at Jackson and then fired another bullet, this time into Boran's head, before allowing Jackson to extricate Evie. Jackson felt the bile rise up and into his mouth as he took in the awful scene now in front of him. For a moment he could only stand there, frozen in horror until he was jolted out of it by Evie's screams. Mercifully the angle she was trapped at meant she couldn't fully see what was left of Boran's head, splayed out on the ground around them. Jackson swallowed hard and darted forward.

"Evie, Evie, are you hurt?" As Jackson crouched down and pulled her out from beneath Boran she couldn't speak. Instead, she flung her arms around his neck and sobbed violently for several minutes.

"I thought you were dead," she eventually said. "I thought he'd killed you."

Jackson rocked her back and forth in his arms. "So did I for a moment!" He looked up at Stanners wondering how he could still look so calm and in control in the face of such carnage. "Thanks boss."

"Just doing my job," Stanners replied gruffly, "although you didn't make it easy you idiot. Running straight up to him like that, didn't exactly go for the element of surprise, did you?!"

Jackson could only shrug his shoulders in response. He still felt like he might vomit at any moment and wasn't entirely certain he wouldn't pass out altogether if he looked in Boran's direction again.

"I couldn't even shoot him from behind because I would have ended up hitting you too. Between you and Hop-A-Long Harry I've got my work cut out!" Stanners' words may have been harsh, but they were delivered with a hint of affection.

Evie still had her head buried into Jackson's chest, but she registered what Stanners had said. "Harry?" she now asked, pulling away slightly from Jackson and looking up at him. "Is Harry okay?"

Jackson nodded. "Nearly lost his leg but yes, he's fine thanks to you." As Jackson was looking at her, he realised that the shadow on her cheek was in fact blood. "Evie, you're bleeding!"

Evie gingerly put her hand up to her cheek and winced. "He hit me. My chest hurts too." She flopped back against Jackson's chest, too exhausted to say anymore.

"You need to get her to hospital, get her checked over," Stanners said to Jackson indicating Evie with a nod of his head. "And you don't look so good yourself."

"I'm fine," Jackson replied though not overly convincingly. "Just not used to seeing people having their brains blown out. How can you look so okay?"

"Well, it wasn't the first time I've had to do that, and I wasn't going to risk him having enough life left in him to still fire his gun. Oh finally, the cavalry arrives! Where the hell were you?" Stanners' attention was taken by the arrival of McAllister and the other operatives.

McAllister surveyed the scene. "Ideally, we wanted Boran alive Stanners. You should have waited."

For a split-second Jackson saw a peculiar look pass over Stanners' face, as if something had suddenly disturbed him, but it happened so quickly he thought he must have imagined it.

"If I'd waited for you and your buffoons my man would be dead. The girl too probably," Stanners snarled, "so don't tell me what I should and should not have done. If you'd done your job properly in the first place, we wouldn't be in this mess!"

"If you'd involved us sooner, before anyone had even set foot in Turkey, we'd not be here at all!" was the angry reply.

"Now is not the time." Jackson stood up, a sharp edge to his voice. "Enough! You can play your blame games in an office sometime but not here and not now! I need to get her to the hospital. Give me the keys to one of your cars," he directed McAllister.

"No!" Jackson was taken aback by how loudly Stanners spoke. "No, she needs an ambulance and you're not in a fit state to drive her anywhere."

"One of my men can take her," McAllister said, "and besides your man needs to stay here, we need a statement from him."

"Which you can get from him later," Stanners said with such a withering look on his face McAllister was temporarily silenced. "Call for an ambulance NOW!"

"Doing it now Sir," one of the Turkish operatives called out, "have said it's an emergency. They have a crew nearby."

"Make sure you go to the same hospital as Hop-A-Long, you'll be guarded there," Stanners told Jackson. "Ye gods, they'll be charging us rent soon!"

"Come on." Jackson helped Evie to her feet, but she was clutching her side and was clearly in pain.

"I think I've cracked some ribs," she said to Jackson, "it really hurts."

"Probably when you were crushed under him." Jackson nodded in Boran's direction but didn't look. "Not exactly lightweight, is he?"

Evie managed a small laugh but winced at the pain in her chest.

"Right, we are going," Jackson announced and, without waiting for an answer, he lifted her up and carried her in the direction of the road. He could already hear a siren in the distance, the Turkish guy wasn't exaggerating when he said the ambulance would get there quickly. By the time he had carried Evie to the road it was already drawing up.

The ambulance crew took one look at Evie and quickly transferred her to a trolley and began attaching her to various monitors. Jackson was relieved to hear the head paramedic speaking to Evie in English, he suspected her knowledge of the Turkish language was as non-existent as his own. As they went about their work, Jackson noticed a movement out of the corner of his eye. A man was moving deftly through the shadows, coming in their direction. Apprehension flooded through him, and he went to reach for his gun only then remembering Boran had kicked it away from him. He looked over to where Stanners was; if he shouted loud enough, he would hear him.

"Quickly," he ordered the paramedic. "Get her in the ambulance and shut the doors. Don't open them until I tell you."

By now the man had reached them, but he had his hands up in the air in front of him, hoping to prove he was unarmed. "Please," he said in a hushed voice, "please, I need to see her, is she okay?"

Although the paramedic was closing the ambulance doors Evie was close enough to hear the voice and recognise it. "Michael, it's my brother, it's Michael."

Michael was now just a few feet from Jackson. "Please, take me with you. You need to listen to me. Evie's not safe yet, far from it."

Jackson was tempted to take a swing at him. He was so angry with this man, the root cause of all that had happened but there was something about the look in Michael's eyes, eyes that were uncannily like Evie's, that made him pause.

"What do you mean?" he hissed.

"Please, trust me. We need to get away from here, now. She's not safe."

Jackson was still not convinced.

"She's my sister, I would never harm her," Michael pleaded.

"You sure about that?" Jackson replied, "Only from where I'm standing, you haven't done a good job so far of keeping her out of harm's way."

"Please," Michael repeated his plea, "they will still come after her. You must believe me."

"Put your arms out, legs apart," Jackson ordered and quickly frisked him. He was indeed unarmed. He looked over to where Stanners was, but he was still arguing with McAllister and the others and oblivious to Jackson's situation. "Okay, get in the ambulance with me, but I swear, you try anything, and I'll kill you."

Jackson banged on the door to signal them to open it. He indicated for Michael to follow him in, there was no way he was letting him in first.

Evie saw Michael and gasped, "What the hell Michael?"

"Oh Evie, I'm so sorry, I'm so sorry," Michael was weeping.

"Save your platitudes." Jackson's voice was still edged with anger. "Explain why she's still in danger."

Michael looked at him as the ambulance sped off. "The man who shot Boran, he's your boss?"

Jackson nodded.

"Can you trust him?"

Jackson nodded again.

"Well, that other man, the one he was arguing with. I've seen him before, I recognised him."

"Go on," Jackson said.

The Gemini Connection

"I don't know his name, but I know he's British and works for MI6. He was Boran's biggest catch to date; Jackson – he works for Boran."

Chapter 34

Jackson stared in horror at Michael. "Are you sure? I think that's highly unlikely."

"Yes," Michael began. "Boran first met him in Erbil, he went there from time to time. He said…."

"Be quiet," Jackson cut in. "We can save this conversation for later. Right now, Evie is the priority." *And the Boss*, he thought to himself. Jackson racked his brains about how to contact Stanners. He tried phoning him but was not surprised when the call went straight to voice mail. He sent a somewhat cryptic text message instead by way of warning but, given that Stanners was notorious for ignoring his phone at the best of times, Jackson felt it unlikely he would see it in time.

Jackson needn't have worried. Stanners may have been a dinosaur when it came to the world of technology, but his instincts honed from decades in the field still served him well. Jackson had not imagined the fleeting look that had passed over his face when McAllister first arrived on his scene. Given that the identity of the man he had just killed was not yet known, Stanners was more than a little curious to know quite how McAllister was able to address him as 'Boran'.

"You're making a habit of this," Stanners said as he entered the hospital side room where Jackson was sitting by Evie's bedside.

"Habit of what?" Jackson asked, relieved to see his boss in one piece.

"Holding vigil at hospital bedsides. How's she doing?" Stanners looked down at Evie who looked pale and ashen against the light blue of the pillowcase.

"Sleeping, at last, thank goodness. She's got three fractured ribs and needed stitches to her face but other than that, she's okay. She was very distressed though; they gave her something to help calm her down and it seems to have worked."

"She's going to have one hell of a black eye by morning," Stanners observed.

"Yep. Boss, there's something…."

"Jackson, there's something…."

Both men began to speak at once.

"Me first," Stanners said claiming seniority. "We need to investigate McAllister. There's something amiss about him."

"How did you? How could…" Jackson stopped mid-sentence.

"Why are you staring at me like I've suddenly grown a second head?" Stanners demanded to know.

"Because I was just about to tell you that McAllister might not be all he seems."

"How do you know that?"

"It's probably easier if I just show you Boss," said Jackson as he stood up. "Follow me."

Jackson fished the key to the relatives' room out of his pocket. The room was just a little way down the corridor, and he had been using it to snatch bits of sleep here and there. He unlocked the door and stood back to let Stanners go in first.

"Boss, this is…"

"Oh, I know who this is," Stanners replied.

"…Evie's brother," Jackson finished unnecessarily.

~~~~~

Not for the first time in recent days, when Evie woke up, she wasn't sure where she was. She was aware of dull pain in various parts of her body and then began to remember what had happened.

"Hi," a voice to her right said and, turning her head, she saw Jackson sitting there.

"Hi," she said, blinking at the bright sunlight streaming into the room. "What time is it?"

"Just after 7am."

"Have you been here all night?" she asked.

"On and off," Jackson replied with a smile. "How are you feeling?"

"Sore, very sore." She frowned as she remembered the events of the night before. "Michael, was he in the ambulance with us? I think he was; where is he?"

For a moment Jackson debated lying, it might be better to let Evie think she had imagined him in the ambulance with them. But he knew that would only backfire when her wits kicked fully back in, and she had a clear memory of him travelling to the hospital with them.

"Yeah, he appeared out of nowhere."

"Can I see him?"

Jackson shook his head. "No, he's not here."

"Where is he?"

"He's safe but my boss has had him taken to what we would call 'an undisclosed location.' We have a lot of questions he needs to answer."

He was relieved that she seemed to accept this at face value. Before she could ask anything else the door opened, and Stanners came into the room.

"Right, I've spoken to the medics and you and Hop-A-Long have both been signed off as fit to fly. His Lordship has to be medevacked so you can go with him, get you out of harm's way. Got it sorted overnight, pulled a few strings. The crew's already here."

"Good morning to you too," Evie said sweetly.

"Er, yes, good morning, I'm his boss by the way, Stanners is the name," Stanners stuttered slightly, much to Jackson's amusement. Evie had managed to disarm him with just one small greeting.

"Coming through, make way, oh shit!" The sound of Harry's voice was followed by a loud bang as he failed to negotiate the door into Evie's room and instead crashed into the wall.

"Jacky boy, could do with some help here!"

Jackson rolled his eyes at Evie and went to retrieve him. "What on earth are you doing mate? Trying to break the other leg? You can't propel yourself around on this!"

Somehow Harry had managed to transfer himself from his bed onto a nearby commode and then, using his good leg to push himself along, made it out of his room and down the corridor to Evie's room. Unfortunately, he had miscalculated the angle he needed to be at to manoeuvre through the doorframe and had sailed on past and into the wall.

"I heard you were here." He grinned at Evie as Jackson pushed him into her room. "You saved my life. Blimey girl, you were brave, Jackson told me what you did. We'd be dead if not for you."

"Well, you more than likely saved Jackson's life when you pushed him out of the way first," Evie replied.

"And the boss saved both our lives last night," Jackson began but was interrupted by Stanners.

"Bloody hell, this is worse than the acceptance speeches at some awful awards ceremony. If you're all quite done with thanking whoever you think saved your life, can I get a word in?!"

"Yes Boss," Harry pretended, and failed, to look serious.

"As I was saying, you two," Stanners pointed at Evie and Harry, "are being flown back to the UK within the next couple of hours. I don't want you going through commercial airports, you'll be taken to a private airstrip and transferred from there."

"I don't have my passport," Evie said.

"You don't need it; you're both travelling under special documents."

"Oh," Evie didn't really understand but her head still felt too foggy to worry about it. She was content to leave the matter in their hands. "Are you coming too?" she asked Jackson.

He looked at Stanners who gave a tiny shake of his head.

"No, the boss and I need to stay here for a couple of days, tie up the loose ends."

The truth was they needed to figure out what on earth they were going to do with Michael and McAllister, but he wasn't going to tell Evie that.

"Will you bring Michael back to England though?" Evie wanted to know.

"Err…" Jackson was relieved that they were interrupted before he had time to answer her.

"Ah, I think this may be one of your team," Stanners stood aside as a young, fresh faced woman in scrubs came into the room.

"Dr Longshaw and Mr Rivers? Hi, my name is Lucy and I'm one of the team who'll be escorting you back to the UK."

Harry only just managed to stop himself from saying "Oh goodie," and instead squeaked out a simple "Hi." To Evie's amusement, Lucy readily returned the huge smile he gave her.

"I've been reading your notes Mr Rivers, and you must be in a lot of pain," Lucy oozed sympathy to him.

"Ah please, call me Harry. Well, you know, the pain is pretty bad but it's nothing I can't handle."

"Says the man who screamed the chalet down when he had a bit of sunburn!" Jackson reminded him.

Lucy tilted her head to one side slightly as she studied Harry's face. "Is that why you have panda eyes?"

Harry was trying to think of a witty reply when there was a perceptible drop in room temperature as an extremely stern looking, well-built woman swept into the room.

"Hah, I see you have met Nurse Morris," she said casting a glance around the room and then indicating Lucy with a rather chubby finger. "She is in training with us, I am Dr Atkins and," Jackson was convinced she narrowed her eyes as she looked specifically at Harry, "I am in charge." She looked Harry up and down before announcing, "I trust you're not planning on using that commode in my presence!"

As Harry visibly shrank back from her, shaking his head vigorously, Jackson couldn't help himself. He let out a small laugh that he tried, and failed, to hide as a burst of coughing.

"Sorry," he said, "got something stuck in my throat."

Dr Atkins gave him a look of disdain and then turned her attention to Evie.

"Now young lady, I see you are a doctor too?" Evie could only nod. "Well, not on my watch, you are first and foremost my patient. You need anything – you ask me. I hate transferring medics," she said to the room in general. "Do you know I had one blow a pneumothorax at 30,000 feet and then tried to put his own chest drain in? I turn round and he's sticking a large bore cannula into his own chest wall! He had fractured ribs too. I'm more concerned about you flying than him," she indicated Harry with a brief flick of her head in his direction. "I want to keep a close eye on your lungs."

Evie was startled by the directness of the doctor's approach but had to admit she felt relieved. For all her brusqueness, Evie felt Dr Atkins was probably a safe pair of hands to travel with.

"And you have well and truly trashed your leg I see. Are you in pain right now?" she was addressing Harry again.

"Yes, it hurts, a lot," Harry whimpered.

"I'll keep you well dosed up on painkillers," she told him. "Nurse Morris will be checking you regularly during the flight and monitoring your pain."

As she saw Harry wink at Jackson, she leaned forward and looked him directly in the face. "We have plenty of drugs available on the plane though I often find suppositories work better at high altitude." She squinted at Harry before adding, "And believe me, I have a very low threshold for prescribing them."

Her last comment finished Jackson off completely. He dissolved into fits of laughter at the look on Harry's face, earning himself a cuff around the ear from Stanners in the process. But it was a gentle cuff and followed by a friendly pat on the shoulder.

Chapter 35

Jackson had been surprised, the night before, when Stanners had said they would keep Michael in the relatives' room at the hospital. He had assumed he would want him in a police cell or even on the first flight back to London under armed guard.

"Surely we can't just keep him here?" he had said to Stanners. "He'll do a runner at the first opportunity."

"Actually, I don't think he will," Stanners had replied. "For starters where would he run to? He's made himself a marked man, both with Boran's cronies and McAllister. On top of that, I don't think he will abandon his sister again. She's the glue that will keep him stuck to us."

"I'm not convinced Sir; he should be locked up properly."

"And what is 'properly'?" Stanners demanded to know. "Think about it lad. If he's telling the truth about McAllister, well we can hardly hand him over to him. And if McAllister has gone rogue, we have no idea who he may have taken with him. McAllister may have branched out alone or be in league with other operatives... ours or the Turks. For now, we trust no-one except each other, okay?"

Jackson still looked unconvinced.

"I can't use one of our contacts to get him into a safe house, they will assume McAllister is in the loop," Stanners continued. "Same applies to asking our Turkish friends to lock him up somewhere. And mark my words, McAllister will know those are the first places to look for him. For now, we have the advantage, we know exactly where he is and nobody else does."

"The ambulance crew saw him get in with us though," Jackson said, "what if they say something?"

"Unlikely, but that's a risk we must take. Hopefully they were too distracted doing their job with Evie to worry about exactly who he was. The mayhem of a shooting might have helped us there."

"We can't let him see Evie though," Jackson pointed out. "That will really draw attention to him."

"Agreed, if she asks where he is say the usual rubbish about an 'undisclosed location.'"

Seeing the persistent frown on Jackson's face, Stanners sighed. He kept forgetting that his men had been out of their depth here. What was second nature for him was completely alien to Jackson.

"Go back and sit with her," he nodded in the direction of Evie's room. "And try and get some sleep whilst you're at it. I'll keep an eye on her brother."

"Thanks Boss," Jackson was relieved to be given a duty he finally felt capable of carrying out.

Stanners had watched him walk down the corridor and into Evie's room; at least she and both his men were still alive. All things considered it could have been very different, but Stanners was no fool. He remembered how David had died, all those years ago. Nobody was safe yet.

~~~~~

As Evie and Harry were readied for the journey home, Jackson had a sudden thought.

"Boss, can we even trust the medevac team? You said to trust no-one."

"Don't worry, I contacted Dr Atkins myself in the wee small hours. I've worked with her before, excellent woman. She and I, we have err…" Stanners coughed uncomfortably, "let's just say we go back a long way."

Jackson raised his eyebrows, "Do you indeed? How long?"

"None of your business lad, I just mention it because I know we can trust her."

"And Nurse Morris? Can we trust her?"

"Yes, I told Rosa, er Dr Atkins, to bring someone she could trust. Don't be fooled by the sweet and innocent manner, Lucy Morris is a highly regarded ex-naval nurse. She's done several tours of duty on HMS this, that and the other."

"But Dr Atkins described her as 'in training'," Jackson was puzzled.

"Only in the sense that this is her first civilian position. I didn't think it wise to advertise her background too much, or Rosa's. I couldn't have any old medical team pitch up, I needed someone I've worked with before and can trust implicitly."

"So, Dr Atkins has worked for us in the past?" Jackson persisted.

"That's classified," was Stanners' only reply.

Jackson chuckled. "So, she's used to dealing with loveable rogues then."

Stanners gave Jackson an indignant stare and was about to admonish him but then thought better of it. As labels went, "loveable rogue" was probably one of the nicer ones he'd been given over the years. "Oh yes," he replied instead, "although even she may draw the line at Hop-A-Long. I might suggest she wear a parachute for the duration of the flight in case she feels the need to throw herself out of the plane at any point!"

Right on cue, Harry's voice echoed down the corridor. "If you could just move my pillow a bit more to the left, right a bit, up, no, down a bit.... marvellous!"

"Are you going to be like this the whole flight?" a slightly exasperated Lucy asked.

Harry was being wheeled towards them on a hospital trolley, grinning from ear to ear.

"Jacko, Boss.... look at me, I'm flying," Harry threw his arms out narrowly missing the wall either side of him.

"You're not even on the bloody plane yet," Stanners rolled his eyes in despair.

"He's been dosed up on painkillers again, hasn't he?" Jackson asked.

"Oh yes," Lucy replied, "can you tell?"

"Feel free to whack him round the head as often as you need," Stanners said sardonically. "I'll pick up any legal costs if he tries to sue you at a later date."

The Gemini Connection

"Ah, you love me Boss, you know you do; but not as much as Jacko does. He saved my life."

"It was the other way round you idiot. You saved mine. That's why you're the one on a hospital trolley with pins in your leg."

Harry looked bemused. "Oh yeah, that kind of makes more sense."

"Good luck," Jackson mouthed to Lucy and then turned his attention to Evie.

She was walking very slowly towards them, Dr Atkins by her side, having insisted she didn't need to be in a wheelchair. Unlike Harry, she was not laughing and joking. She still looked very pale and a little afraid.

"I wish you were coming with me," she said as she drew level with Jackson.

So did he, but instead he could only nod and say, "I know."

"Will I see you once you're back?"

"Of course, the boss has arranged for you both to stay together somewhere until everything here is sorted. We'll catch up with you there, I promise."

"And Michael?"

On that score Jackson could make no promises. "We'll do our best," was all he could manage to say as he kissed her on her forehead wishing he could freeze time at that moment. Instead, he briefly rested his chin on top of her head then stepped back and watched her walk away.

~~~~

"Right, start talking."

With Evie and Harry safely on their way, Stanners and Jackson were back in the relatives' room with Michael.

"Is Evie safe?"

When the two men remained silent, he asked again, "Please, I need to know. Is she safe?"

"Yes," Stanners eventually replied. "I've heeded the warnings you gave about her safety but forgive me if I don't feel inclined to discuss exactly where she is at the current time."

"This is all my fault," Michael said looking up at the ceiling.

"That has to be the understatement of the year," Jackson growled, clenching his fists into tight balls. "What the hell were you thinking when you dragged your sister into all of this?"

"Jackson…Jackson," Stanners had to say his name twice to get his attention. When Jackson finally looked at him, he did a calming motion with his hand.

Jackson nodded and cleared his throat. "You told me that Boran recruited McAllister, are you sure? How do you know?"

"Yes, I'm sure," Michael replied. "Boran boasted about it to me. That he had recruited a British intelligence officer he met in Erbil. It's in northern Iraq."

"I know where Erbil is," Jackson snapped. "When was this?"

"About eight or nine months ago. Boran often visited Erbil, he said it was a good place to buy things."

"What sort of things?"

"Cheap phones, laptops, medicines. I sometimes went with him to restock our drug supplies."

"Why Erbil?"

"Boran said he had lived there as a boy. We went to other places too, but Erbil seemed a favourite."

Michael looked from Stanners to Jackson, but the two men simply stared back at him waiting for him to continue. "On this occasion we were there together, and he told me he was off to meet a new contact. He said the man was British and had been involved with advising on the security for a group of British and American archaeologists. They were visiting the various ancient sites IS had desecrated. They wanted to see what was left of them, try and salvage what they could and get them back into the museums in Mosul."

"Spare us the lecture on archaeology," Stanners barked. "How do you know this contact was McAllister?"

"I was curious when Boran said he was British, so I followed him. I saw them together in one of the marketplaces. I didn't dare follow them for too long, but I noticed that the man had severe metatarsus adductus."

Jackson and Stanners stared at him blankly.

"Pigeon toes? Where you walk with your feet turned in?"

"What the hell has that got to do with anything?" Jackson's patience was nearly gone.

"He has a very distinctive way of walking; you must have noticed?"

Stanners was slowly nodding his head, "Yes, he does."

"Well, I might not have seen much of him in Erbil but when I saw him last night, I knew it was the same man. Not only was he the right height and build but his gait, his walking, it had to be him."

Stanners sat back in his chair and rubbed his chin; he looked at Michael and then at Jackson.

"I'm telling you the truth," Michael cried, thinking he had not been believed. "Evie will not be safe whilst McAllister is around. And neither will you."

Stanners carried on rubbing his chin. "I do believe you Michael," he finally said. "I've already been looking into McAllister's record. He was in Erbil at the time you said, and for the reasons you said. And he knew who Boran was when the rest of us didn't."

Relief flooded through Michael. "So, have him arrested. I will testify in court to everything I just said. He will go after Evie; I know he will."

"But why?" Jackson wanted to know. "He has no real connection to her. It was my boss who killed Boran."

"Because both she and I will be seen as the root cause of Boran's death. More so than the man who pulled the trigger even. It's a warped ideology. Revenge is, was," Michael corrected himself, "revenge was everything to Boran. He saw himself as the righter of wrongs. He would make a whole family pay for the crimes of one man. 'Wipe out the evil seed' was how he phrased it. He was drunk on his own power in the end and that was why I wanted out."

Michael continued at length, repeating everything he had told Evie. From the Kabul bomb right through to the events of the last few days, but he left out one crucial detail. He omitted to tell them how he had convinced Boran to let him contact Evie in the first place.

Jackson was struggling to keep up with all the information spilling out of Michael. Stanners however had not missed a beat.

"So, you told Boran you wanted to contact your sister and he just said yes?"

Michael shifted uncomfortably in his chair. "I let him believe she would want to join us."

Stanners was silent for a long while. Eventually he spoke, "No, not buying it. There was something else. The man you've described vetted every recruit personally, but he was happy for you to just message your sister, a sister who thought you'd been dead for two years, and say 'Hey Evie, come and join us!'"

He leaned forward in his seat and scrutinised Michael's face. "What did you really tell him?"

Michael swallowed hard. "He was desperate for a wife. I said she would want to be his wife, he believed me."

Jackson moved so fast that Stanners could do nothing to stop him. He had Michael pushed up against the wall and was screaming into his face before Stanners had even stood up from his chair. "You pimped your own sister? I'm going to kill you, right here and right now. You son of a…"

With a strength Stanners didn't realise he still possessed he managed to pull Jackson away. "Sit down," he ordered. "NOW! This is helping no-one."

He pushed Jackson back down into his chair. "Cool down, and quickly!"

Michael was the first to speak. "You're right, I betrayed my own sister. I will never forgive myself. Never! That's why I'll do whatever it takes, you can lock me up and throw away the key after I've testified."

Stanners let out a deep sigh. "You can't testify."

Michael looked stunned. "Why not?"

"Think about it. It will be your word against that of a MI6 officer who, on paper at least, has an unblemished record. Even if I go straight to his superiors with all you've told me they will probably throw me out of the room. The very best I could hope for is a half-hearted investigation that is bound to end in exonerating him. I need hard evidence; proof from multiple sources; witness statements. Your testimony is not going to cut it. You carried a bomb into Kabul University. You claim it was unwittingly and yet you chose not only to stay, but to join, the man behind the attack. You allowed your family to believe you were dead for two years before dramatically reappearing and nearly causing the deaths of your sister and two of my best men in doing so."

Jackson made a mental note to relay the "best men" part of Stanners' speech to Harry at the first opportunity.

"Michael, who would you believe?" Stanners asked. "Yourself with that history? Or the upstanding MI6 guy with the funny walk?"

Michael stared down at the floor, he knew Stanners was right.

"But McAllister will go after Evie, we have to protect her," he heard Jackson say to Stanners.

"I know, but you must see what we are up against," Stanners replied.

"Well, you're onto him now. You can start looking for that hard evidence."

"Lad, that could take months if not years."

"Well, witness protection then? For Evie?" Jackson was grasping at straws.

Stanners shook his head. "On what grounds though? It wouldn't be granted."

Michael raised his head; he was surprised at how calm he suddenly felt. "Everything you say is true. Everything. You're right, nobody will believe me. And going through the right channels will take years. But I am telling you, McAllister will kill Evie. And he'll cover it up so well that even her death won't give you the evidence you need."

Michael looked from one to the other of them. "But the bottom line is, he needs to be removed. You're both assuming you must play this by the book. But you don't. There is another way."

Chapter 36

Evie shifted uncomfortably in her seat. Her ribs were aching, and every breath caused her some pain. Seeing her grimace Dr Atkins came alongside her.

"How are you doing young lady?" she asked.

"Sore, but I'm okay."

Dr Atkins popped a pulse oximeter onto her finger to check her oxygen levels. "98%, I'm happy with that. Try walking up and down a little bit. I know it's a small aircraft, but it will help. Lucy might appreciate a bit of respite from chatterbox there!"

Evie smiled; Harry's initial drug induced euphoria had dissipated but he was relishing the one-on-one attention he was getting from Lucy. Although from what Evie could see, Lucy didn't need to be rescued – she seemed quite happy. She made her way across to where Harry was lying; unlike her he was confined to a stretcher with his bad leg supported by various orthopaedic cushions.

"How are you feeling?" she asked him.

"Ah, not bad. The leg really hurts though."

"I'm not surprised, you're lucky you didn't lose it altogether."

Harry grimaced. "Yeah, don't think I realised at the time how bad it was. How are you? You've got a cracking black eye!"

It was Evie's turn to grimace. She touched her face carefully. "Hmm, at least it will fade. You're going to be left with an awful lot of scarring on your leg."

"Don't sugar-coat it for me, will you?" Harry complained.

"That was the sugar-coated version," Evie grinned.

"Well, if nothing else, I can show the scars off for sympathy. Just hope the boss lets me tell people I got them in the line of duty. Knowing him he'll make me say 'That's classified' if anyone asks how I got them! How am I meant to impress the ladies if I have to say I got them falling off a ladder or something equally stupid?"

Evie laughed. "You're incorrigible."

"Yeah, but you love…"

Evie didn't let him finish, "Oh shut up!"

"You know it's true though."

Evie smiled at him before letting out a big sigh. "I can't believe I was living such an ordinary life just days ago."

"We all were," Harry reflected.

She groaned as she remembered what had happened in Paris. "And I still have to sort out the hideous mess I'm in at work thanks to Matt."

"Seriously, don't worry about it," Harry replied. "Once you have a new phone, I'll upload just enough footage to make it look like you did the recording and

The Gemini Connection

then all you'll have to do is show it to your boss. It clearly shows Matt injecting himself and attacking you."

"Thanks Harry, I appreciate it."

Harry studied her face for a few moments. "I have to ask, you're clearly a bright girl. And brave. And pretty…"

Evie was taken aback. "Are you hitting on me?"

"Good grief no, Jackson would have my guts for garters."

Evie blushed and tried to hide the startled look she knew was spreading across her face at his comment about Jackson.

"I'm just wondering," Harry continued, "why you hooked up with a lowlife like Matt when you could do so much better? Do you love him?"

"No," Evie looked down at her hands.

"Why then?"

Memories of her father flooded her brain and she shuddered. "I think, I thought…" she began and then went silent.

"Ghosts of relationships past?" Harry conjectured.

"Something like that," she answered.

The answer seemed to satisfy Harry. "Well, Jackson is a good bloke, one of the best. You'll be alright with him."

"Excuse me?" Evie could not hide her startlement this time.

"Oh Evie, he's fallen for you, big time. I know him better than he knows himself sometimes. And besides," Harry paused for effect, "I saw you both, that night in the chalet in France. You were asleep together on the sofa and you were all curled up across his chest."

The Gemini Connection

Evie blushed. "Oh," was all she could think of to say. She remembered Jackson putting his arm around her when she had gone downstairs, unable to sleep. It was true, they had both fallen asleep, but she hadn't appreciated they'd been seen by Harry.

"I've got a photo somewhere," Harry jested and pretended to pat down his pockets searching for it. "Only joking! To be honest, I didn't think he would ever look at a woman again after what Claire did to him. But I reckon I was wrong. How do you feel about him?"

"For goodness' sake, are you always this blunt?"

Harry grinned. "Yep. And you haven't answered my question."

"And I'm not going to!" Evie replied, but Harry noticed she was blushing a little again.

~~~~

"You must see this is the only way," Michael pleaded. "And it's the only way I can make amends; I can't live with what I've done. I am begging you to let me do this."

"I don't like it Boss," Jackson began arguing with Stanners. "There must be a better way."

Stanners looked at him. "Well, if you can think of one then enlighten us."

"I can't do it, I really can't," Jackson said in anguish. "How can I ever face Evie again if I do this?"

Michael put a hand on his arm. "She'll understand, eventually."

Jackson was still unconvinced, and Stanners could sense the conflict in him. "Look lad, if there was any doubt about McAllister, any at all, I wouldn't countenance this. But I'm convinced Michael has told us the truth. McAllister isn't the brightest lightbulb in the pack, he's an arrogant little shit and he sealed his fate this morning."

Two hours earlier, Stanners had met with McAllister at the Turkish headquarters. Wisely, he insisted on having two of the Turkish staff present as a precaution. He had decided to play his role of doddering, out of touch, old fool to the max and then sit back and see what McAllister gave away.

"So," Stanners began, "do we know yet who the man I killed was?"

He saw a brief look of relief pass over McAllister's face. At the time of the shooting, Stanners had not said anything when he had made his rookie mistake of calling Boran by name, in fact he had not even seemed to notice. Considering the question Stanners had now just asked him, McAllister was falsely reassured.

"No," the reply came from one of the Turkish men "but we are still working on that. We've run facial recognition our end and we're getting nowhere. We can't explain it, he should come up on a database somewhere, not least because he must have travelled. Even a fake passport would still have his photo in it."

"Unless he was disguised from the outset," Stanners said. "False nose, dyed his hair, fooled the computers."

"Very likely," McAllister replied, "that may well be what's happened."

Lie number one, Stanners thought. Modern software was not going to struggle with such an inept disguise, he had learnt something from his boys over the years.

"Did you check our databases?" Stanners threw the question at McAllister.

He nodded his head. "Nothing."

"Any thoughts at all on who he is?"

"No, I have no idea."

Lie number two.

"What about the girl?" McAllister asked. "She must have known who he was."

Stanners shook his head. "She was badly injured, hasn't been able to talk to us yet."

McAllister looked aghast. "But I saw her walk with your man to that ambulance. How can she now be unable to talk?"

Stanners shrugged his shoulders. "No idea, they got her to the hospital, she collapsed. Been unconscious ever since."

McAllister fell for it. "Which hospital is she in as a matter of interest?"

"Same one as my other man, why?"

"Oh, just curious."

Like hell you are, Stanners thought, *Lie number three.*

"And Michael Longshaw? The man at the heart of all this?" Stanners said aloud. "Where is he?"

McAllister frowned. "Well, that's the mystery, isn't it? One of my men is convinced he saw another man get in that ambulance with the girl and your man. Yet, when I asked the ambulance crew about it, they were adamant there wasn't anybody else."

"Really?" Stanners opened his eyes wider to feign innocent surprise. "Well, somebody's got it wrong." He smiled inwardly, his discreet word with the relevant ambulance staff had paid off.

"Do you know where Michael Longshaw is?" McAllister demanded to know of Stanners.

"Me?" Stanners pretended to be shocked. "It was your job to find him, not mine. How would I know where he is?"

Just then his phone began to ring. "Excuse me," he said pointedly, "I need to take this. Hello?"

"It's me," Jackson's voice came down the line, "you said to phone you at this time?"

"Has she indeed? Great news," Stanners replied. "I'm on my way."

He pushed his phone back into his pocket. "Sorry, I need to get back to the hospital, she's awake." Without giving any further explanation, he stood up and left the room.

~~~~

Stanners was not in the least surprised when McAllister raced after him and insisted on going to the hospital with him. "I need to see her first, she is our asset now."

"Well, she was ours first," Stanners said.

"Yeah, and you and your men ballsed it all up, didn't you? So, I will take it from here."

"Whatever," Stanners used his best disinterested voice, "but go easy on her."

"Don't tell me how to do my job," McAllister growled.

"Oh, I wouldn't dream of it," Stanners replied obsequiously.

If Harry and Evie had not been at 30,000 feet and well into their journey, they probably would have heard

McAllister screaming in frustration when Jackson greeted him and Stanners in the hospital foyer saying he had bad news. "What do you mean she's back in theatre?" McAllister demanded to know.

Jackson shrugged his shoulders. "Just that, she woke up and started talking but then said she was in agony. Next thing I know there's staff everywhere and somebody's yelling that she's bleeding from her liver or something and she's whisked back to theatre."

McAllister was at boiling point. "Right, you two morons, I want you out of here now. I'll take it from here. You're off this case so get on the next plane back to London. I'll deal with the girl."

"No, I need to stay with her, she trusts me," Jackson pretended to plead.

"I don't give a monkey's arse who she trusts. Get out of here now or I'll make sure you have no jobs to return to."

Stanners let out a long sigh. "Come on, he's right. It's for MI6 to deal with now."

He'd seen and heard enough, McAllister had to go.

~~~~~

"So, you must see this is the only way?" Michael again asked Jackson.

Stanners looked at him. "Jackson, I know you didn't sign up for this, not your pay grade and all that. But the reality is that if we don't let Michael do this, Evie and goodness knows who else will fall victim to McAllister. Sometimes two wrongs do make a right."

The Gemini Connection

Michael let out a hollow laugh. "Boran used to say something like that. Only he said a wrong can sometimes right a wrong." He looked up at the two men. "Ironic, eh?"

Silence descended in the room for several minutes until it was broken by Michael.

"Right, give me his number." Stanners handed him a piece of paper.

Michael slowly dialled it. When McAllister answered he repeated the words he had already rehearsed a thousand times in his head.

"It's done," he said to them both before turning to Jackson and handing him a letter. "When this is over, please, please, give this to Evie. It explains everything."

"We can't do that..." Stanners began, "we can't leave written evidence behind us."

"It's in our own language. Nobody but Evie will ever be able to understand it. Please."

Jackson nodded and silently took the letter from Michael.

Chapter 37

"It's terrifying to see how easy this is to do," remarked Jackson as he watched Michael deftly assemble the device from the items he had sent him out to buy.

"Well, you can't live alongside Boran for two years and not learn a thing or two."

Jackson let out a heavy sigh and Michael looked up at him. "You don't want to do this do you?"

"Of course I bloody don't. Would you want to if you were in my shoes?"

"No, but I'd make peace with it for Evie's sake."

Jackson shook his head. "I'm a computer geek, I don't kill people."

"Well, technically you're not going to be killing anyone."

"I might as well be."

"See it as saving innocent people instead."

Jackson shrugged his shoulders but said nothing.

"Besides," Michael said, almost to himself, "it's high time one of the men in my family did something right by Evie."

"What do you mean?" Jackson didn't understand.

Michael studied him, weighing up how much to say. "Will you look after Evie when I'm gone? She'll need you."

"If she'll let me," Jackson replied.

"You're a good man Jackson, I can tell, and Evie needs a good man in her life. Our father was pure evil, that's all you need to know."

Jackson nodded, he understood perfectly.

Michael sighed. "I think my decision to join Boran was driven by some deep desire to exact revenge on authority figures. Specifically, the ones who pretend they are righteous and upstanding and hide the fact that they are perverted monsters at home. If you scratched the surface of McAllister's background, you'd find something. I bet he was bullied and abused as a boy, probably because of the way he walks. Boran was exceptional at spotting people carrying the sort of wounds he knew he could mould to his advantage. But I never thought it would get this far, I really didn't. Please believe me. I love Evie with all my heart, but I know I failed her. Completely and utterly failed her."

"Yeah, you did," Jackson said, but there was no malice in his voice.

Michael finished what he was doing and stood up. "Right, let's see how well this fits me." Jackson flinched as Michael fastened the belt around his waist. "Don't worry," Michael reassured him, "it's not primed yet."

McAllister had almost fist pumped the air when he got the call from Michael. "How did you get this number?" he had demanded to know.

"From Boran of course," Michael had calmly replied. "I want to meet you."

"Why?"

"Because I was Boran's right hand man and now I'm taking over."

"You ran off with your sister," McAllister said cooly, but Michael had his reply ready.

"I ran *after* my sister, she wanted to be with Boran, but those MI5 jerks ruined everything. And now she's dead."

"Evie is dead?"

"She died on the operating table this morning and I want revenge on the men who killed her. Boran told me all about you McAllister, I know you'll want in on this."

"Agreed," McAllister replied. "Where are you now?"

"The City Hospital, be here in half an hour. I'll meet you outside the main entrance and we'll talk then."

Stanners had been right when he said McAllister was not the brightest recruit to MI6, he was fool enough to agree to Michael's demands.

~~~~~

Jackson pulled the baseball cap down low over his forehead, pulled up the collar of his recently purchased cheap shirt and donned the sunglasses he'd bought in the hospital shop. He got into the driver's seat of the taxi that Stanners had somehow acquired and glanced at Michael, already waiting outside the hospital entrance. Michael gave him a small nod and Jackson drove off out of sight.

"So, your sister is dead?" McAllister greeted Michael with the brutal observation.

Michael nodded. "Yes, but we can't talk here. I'll order a taxi; you can choose where we go."

McAllister laughed. "Thanks, but no thanks, I'm not getting into a car you've organised. I'll do it myself."

Michael shrugged his shoulders nonchalantly. "Fine by me."

Michael had to hand it to Stanners, he knew exactly how to play McAllister. When the taxi drew up ten minutes later McAllister, assuming it was the one he had ordered, got straight into the car. Jackson held his breath, but McAllister wasn't interested in the driver.

Leaning forward, he barked the name of a street at Jackson but didn't take his eyes off Michael. "Don't try anything stupid, I have this." McAllister made a downwards motion with his head and Michael looked to see he had a small gun pointed at him. Michael almost wanted to laugh out loud, as if that was going to be of any use against what he had strapped around his waist, hidden underneath his untucked shirt.

"There's no need for that," he hissed, "we're on the same side."

"Just a precaution," McAllister replied.

"Where are we going?" Michael asked.

"A crowded bar, always way more private than a quiet place. First mistake most people make, they assume quiet is better but try listening in on a conversation where there are loads of people talking, it's impossible."

The Gemini Connection

"Clever," Michael murmured as he fixed his gaze on the road ahead.

It was a good five minutes before McAllister realised they were heading in the wrong direction, away from the city.

"Hey, where are you going?" he demanded to know.

"This way quicker," Jackson replied in what he hoped sounded like the broken English of a Turkish taxi driver.

McAllister wasn't persuaded. "What's going on? Turn this cab around."

Jackson didn't reply, he instead put his foot down and headed for the piece of wasteland he and Stanners had chosen a few miles away from the hospital. Thrown back into his seat, McAllister lost his grip on the gun and Michael deftly grabbed it from his hand. "You won't be needing this," he told him.

When Jackson reached the designated spot, he skidded the car to a halt and glanced back quickly at Michael. He was astonished to see how calm Michael appeared, but he also looked so much like Evie it made Jackson falter. He came close to aborting the whole plan.

"Go!" Michael's voice shook him out of his stupor.

Jackson did as he was bid and jumped out of the car. As he slammed the driver's door shut, he hit the car's central locking button on the key fob and began running.

"What the...." McAllister was realising too late he had been ambushed. He tried helplessly to get the car door open. "You bastard!" he screamed at Michael. "Your sister's not dead at all is she? I am going to find her and make her suffer in every way imaginable. Scum like you and her, you don't deserve to be alive." McAllister's face was contorted with so much hatred that if Michael had felt any hesitation about what he was about to do, it dissolved instantly.

"I think you'll find I'm the one with all the power but thank you."

"What the hell for?" McAllister demanded to know.

"For making this so easy for me," said Michael as he closed his eyes and thought of Evie.

"Forgive me Evie," he murmured as he reached under his shirt and flicked the little switch.

~~~~~

Jackson was still running across the wasteland to where he knew Stanners was waiting when he heard the deafening bang behind him. He had not expected it to be so loud and he almost threw himself to the ground thinking he would be hit by flying debris.

"Well done lad, that wasn't easy," Stanners said as he fell into the passenger seat and they drove off at speed, but Jackson couldn't hear him - his ears were still ringing from the explosion. He looked back over his shoulder at the burning car he had been in just moments before and began hyperventilating.

"Pull over!" he cried out.

"We need to get to the airfield," Stanners replied. He looked sideways at Jackson and grimaced; his breathing was ragged, and his face, beaded with sweat, was green.

"On second thoughts…" Stanners swerved the car onto a grassy verge and Jackson only just got out in time. He vomited profusely over the side of the road and then his vision blurred, and the world began to go black. He slumped to the ground and Stanners had a sense of déjà vu from when he had collapsed at his feet with appendicitis.

"Come on lad," he said hoisting Jackson to his feet, "let's get you home."

~~~~

Jackson did not speak for the entire flight back to the UK. He barely registered anything going on around him and did not question how Stanners had managed to arrange such a speedy exit from Turkey. He didn't ask where they were flying to and, when they landed at the same RAF base that Evie and Harry had, just 24 hours earlier, allowed himself to be led off the plane by Stanners as if he was a small child. Stanners suggested they go straight to see them, but Jackson had simply stared at him blankly and remained mute.

Stanners asked the officer escorting them from the plane to guide them to a private room instead and bring Jackson a stiff drink.

"And the same for you Sir?" the officer asked. At that moment, Stanners would have given anything for a decent malt whisky. He nearly faltered and ordered one.

"No, thanks," he managed to say instead, "just water for me."

He pushed Jackson down onto a small sofa and wiped his own forehead with the back of his hand. "How are you?" Stanners began awkwardly. Jackson dropped his head and began studying his hands as if he had never seen them before.

"Talk to me," Stanners tried again, this time drawing up a chair and sitting directly opposite Jackson. "You've not said one word since you pebble dashed the roadside."

Very slowly, Jackson lifted his head and looked his boss directly in the eye. "I killed Evie's brother," he spoke in such a whisper Stanners could barely hear him. "I killed them both."

"No, you didn't," Stanners said sternly. "Michael made a choice, a very hard choice, but nevertheless it was his decision."

"I was the one who locked them in the car," Jackson's voice faltered.

"Michael knew what he was doing. You will never know how many lives you and he saved today by your actions. With McAllister gone rogue who knows what he would have done? He was privy to deeply sensitive information; he could have created merry hell before we finally caught up with him."

The officer came back into the room with a small tray of drinks.

"Ah, thank you," Stanners took the brandy. "Drink this," he ordered Jackson, "and then we'll go and see Evie and Hop-a-Long."

Jackson took the glass and shook his head. "She'll never forgive me. When she finds out Michael is dead, she won't want anything to do with me."

"Jackson," Stanners tried to persuade him, "Evie will want to see you, she needs you. You can't abandon her now."

"I'm not abandoning her; I'm protecting her from the pain she will feel every single time she sets eyes on me."

The Gemini Connection

"Let me do the talking, there's a limit to how much we can say anyway, you know that," Stanners said. "Come on, drink that down and then on your feet."

Slightly to his surprise Jackson did as he was told, and Stanners asked the officer to take them to the base's medical centre where Evie and Harry had been temporarily ensconced.

Evie looked up anxiously as they entered the clinic room. She was sat on a low chair under the window and Stanners was struck by how very young she was. Only then did he register that Michael was, of course, the same age. Just 28 and he had made the ultimate sacrifice.

Harry, laid on the bed and propped up by various pillows he was taking great delight in having rearranged by Lucy at every opportunity, took one look at Jackson and knew something was seriously wrong.

"Mate, you look like shit, what happened?"

Before he could answer, Evie leapt out of her chair. "Jackson!" she cried and ran to him. She threw her arms around him, but he didn't reciprocate and remained rigid in her embrace. She let her arms fall back to her sides and backed slowly away from him.

"What is it?" she asked.

Silence filled the room as she looked from Jackson to Stanners and then back to Jackson.

"Evie," Jackson began but his voice broke almost immediately.

"Where's Michael?" she asked, guessing correctly that something had happened to him. "What's happened?" Still, they remained silent. "Tell me!"

Stanners moved towards her and placed one hand gently on her shoulder. "I'm very sorry Evie, but Michael is dead."

"No, NO!" Evie sobbed. "He can't be. I would know, I'd feel it. We're twins, we're soul mates. No, you're wrong, you must be. He's only just come back to me. I can't lose him again." She looked at him in desperation. "What happened?"

When Stanners didn't answer, anger began to rise in her, and she shrugged his arm off her shoulder. "What happened?" she was screaming now, and the sound brought Dr Atkins running into the room.

"He was killed earlier today in a confrontation with one of Boran's men," Stanners said eventually. He looked at Jackson who was stood stock-still next to him. His face was etched with so much fatigue and guilt he might as well have had the truth written all over it. Stanners knew then that Evie would not accept his answer.

She didn't. Evie looked Jackson directly in the face. "What happened?"

Jackson looked down at her. He was convinced her eyes had seen deep inside him and found the truth lying there.

"Did you kill him?" she asked him.

"He's dead Evie, I'm sorry, he's gone…." Jackson's voice tailed off.

"Did you kill him?" she asked again.

Evie searched his face for the answers he wasn't giving her. "You promised me, you promised me you would get him home. You promised me, you promised me." She repeated the same words over and over until deep guttural sobs made her whole body start to shake. Jackson moved forward to try and hold her, but she pushed him away from her.

"Get away from me," she screamed before collapsing onto the floor. It was Dr Atkins she allowed to hold her. Rosa dropped down onto the floor next to her, wrapping her arms around her as she did so. Evie held onto her as if for dear life. "I've already grieved for him once; I can't do it again. I can't do it again," she sobbed into Rosa's arms, "I can't."

"Evie," Jackson looked down at the two women huddled on the floor. "Evie please!"

But Evie was too lost in her own sorrow to even hear him.

"Leave her to me," Rosa said looking up at him. "I'll take care of her."

As she helped Evie to her feet, Jackson made one last attempt. "Evie…"

This time Evie heard him, and she turned to face him. "I never want to see you again." She said the words slowly and deliberately and, as Jackson watched her leave the room, with Dr Atkins' arms around her and not his, he felt his world begin to shatter. It was a feeling he had known before, but this time was different. This time, he didn't think he would ever be able to rebuild it.

Chapter 38

4 weeks later

"William, come in," Rosa opened her front door wider for Stanners.

"How is she? Is she ready for this?" he asked.

Rosa smiled. "Much better. I swear, she slept for a week when I first brought her here then she spent the next week either crying or staring into space. But she's on the up now, she said she was happy to meet with you."

In the aftermath of the revelations at the airbase, it was clear that Evie was in no fit state to be left alone. Rosa had asked her if she could go and stay with her mother for a while, but Evie flatly refused.

"I don't have that kind of relationship with my mother," Evie had told her. "I wouldn't confide in her about what I ate for dinner, let alone deeper stuff."

"Well, how about moving in with me for a couple of weeks?" Rosa had suggested.

"Really? Do you mean that?" Evie had been taken aback by the unexpected kindness.

The Gemini Connection

"We medics have to stick together," Rosa had said with a smile, "of course I mean it. Not my London pad, I have a small house down in Sussex, inherited it from my parents. It would be a good place for you to recuperate."

And so, for the last month, Evie had been living with Rosa and the two women had begun to forge a strong bond. Rosa's forthright, no nonsense manner suited Evie perfectly. The older woman had seemed to know intuitively the best way to help her. She had let her sleep by night and doze by day the first week and whenever Evie woke up crying from another nightmare, Rosa was on hand to hold her and comfort her. By the third week, the two of them were going for long walks and the colour finally came back to Evie's cheeks.

Evie was intrigued by Rosa's background although she didn't give much away. All Evie knew for sure was that, like her, Rosa had trained in anaesthetics but as an army doctor. Rosa had joined up straight out of medical school and done various tours of duty in Bosnia, Iraq, and Afghanistan. On leaving the army, she had worked as a medevac specialist and at some point, she had clearly crossed paths with Stanners but as to the how, when, and why she didn't say.

"Much as I hate the phrase, I have to say, 'It's classified,'" she told Evie one afternoon when they were sat together in the garden. "Those words! They hide all manner of sins!"

"Had you met Jackson or Harry before?" Evie asked her.

"No," Rosa laughed, "and let's face it, you'd remember if you had met Harry before, wouldn't you?"

The Gemini Connection

"Oh yes," Evie grinned. "He's impossible, but I couldn't help liking him in the end. Even if he does act like a deranged chimpanzee on amphetamines!"

"And Jackson?" Rosa said gently, but Evie's face was already clouding over.

She sighed. "I, he, I...." she couldn't continue, and Rosa noticed that her eyes were welling up with tears.

Rosa stood up. "I'm getting us a glass of wine," she said but as she turned to go into the house Evie suddenly grabbed her hand.

"I care about Jackson; there I've said it. But how can I even be in the same room as the man who killed my brother? How could we ever get past that?"

Rosa sat down again. "I genuinely don't know exactly what happened in Turkey Evie, but I do know Jackson was a broken man when you last saw him. The service, they demand so much of their people. Many fall by the wayside as a result and it's compounded by the fact that they are sworn to secrecy. Honestly, it's not just us they keep in the dark. People can be working in one office and be completely clueless as to what the people next door are doing. I suspect that whatever happened, he didn't kill Michael in cold blood."

"But's that the problem, isn't it?" Evie replied. "I don't know if Jackson is a ruthless killer. And if he can't ever tell me what happened, then there's no future for us, none at all."

~~~~~

"Hello Evie, you look a darn sight better than when I last saw you."

The Gemini Connection

Evie looked up and smiled as Stanners joined her in the garden.

"The black eye's gone I see. Has Rosa been looking after you well?"

"Yes, she's been brilliant," Evie replied, "and how are you?"

Stanners eased himself into a garden chair next to her. "Yes, I'm well thanks. Well, sort of. The office isn't really the same at the moment, but we'll get there."

In truth, no-one was more surprised than Stanners that he even still had a job. After taking the fallout for Vivian's sabotage, followed by the complete and utter mess that had happened in Turkey, he was fully expecting to be let go with immediate effect the moment they had returned to the UK. But during his absence, Vivian had gone to the top brass and told them that it was she who had accessed their databases and deleted information. She hadn't intended to confess; she still felt ambivalent towards Stanners and being retired off early with no golden handshake seemed a suitable ending for his career. But then she had received a message from a drugged-up Harry in his hospital bed in Turkey. He should not have been messaging her at all but, in his morphine induced state, he had sent her a garbled message saying how he and Jackson had nearly died and then waxing lyrical about how the boss was there with them.

When Vivian had received his message, she quickly deleted it and rang Stanners telling him to check Harry's phone. Stanners had acted swiftly and commandeered the phone off Harry. "You can have this back when you're sane," he had told a sulky Harry, "although who knows when that will be!"

After that, Vivian could no longer square her conscience. Whatever was going down in Turkey, those boys would need Stanners by their side, and she could not reconcile harming them as well as him. When Stanners was called to meet with his superiors he was expecting to be hauled over the coals and then ejected from the building. Instead, they seemed to grudgingly admire him for trying to protect Vivian and told him she had exonerated him. He had then spent hours being debriefed over events in Turkey but whilst everything he said was true, it was not the whole truth. He stopped at the point when McAllister had told him and Jackson to get out of the country and return to the UK.

"So, we did," he had explained. "He said we'd done more than enough damage and finding Michael Longshaw was for him and MI6 to do now. I don't think he liked us very much," he couldn't resist adding.

Stanners feigned shock and surprise when he was told that McAllister was dead, and that work was ongoing to identify the other man found dead at the scene.

"We expect it will be Longshaw," he was told. "We are working on two separate theories. Either they were both killed by an unidentified assailant, or we are looking at a murder-suicide scenario. We've instigated a media blackout on it. McAllister's death will be announced as an unfortunate car accident whilst on assignment in Turkey."

Stanners had managed to look stunned. "Well, I guess CCTV camera footage of where it all happened will help you get answers."

The Gemini Connection

"Unfortunately not, the patch of land where they were killed isn't covered by any cameras. In fact, there's nothing else there at all; no buildings, no passing traffic, so no witnesses. Whoever chose that location chose well."

"Didn't they?" Stanners replied, basking inwardly at the compliment they didn't know they had just given him.

"How's Harry?"

Evie's voice brought Stanners back to the present.

"Driving me insane. When he's not at physio, he's back in the office with some huge contraption on his leg. I kid you not, talk about milking it. The lad's got celebrity status, he'll be selling signed photographs of himself next!"

Evie giggled. "I hear from Rosa that he and Lucy are seeing quite a bit of each other too."

"Girl must need her head examined!" Stanners snorted.

"Ah, you've got a soft spot for him really haven't you Mr Stanners?"

Stanners smiled. "Yes, I have but for pity's sake, don't ever tell him! I'd never live it down."

Evie burst out laughing and looking at her, he could see why Jackson had fallen for this girl. They sat in companiable silence for a few minutes before Evie finally asked, "And how's Jackson?"

Stanners sighed. "Not good Evie. He tried to come straight back into work after we got back but he wasn't up to it. In the end I got him signed off for a couple of months."

"Did he kill Michael?" she asked boldly.

"No, he didn't. But he was there. I put too much onto his shoulders Evie, and it broke him."

"If it was too much for him, why did you do it?"

Stanners shrugged. "Circumstances. No other options. For the greater good."

"I'm afraid all those answers are very clichéd."

Stanners nodded. "I know. He didn't sign up to do the things I asked of him, but he did sign up to MI5. It's a bit like being a cook in the army. You might be there to prepare food and feed the troops, but you're still trained to fight. At the end of the day, when you work on a battlefield, you might get caught up in the war."

"Where is he now?"

"Paris."

"Paris? Why Paris?"

"Because he said that would be where he'd feel closest to you. He's staying in the same apartment you were in with him."

Evie was stunned. "What? I mean, how could he even book it again?"

Stanners laughed. "Hop-A-Long of course. Some poor sods will have had their Parisian mini breaks ruined when their bookings were cancelled but Jackson now has it for the whole month."

Stanners studied her face. "He needs you, Evie. And I think you need him."

Evie shook her head. "It's the not knowing. Please, can't you tell me what really happened in Turkey?"

The Gemini Connection

Now it was Stanners' turn to shake his head. "I'm not sure you would believe me even if I did, you would never know if I was telling you the truth and without that, I can see there's no way forward for you where Jackson's concerned. But there is one person I know you will believe."

Evie frowned. "Who?"

"Michael." Stanners pulled a letter from his inside jacket pocket. "Michael wrote this to you before he died. He entrusted it to Jackson to give to you. He in turn gave it to me. I asked Rosa to let me know when she thought you were ready to receive it. He explains everything Evie. I'm sorry it's open, Michael said it was in your own language, but I had to be sure before giving it to you. We can't risk anybody else knowing what happened. Once you've read this, there will be no going back for you. You can't unknow it," he warned her.

Evie held out her hand. "Give it to me, please."

Stanners handed her the envelope, and she gently clasped it to her chest. "Thank you," she whispered.

"Before I go, I have a few other things for you. Here's your passport back and a new phone. Harry said to tell you he's uploaded the footage you need for work. You'll find our numbers in it too."

"And there's this." He handed Evie a key.

"What's this for?" she asked.

"When we retrieved all your various belongings from Turkey, Jackson still had the keys to the Paris apartment. I took the liberty of having a copy cut, just in case."

"In case of what?"

Stanners stood up and readied himself to leave. "Just in case. Take care Evie." He stooped down and kissed her lightly on the cheek. "I'm sure I'll be seeing more of you."

The Gemini Connection

Epilogue

Evie sat alone in the apartment, staring out of the window. Silent tears streamed down her face as she looked out onto the Boulevard Saint-Michel, the towers of Notre-Dame visible in the distance. She looked down again at the letter in her hands, the ink smudged by her tears. At least she now knew the truth. She began to read it once again....

Dear Leenie,

By the time you are reading this I'll be gone, and I know you will have so many unanswered questions. You will probably be looking for someone to blame for my death, but you need to know that I, and I alone, am responsible.

I've made so many mistakes Leenie; from joining Boran in the first place to letting you believe I was dead for so long and then using you as bait to try and come home. But my death this time was not a mistake and I truly believe I finally did the right thing. You were never going to be safe whilst I was alive. Boran had successfully turned a British agent, that was how he knew when you had arrived in Gaziantep and which coffee shop to find you in that fateful night.

Boran's death won't have meant the end of his group. On the contrary, he is more dangerous dead than he ever was alive. The next leader would have risen up swearing revenge on those who had killed him. That would have included you, me and the men who were protecting you.

The Gemini Connection

I am ashamed of what I became over the last two years, and I cannot justify it. When I saw you in that ambulance Leenie, so close to being killed yourself, I knew what I had to do.

Stanners and Jackson took a lot of convincing, especially Jackson. He was desperate to find another way, a better way but there wasn't one. In the end I persuaded him by giving him a stark choice; he could have only my death on his conscience or mine, yours and countless others. I didn't spare him any of the details of what could happen to you if he didn't go along with my plan.

The only way I could truly protect you was to die a death that swore allegiance back to Boran and the group. I asked Jackson to film my suicide video in which I claimed to have located the agent who killed Boran. I promised to kill him for what he had done and accepted I may die with him. When they see it, the group will no longer see me as a deserter but as one who was prepared to die a martyr's death. By professing my loyalty to Boran and appearing to avenge his death, you will be safe.

Leenie, I couldn't protect you from evil when we were children, but I can protect you now. Please don't blame Stanners or Jackson for my death; this is my choice, my decision. It will not rest easy on either of their shoulders, but I fear it will take a greater toll on Jackson. Believe me when I say to you what I said to them – there is no other way.

Jackson is a good man Leenie, and I can see how much he cares for you. You will need him when this is all over and he will need you too. You put that gun to your

The Gemini Connection

own head to save both their lives, but I think it was Jackson you were referring to when you said, 'I really care about him, I will do it.' It's clear to me that he loves you. As do I.

You are the better half of us Leenie, you always were, and you always will be. Never forget that.

With all my love, now and forever.
Clocal. XXX

Evie looked at her watch, it was just gone five o'clock in the afternoon. She dried her eyes, folded the letter, and put it back in her handbag.

She could hear footsteps now; first reaching the top of the stairs and then becoming louder as they came down the corridor. There was a clinking noise as a key was placed into the lock followed by a small exclamation of surprise at the realisation that the door was already unlocked. As the door was slowly and cautiously opened Evie stood up. She turned away from the window to face the man coming into the room and a smile lit up her whole face. "Hello Jackson," she said.

The End

The Gemini Connection

The Gemini Connection

Acknowledgements

Thank you to my fellow "RRR" writers, this story would never have made it into print without you all.

Ann, Carol, Caryl, George, Liz, Lynn, Martyn, Paul, Sally, and Sue – you are the best writing group a girl could wish for. Week by week you listened and critiqued and encouraged. I'm sure you will all spot things in the text and think, *I remember saying that!* I promise I did listen when you also pointed out the things that didn't work - remember the initial prologue that gave the entire plot away? – so you may just spot some omissions too. Hopefully their removal improved the end result.

Special thanks to Martyn who came up with the idea for the title when I couldn't get beyond "Dear Evie", not the most original title for a novel that begins with reading a letter.

Thank you to my "Book Club - but we don't read books anymore" girls Ali, Julie, Sam and Yvonne who read the first few chapters and told me to go for it.

Thank you to Ariadne Tomé, for designing the cover (and not laughing at my stickman drawings when I attempted to show you what I wanted!) You are very talented.

Thank you to Samantha Lockhart-Fleming, for proofreading my initial draft so thoroughly, and then going through it all again.

Thank you Sue and Peter for reading the first proof version and being so positive about it. You gave me the boost I needed to publish it.

And finally, thank you reader, I hope you enjoyed it.

You can see more of Ariadne Tomé's work at:
Instagram @ariadnes_arts

The Gemini Connection

The Gemini Connection

About the Author

Julie Hamstead is a doctor by day but, since joining a local writing group, she also likes to pretend she is a novelist by night. She lives in the south of England with her family, various cats and the occasional dog borrowed from a friend.

The Gemini Connection is her first novel. She is now working on her second in which the protagonists will all – hopefully – return.